Airavata

Various Authors

Ukiyoto Publishing

All global publishing rights are held by

Ukiyoto Publishing

Published in 2021

Content Copyright © Meera Bharat

Cover By Satinder Ahuja

Concept by Dr. R. Lakshmi Priya

ISBN 9789370097285

Edition 1

All rights reserved.
No part of this publication may be reproduced, transmitted, or stored in a retrieval system, in any form by any means, electronic, mechanical, photocopying, recording or otherwise, without the prior permission of the publisher.

The moral rights of the author have been asserted.

This is a work of fiction. Names, characters, businesses, places, events, locales, and incidents are either the products of the author's imagination or used in a fictitious manner. Any resemblance to actual persons, living or dead, or actual events is purely coincidental.

This book is sold subject to the condition that it shall not by way of trade or otherwise, be lent, resold, hired out or otherwise circulated, without the publisher's prior consent, in any form of binding or cover other than that in which it is published.

www.ukiyoto.com

This title is produced in Association with Pachyderm Tales

www.pachydermtales.com

Foreword

Gaja, Hasti, Elle, Elephant… A creature so large that your imagination can make you roll out in any direction and space and that is exactly what these amazing little stories are all filled with.

There are stories from present, Mythology, Animals in action, dreams vivid. Wow, it just triggered off my thoughts and I must say, it can liven up your time any day. Characterisation of an animal is at times tricky and when that is mixed with imagination, magic fills up the air in many ways.

The various amazing storytellers have weaved magic by bringing in day to day issues in a beautiful way, weather it is about, freedom of mind, to being different, to being caring, to be concerned about nature, you could name it and the stories are filled with it. Then there are stories that will teach you a little about history, geography as the plots is created in different parts of this beautiful country. Each of the story has a twist and a tale for the child and the child in you to light up. It is not just the moral in every story, it is just the sheer flow of ideas and thoughts that will catch you with Aww.

Spend in the time with your child and the elephant in these stories will transport you to a different world with wonder and joy. Hats off to the amazing storytellers from across the country. I would say worth every moment you spend. I simply loved it!

Sidhartha Satpathy (Sid)

Author and story teller

Compiler's Note

Airavata, this name just surfaced on top of our mind when we were planning a title for our upcoming Anthology with an Elephant as a theme or rather the Protagonist. We wanted to see "an elephant," in different shades of prosperity. When we imagine an elephant, our hands take the form of the trunk and we sway with grace, flushing out the happy hormones and letting the neurons within us to dance. Whether it's in our school days or as a parent, I think most of us love to share stories related to an Elephant. The very mention brings out not the gigantism but the grace of carrying our mind and body gracefully just like an elephant.

Have you ever watched an elephant dancing in rain?

Have you imagined elephants smelling the flowers?

Have you seen them fighting or crying?

An elephant is just not an animal alone, it is carrying on its shoulders elephants of stories and experiences to share with us. It doesn't like it to be played as an animal in schools during the fancy dress competitions alone, it wants it to be heard! They have thoughts and emotions too. They aren't a mere object to be identified as, "e for elephant," nor as a picture to be coloured in the crafts or drawing classes. They want us to hear about their evolution, what is family to them, what it is being a friend, what it is being grounded in spite of their heights of growth, what it is being treated as an object of display in a zoo, what it is being vulnerable, what it is loosing a part of them to the Human's thirst, and, why they behave the way they do when harmed or when we step into their boundary? The stories are endless.

How can an elephant add prosperity? "How" as such might take several books to be answered. To me, they are just a prosperity in different shades and each shade has its own story to be shared. Why Airavata as a title might be your next question.

Airavata, as the name goes, is a white Elephant with more than one head, some say 3-5, some say even 3-30. It can be in any number, as per different schools of thought. The thoughts might vary but the emotion for an elephant remains the same. In today's scenario, can we spot or get an opportunity to see an Airavata, well, not in real though, but we thought we could bring that visualization of yours through our writers in this anthology. Each and every story shared carries its energy, love and happiness and gratitude. Gratitude as a word is easier said and felt, than actually practicing the same. I feel that we could feel the gravity of this word in an elephant's eyes. They bring us the reality about consciousness and awareness, I don't know if this is the reason we call him Lord of Consciousness, The Lord to whom we offer our prayers before starting a work or a new beginning in our life, The Lord known for his humbleness, The Lord who teaches us to be one under all circumstances of growth in our life..

This Anthology also brings several elements to awakening our consciousness and to be aware about what we do and how we do certain things. An Airavata more than being an animal, is The Conscious mind within us, alerting us constantly to be aware about our Thoughts and emotions and align them in a way that would give 'Bliss' as an outcome. As you pick this read we are sure you will be delighted to read each and every story and story-poem woven by our writers. May the Airavata sway its prosperity through our writers your way!

Airavata is a collection of weaves brought to you by Children and Adult writers.

Also, wish to share that two of our Editors are also part of this Anthology, our process of selection or editing have been transparent that it has been reviewed at every stage and it's a teamwork that we bring to you.

Meera V

Founder of Mayakatha

Notes of the Editors

Deepti Sharma

It has been an incredible experience editing Airavata, an anthology in children's fiction space, however adults would equally enjoy these heart-warming stories about the most adorable elephants. The moral values carved out in every story will make you pause and think, inculcating empathy and love for animals. A definite must-read for children.

Thank you,

Deepti Sharma

Preeti S. Manaktala

I came across this beautiful project and was instantly attracted to it. The delight of seeing an elephant in all its glory still makes me jump with joy. God's most magnificent beings on this earth that makes everyone, both young and old, stop in their tracks and watch !

Elephants! These huge animals and highly sensitive beings, makes me wonder at times, what they think of us as humans !

It was a sheer delight going through all the stories. They have myriad shades and flavors of sentiments and feelings. Each story powerfully connects, exhibits and explores the world of elephants. I am in awe of the imagination used by the writers to create characters and sketch the plot of their story.

Thank you

Preeti S. Manaktala.

Shristee Singh

Elephants can not only be cute but also valorous! That's what I learned from the stories penned by children on Airavata. From the land of mythology to the jungles the children have beautifully crafted stories that speaks volumes about their imagination and innocence. Editing for Airavata came with a challenge in the festive season of Vijaydashami. Nevertheless it was a beautiful learning experience. Editing stories for children was not easy but I have tried my best to keep them as original as they have come from the innocent hearts. My best wishes to the little writers. Hoping to read their novels soon as they grow in their journey.

Thank you,

Shristee Singh

CONTENTS

Enlightened Gajju 1

Faith moves mountains 4

Meghnad 7

Together forever… 17

Musical Tale 26

Airavata Maharaj ki Jai! 29

Renu in Haritham 35

The Tug of War 46

A Pure Love Story 51

All in a Night's Time 62

The Little Zola 73

Yaanai kutty and Mooshak 79

Little Gobu 87

The Elephant and the Snail 92

When an Elephant Comes To School 97

Imaginations Run Wild 104

In Pursuit of Peace and Harmony 108

The Albino Princess 114

Gappu's Homeward Journey 120

Airavata goes to the Lake 124

The Memorable Birthday 128

True Friendship Never Ends 135

Rathi and Damayanti 139

25 Days Around the World 145

Jumborina and Rose Fairy 151

Airavata 162

Sumukha's Saga 166

Love beyond 171

Love Knows No Bounds 181

The Dancing Elephant 185

The Elephant in the Room 188

Pintoo in the Temple 194

Kokkitu's not-so-secret Gift 202

Little Jumbo's 208

The Fall of Insunisi 209

Eela's Experience: Exasperated-to-Elated 218

Heroic Han 222

Jumbo's Happiness Formula 227

A Case of Collective Nouns 231

Chadanese Reunion 244

Not all of them… 249

Daredevil Pintu 252

Kuki & the Elephant 260

The Night-flower Quest 263

The Compiler 267

The Editors 268

The Illustrator 271

Enlightened Gajju

Aparna Menon

Once upon a time, in the kingdom of clouds, there lived an elephant named, Gajju. He was the first cousin of Lord Indra's elephant Airavata. Gajju had two white pearl-coloured tusks and two ears hanging like big fans. His beautiful small eyes and broad body made him noticeable among others. He strode with grace on his four legs and short tail in between. Now, Gajju was different from other elephants. He was a very handsome elephant as he had distinctive white spots all over his lovely grey skin. To top it all, he was born with a magical trunk. Gajju's magical trunk had the power to suck up all the water in the watery underworld and spray it into the clouds, which in turn fell as rain on Earth.

One day, a specific region on Earth faced severe drought, and the grief-stricken humans prayed to Lord Indra for rain. But as Indra's power had depleted due to his recent illness, he could not fulfil such a wish. Indra was in a dilemma on how to satisfy his devotees. Further on, he had too much pride to show his weakness to the humans. So, as he sat pondering for a solution, his aide Airavata suddenly remembered his cousin Gajju's power. Airavata suggested that Indra should go and meet Gajju and seek his help. The next day, at the crack of dawn, they both set out to the kingdom of clouds.

Gajju was meeting his cousin after a decade and was delighted to see him. After exchanging pleasantries, Airavata explained Indra's position and urged Gajju to help them out this one time. Gajju loved his cousin Airavata too much to turn him down, so he readily agreed to help Indra. But there was a problem. Gajju had recently sucked up all the water from the watery underworld, and it was too soon to go there again for more water. So, he needed a new source of water.

Indra suggested Gajju to take water from a vast lake in the kingdom of Bhrampur. This village was blessed with water in abundance, and therefore,

2   Airavata

even if Gajju took some, it would not harm the people inhabiting there. However, there was a big hurdle yet to be tackled. In this lake, there lived a demon crab named Creek. This crab was so giant that it could catch any creature, even as big as elephants and kill them. Hence, no creature dared to go near that lake.

Indra had already warned Gajju about Creek's presence and asked him to be careful. Gajju chose a quiet afternoon while Creek was snoozing. He extended his trunk and started quickly sucking up the river water. But soon, Creek felt the pressure of the river water decreasing, which woke him up. He was in a terrible mood and soon sighted Gajju's trunk. He stung the trunk and clutched it so tightly that Gajju started to bleed. He trumpeted in pain and helplessness and called out to Indra for help. Gajju cried,

"Gold-clawed creature with projecting eyes,
Lake-bred, hairless, clad in bony size,
He has caught me! Hear my woeful cries!
Lord Indra! Don't leave me - help me rise!"

But Indra ignored Gajju's cries and cowardly made for a run. However, Airavata could not leave his cousin in danger. He decided to reason out and talk to the crab. He began pleading and asked Creek to let Gajju go. Airavata said,

"Of all the crabs that are in the sea,
Bhrampur or the Indian Ocean be,
You are best that I know of thee:
Hear me Creek, and let my cousin go free!"

Hearing Airavata's pleasOP67 made the evil Creek dig deeper into Gajju's flesh. Unable to bear the excruciating pain any longer, Gajju began to give up as he felt he had expended all his strength. Airavata asked Gajju to pray to Lord Vishnu. With folded hands and earnest heart, Gajju prayed,

"Oh Lord Vishnu, I call out to you
I seek shelter at your feet which is blue
You are in all hearts through n through
Enlightening every soul's view
I am in danger so large and undue
Please protect me from being chewed
Oh, supreme one, come and relieve me soon."

On hearing Gajju's earnest prayers and plightful calls, Lord Vishnu rushed to his rescue. He noticed that Gajju had already lost a lot of blood and was almost unconscious. Lord Vishnu used his sacred discus, the Sudarshana Chakra, to separate Creek's head from its body. Lord touched Gajju's trunk, and in seconds, all his wounds were instantly healed. Gajju bowed before Lord Vishnu in reverent gratitude while shedding tears of joy.

Soon Gajju's expression of joy turned into that of disappointment. Noticing this, Lord Vishnu asked him, *"What is the matter Gajju?"*

Gajju openly expressed his disappointment regarding Indra. Gajju said, *"Lord, how could Indra seek help from me and yet abandon me in time of need?"*

Angry at how Indra had fled the scene without a second thought, Gajju decided to return all the water he had sucked up back into the river. He did not want not to help Indra anymore. However, Lord Vishnu said to him,

"It is hard when you find injustice around you. But you must not let injustice smear the good deeds that can be done by you."

Lord Vishnu added that the people's need was more significant than one's personal emotions and advised Gajju to fulfil his promise to Indra and shower rain. Gajju could not turn down the Lord and hence decided to help the humans by releasing the water to the drought-stricken land. Lord Vishnu blessed Gajju to achieve Moksha and join him in Vaikuntha, the Supreme Abode of the lord, in return for his good deeds. Gajju's happiness knew no bounds, and he sang a hymn in praise of the Lord.

"त्वमेव माता च पिता त्वमेव त्वमेव बन्धुश्च सखा त्वमेव ।
त्वमेव विद्या द्रविणम् त्वमेव त्वमेव सर्वम् मम देव देव ॥"

Singing this hymn, the handsome Gajju cheerfully returned to the clouds, where he lived happily ever after. He continued to help those in need until he attained Moksha.

***

Aparna Menon is an alumnus of Cardiff University, U.K, where she completed her LLM in Commercial Law. She is a passionate writer, reader & health enthusiast. Some of her works being, "Open Source and the Law" co-authored 1st edt. 2006, edited," Morality of Profits" by Sanjeev Raman, aired her poem on Tony Cranston's, "Talking Stories" East London Radio, published a story on www.readomania.com/story/the-prince-in-pursuit-for-wisdom and contributed on creative platforms like Mayaakatha, where Stories dance and Storipur. Aparna has featured in the magazine Stay Fit (March 2019).

Faith moves mountains

Nithya Rajagopal

It was a hot summer day at the foothills of Maruthamalai in Coimbatore. Muthu was tired after a day of heavy labour. Despite fifteen years of working as a mason, he did not know that renovating a temple could be so exhausting. "You need to keep your thoughts pure when you step in for work. Remember, people come there to seek the blessings of the almighty. Every brick you place should be made of good thoughts. You are renovating God's house!" his wife told him. This, coupled with the tremendous concentration required to carve on concrete, took a toll on him every night. Every night, he slept like a log, unaware of what was happening around him.

The Jambulingam Temple, an abode to Lord Shiva and Goddess Parvati, was hundreds of years old and was being renovated by the villagers. Muthu and ten other workers, who hailed from neighbouring villages, lived in makeshift tents at the small, ancient temple gate and worked with the temple authorities for the renovation.

"Ok now come with me and carefully place it where I tell you to!" the priest pointed to a statue and told Muthu. The weak and thin Muthu carried the heavy granite statue of an elephant and placed it at the spot indicated... He secured it in its place with a layer of cement.

"Do you know who this elephant is? Airavata, the vehicle of Indra. It has magical powers and was gifted to Karthikeya on the occasion of Karthikeya's wedding with his daughter! " The ageing priest told him."After a few days, the sculptor will instal a statue of Karthikeya here!" he added.

"Oh, this is not Ganesha then? I was misled by the elephant face" The innocent man was surprised. He did not remember seeing the statue of an elephant in any temple earlier.

"No you silly man", the priest laughed. "Since you do not belong to this village, you will not be allowed to touch or place the idol of Ganesha!".

6   Airavata

Muthu felt a little disappointed. He stood looking at Airavata when the priest left and smiled. The sthapathi (the sculptor) had carved beautiful jewellery, and a face that made it seem like Airavata was smiling. In the lonely corner of the temple where Muthu was assigned work, the arrival of Airavata felt like he had company. From that day on, he greeted Airavata every morning, spoke to him when he worked, offered him his Kanji for lunch, and wished him good night when he wrapped up for the day.

As the work on the temple progressed, many devotees sponsored silver and gold jewellery for the deities. These were placed in a giant locker inside the temple's main hall, which was secured by a heavily padded lock. Only the temple authorities were allowed there. The day after the village fair, when the priest opened the door to the main hall, he found the locker open and the jewellery missing. "Oh Lord Shiva! What has happened?" the priest yelled. "Someone has stolen from the temple" He ran out weeping.

Soon the Panchayat was assembled, and everyone who was in the temple the previous evening was called upon for enquiry. As he was the last person to leave the temple and the only labourer who did not attend the fair, Muthu was blamed for the robbery. The poor man wept, denying his involvement in the crime."No sir. I didn't do it. I was too tired and I slept early!" He pleaded innocence. "But you are not from our village. I am certain you would have done this," they said and searched his clothes for the missing jewellery. Muthu felt humiliated. "I don't think he would hide them in his clothes! Let us search the wooden box where he stores his things," someone suggested. He wept, praying to Airavata, seeking help from him. "Airavata! They say you have magical powers. You have seen me everyday. Do you think I would do something like this?" The entire group headed to the little shack outside the temple where the labourers lived. They emptied the box, only to find nothing. "Maybe he has smuggled it off to his village! One of us should go there and check," the head of the Panchayat ordered. "Meanwhile, tie this man to the tree so he does not run away! How dare he set his eyes on the property of the Lord!".

So Muthu was tied to a tree outside the temple. He was not given food or water. The poor man wept all night, seeking help from Airavata, his only witness. Meanwhile, a few villagers rushed to his village to find out if the jewellery was there in his house.

That night, a herd of elephants from the neighbouring forest ran into the village, creating a ruckus. They broke the walls of a few houses located on the outskirts. "The jewellery is here! It is here!" a little boy shouted when he saw a bagful of gold and silver strewn amidst the rubbles of a blue coloured house, that of the priest!" On hearing the news from the locals, Muthu's co-workers untied him before running to see what had happened. An overwhelmed Muthu ran into the temple with tears in his eyes. He hugged Airavata, the miracle elephant, his saviour.

***

Nithya has written three sets of short stories and a novella so far, all of them with a Desi / Indian touch. Her most recent work is The Ultimate Kasi Yatra, a novella. ThanThanaThom, my first, is a collection of short stories set in Tamil Nadu. Over a Samosa, published by Readomania, is a set of ten flash fiction stories. A Ticket to Love tells the tales of four people who embark on unusual journeys.

Meghnad

Papia Ghosh (Pal)

Airavata

Chapter -1

Kalikapur was a 'jewel in the crown', surrounded by deep dark forests where the warm sun rays were forbidden entry. The heartbeat of this tiny village was 'Golpo Dadu', who lived in a tiny hut on the western edge of the village. Every evening, as the sun rode its golden chariot across the dark orange sky, the village children sat around him under the ageless peepal tree and begged him to tell them a story.

"Tell us a story, we want a story," they chortled, the cacophony of their voices merged with the chirping birds as they returned to their nests.

Golpo Dadu's dark face broke into a bright toothless smile since these children were a part of his heart. He waited for the children to settle down, took a deep breath, and then, he began his tale. His stories always started with a rhyme spun out of the dusk, which slowly unfurled its wings.

> " Long, long, ago there lived a mighty king.
>
> About his conquests, many a pagan did people sing,
>
> King Vikramjit of Vikrampur was indeed very brave,
>
> In his kingdom, there was not a slave,
>
> The mighty king never lost a battle,
>
> His enemies in fear would rattle."

Golpo Dadu cleared his throat as a hushed silence fell over his enchanted audience.

He continued, "King Vikramjit had a pet elephant named 'Meghnad'. The elephant was as dark as the new moon night, but he was no ordinary elephant. Meghnad lived in a well-guarded special stable, just next to the king's palace. Every morning, the king fed the apple of his eye with his own hands although Meghnad had a mahut named Mohan. The animal and his mahut got along very well. Before the king's arrival in the morning, Meghnad was taken to the Saraju River for a bath. After a good rub down, Mohan anointed the elephant's forehead with beautiful colourful sketches with his artistic fingers.

Airavata

Although it tickled, Meghnad stood patiently as Mohan embellished his pet with new paintings every day."

Golpo Dadu was tired, and he wanted to retire early to bed. It was so dark that they could not see each other's faces. He urged the children to run home since he could hear their parents calling out their names. Usually, the villagers had an early dinner, and a tranquil blanket of sleep soon covered the village.

Chapter – 2

The next day, the eager children gathered around the peepal tree earlier than usual. The fingers of dusk hadn't clutched the dying sun yet, and Golpo Dadu peered at the hungry faces, eager to begin.

"Meghnad floated in the sky,

With his beloved king, he did fly.

The elephant had wings,

So the legend sings.

When King Vikramjit entered the battlefield with Meghnad, he never lost a battle. The elephant trumpeted as loud as thunder, validating his name, 'Meghnad', which meant 'roar of the thunder.' Hearing his loud battle cry, the elephants and horses of the attacking army deserted the battlefield in fear carrying their soldiers away. Therefore, half the battle was won even before it began. Meghnad had the king on his back and flew over the enemies who remained on the battlefield to fight back. King Vikramjit was a skilful archer, and he shot arrows at his enemies as he flew over them. So, the king remained unharmed, but he could kill all his enemies. Thus, no one dared to attack the kingdom of Vikrampur, and the invincible King named himself 'Rajadhiraj' or 'the King of Kings.'"

Suddenly a clap of thunder startled Golpo Dadu and his little followers. "That must be Meghnad, hearing our story," Dadu chuckled. Big drops fell from the heavens on the children as they looked up to the dark sky where the afternoon sun was covered by angry slate clouds. "Run home!" urged Dadu. The children got up reluctantly and ran home while Golpo Dadu wobbled back to his hut.

Chapter 3

"Dadu please begin your story," the children pleaded. Not a single child in the village missed the story sessions of Golpo Dadu.

Dadu cleared his throat and began,

"Every year Vikrampur welcomed the rains,

So that the fields were covered with ripened grains,

To Lord Indra, everyone prayed,

Airavata

The King of Heavens, in turn, blessed every glade.

Vikrampur welcomed the monsoons by worshipping Lord Indra every year. A beautiful temple stood at the centre of the kingdom where the people prayed on the first day of the month of Shravan to appease the King of the Heavens. Rajmata Nandini was the first to offer her prayers, followed by the King, the Queen, and all his subjects. They all walked barefooted to the temple with offerings of flowers and sweets.

So that year was no different. The village woke up to the loud trumpet of Meghnad, who reminded the villagers of the special day. All the villagers woke up early, bathed and got ready to follow the royal family to the temple. There was a flurry of activities in the palace, as everyone dressed up in their finery. They decorated their hair with flowers of every hue, wore their most delicate ornaments and were ready to go.

Rajmata Nandini was getting ready. She wore a beautiful white silk saree and very few ornaments. A small diamond tiara shone in her long salt peppered hair. She smiled at the golden hand-held mirror, humming a song to herself. Just as she was about to keep the mirror on the dressing table, it fell from her hand, and the glass smashed into a thousand pieces. "O dear!" she cried. The servants came running, hearing her cry. "It's a bad omen," the Queen muttered in fear.

Just then, King Vikramjit entered her room. He took his mother in his arms and comforted her. "I will make a beautiful mirror for you," he promised. But Rajmata Nandini had tears in her eyes, "This was the last gift from your father who left us so many years ago," she wept on her son's broad shoulders. King Vikramjit dried her tears gently and tilted up her face, "We must go," he said. "The whole kingdom is waiting for you."

Rajmata Nandini steeled herself. She stepped outdoors with her offering of jasmine flowers and the special sweets she made with her own hands. The subjects shouted in joy, but above the cacophony, you could hear the loud trumpet of Meghnad, who swayed his trunk in excitement.

Rajmata began to climb down the flight of steps as the subjects cheered when suddenly her silk saree got entangled in her feet, and she stumbled down the long flight of white marble steps. The crowd was petrified while the King ran to rescue her. But alas! It was too late. The lifeless body of Rajmata lay in a pool of blood at the bottom of the steps. The white marble steps were stained with her death. The Raj Vaidhya or the Royal Physician cradled her head on his lap. He found that her body was still warm, but there was no pulse.

In a moment, the colourful celebration was overshadowed by the sorrow of a funeral. Meghnad put his trunk around his king, and they wept. The King of Kings and his favourite elephant were inconsolable. Rajmata's mortal remains were carried to the palace, and the King's officials started planning a state funeral. An eclipse of misfortune covered the land, and so, no offerings were made to the King of Heavens that year."

Golpo Dadu sighed deeply. A deafening silence engulfed the dusk as the children had unshed tears glistening in their eyes. "Go home today," he urged, clearing his throat, which was also thick with emotions. While the other children dragged their heavy feet, tiny Bholu, who was sitting behind everyone, ran into Golpo Dadu's arms and wept. He had lost his mother very recently. The old man rocked the little boy in his ageing arms and kissed away his salty tears. "Come home with me and we can have dinner together," the old man urged. But Bholu shook his head and walked away with tear-stained cheeks.

Chapter 4

Although the overcast sky grumbled and rumbled, the children gathered around Golpo Dadu to hear what happened in the kingdom of Vikrampur.

Little Bholu sat a little closer to Golpo Dadu today, and perhaps it gave the child a sense of security. The old man patted his head and began spinning his tale,

"The dark clouds covered Vikrampur's sky,

But gusts of the gale made them fly,

Not a drop of rain fell on the land,

Strong winds covered the earth with fine sand.

Since the monsoons were round the corner, everyone awaited the rains, for crops were to be sown, and the ponds and lakes were to be filled. People looked at the dark clouds anticipating heavy rainfall, but something strange happened. Whenever the sky was covered with grey clouds, gusts of strong wind blew them away. It rained beyond the kingdom of Vikrampur, but not a drop fell within. Thus, Vikrampur was surrounded by heavy showers, but there was no rainfall in the kingdom. Instead, the storms brought in fine grains of sand, and they filled the fields!

King Vikramjit was very worried. Although the king was still grieving over the sudden death of his mother, he knew that no rains meant no crops. He understood that Lord Indra was offended since no offerings were made. As he was feeding Meghnad, the king was absent-minded, for he knew that there would soon be a famine. All the ponds and most of the lakes had already dried up, so the people faced an acute water crisis.

Meghnad put his trunk around the king, for he knew that something was not right. "I wish Lord Indra would forgive us. Meghnad, can't you help us? Can you go to the heavens to meet Lord Indra?" the King pleaded. The elephant shook his head. He was ready to give up his life for his Master."

Golpo Dadu paused to catch a breath. "Go home," he urged, "It is going to rain very soon." "We want to hear more, please, please Dadu," the children shouted unanimously. Just then, a loud thunderbolt struck, and the children shrieked in unison and ran pell-mell. Golpo Dadu hobbled back to his hut as fast as his old legs could carry him.

Chapter 5

It was raining quite heavily throughout the day, and in the afternoon, there was a light drizzle. The children came running to the peepal tree where Golpo Dadu stood with an umbrella. "Come into my hut," he urged. "Be quick! The ground is wet here." The children did not need any further invitation, and they ran behind him. Soon they huddled around Golpo Dadu, who lit a lamp to dissipate the darkness. As the skies broke down into a fresh downpour, Dadu cleared his throat and began,

"Meghnad had magical wings,

So the legend sings,

He whooshed into the sky,

His master the King watched with a sigh.

As King Vikramjit poured his heart out to Meghnad, the intelligent elephant listened attentively. He bowed before the King as if to say that he was ready, and then Meghnad whooshed into the sky. The King stood rooted to the spot with a deep sigh as the elephant grew smaller and smaller, and finally, he disappeared.

When Meghnad reached the dark clouds, he found that Lord Indra's white elephant Airavata was blowing away the dark rain-laden clouds as they were about to float over the skies of Vikrampur. Meghnad let out a loud trumpet which startled Airavata.

"Now what do you think you are doing?" shouted Meghnad. "It is my Lord's order," called back Airavata. "You better stop if you value your life !!" shouted Meghnad.

The two elephants began wrestling with each other, which shook the heavens. Meanwhile, the dense dark clouds floated over Vikrampur, and the people of the kingdom shouted in joy as drops of rain drenched the parched earth.

Meghnad defeated Airavata and was about to strangle him when the heavens boomed. "Stop!" someone shouted, and to their surprise, Lord Indra appeared. Meghnad slowly released Airavata and bowed before the Lord.

"Airavata, can you recognize your brave son?" Lord Indra said with a smile. "This was the baby you had abandoned in the forests of Vikrampur because he was black in colour," he said.

Airavata hung his head in shame. There were tears of regret in his eyes. "Forgive me, my son," he wept. Meghnad couldn't believe his ears. Father and son hesitantly embraced each other, and it seemed as if day and night had met.

"Come to my palace brave Meghnad and stay with me," invited the King of the Kings. Meghnad bent low and shook his head. "I cannot be my Lord. Vikrampur is my home and King Vikramjit is my master and my father. He loves me more than his own child. I can't leave him."

Airavata

Lord Indra was impressed by the honesty and integrity of the young elephant. "Please bless our kingdom with wealth and prosperity," pleaded the elephant.

"Don't you want anything for yourself," the Lord inquired with a smile. Meghnad shook his head. Touched by the humility of the elephant, Lord Indra blessed him. "You will be the strongest magical elephant on Earth."

Thus, the King of the Heavens blessed Meghnad and the Kingdom of Vikrampur. Airavata was so proud of his son. "Forgive me," he begged again. "I just judged you by your external appearance. I am so proud of you. Whenever you are in trouble, just call your father and he will be there by your side."

Meghnad embraced his father. "Do come to visit me from time to time," he pleaded. "Sometimes I feel so lonely." "I will, I will," promised Airavata.

Soon Meghnad returned to Vikrampur, where the whole kingdom along with their King stood in the rain to welcome their hero. King Vikramjit embraced Meghnad amidst loud cheers, and their tears of joy mingled the rains. The King made a statue of Meghnad just outside their temple. If you visit Vikrampur, you will see the temple and the statue of Meghnad."

"Can we go there Dadu?" asked Bholu. "Of course, you can if you know the way," replied Dadu with a toothless smile. "Dadu take us there," the children chortled while the skies overhead sighed with relief, allowing the children to go home.

"Run along," urged Golpo Dadu, "We can plan a trip to Vikrampur tomorrow."

***

Papia Ghosh is a post graduate in Economics with a flair for writing poems and short stories. She is currently working as a Senior Instructor at Word Munchers.

Together forever...

Shristee Singh

'Fire in the mountain run, run, run!' Yelled little Gaj beaming with joy as he saw the glow worms come out one by one around the forest trees. He ran playfully with his trunk swaying to and fro like a pendulum. Running under the canopy of the dense forest, his joy knew no bound upon seeing the glow worms shimmering in the darkness. There was something mystical about them that he loved.

Gaj would eagerly wait for the golden ball to become orange and hide behind the giant trees. When birds took shelter in their nests, hyenas howled, and the owls hooted, glow worms would come out, twinkling like a cluster of stars in the pitch darkness of the forest. They danced literally, performing an opera while crickets stridulate, playing background music for them in the dense forest. Gaj would look at them and then the stars above. He would watch them mesmerized for hours.

He loved the jungle, which was inhabited by his huge family for thousands of years. He lived in peace there with his parents, aunties, uncles and cousins. The scented trees produced sweet-smelling flowers and fruits, the wildflowers adding colour to the verdant carpet and the springs' gurgling sound, and the songs of the exotic birds and animals added hue and music to the jungle. Indeed, it was a perfect retreat for all of them!

'Gaj… Gaaaaaj,' cried Jugni, making him come out of trance.

Gaj turned around to see Jugni hovering over him. Jugni was a little glow worm who had besotted him with her sparkling tail. Unlike Gaj, who had four legs to walk, Jugni was blessed with wings that could take her anywhere and everywhere. Gaj was always in awe of her! Sometimes, her ability to fly and shine made him feel jealous, but whenever he saw Jugni's sweet smile, his jealousy evaporated in thin air.

'Let's go!' Jugni said, flapping her tender wings in front of his face. Gaj's pupil dilated, seeing the light coming from her tail. He knew his friend was here for some adventure.

'Amma, I am taking Gaj for a walk.' Jugni buzzed near Gaj's mother's giant earlobes. Amma smiled, looking at the confidence of the tiny beetle. She knew how her son loved the company of the glow worm.

'Don't go very far dear!' She said amicably, fondling Gaj's head with her trunk. Amma's calf was growing up and needed to explore the woods on her own. However, she always kept her watchful eyes upon him wherever he went.

Flying before Gaj, Jugni moved with the poise as though her little illuminating tail was just a perfect torch to show the way in the dark night.

'Let's go towards the pond!' Jugni beamed with excitement.

'Ehhh… So that you can admire the reflection of your glowing tail.' Gaj smirked.

'Oh dear! How I wish I could do that. But the pond has become like a puddle now. There's hardly any water there.' Jugni said.

She was right, Gaj reflected. There was now not even enough water for him to sit and sink his large body in it. Remembering the good old days when his whole family would swim in it and play with water, splashing it on one another with their trunks, he sucked in some water and sprayed it on his back, getting temporary relief from the heat.

Jugni loved the lotus growing in the pond. She hovered over the close buds of lotus, looking for a safe place to land. While Gaj stood on its bank, his gaze followed her. The water in the pond was pristine. It was a sight to behold when millions of stars played peek-a-boo on its surface. However, tonight, the sky was covered with a thick smoky cloud forming a curtain that did not allow the stars to peep from above.

'What happened, Jugni?' Asked Gaj as he noticed Jugni's face turning pale.

'Shhhhh… can't you see!' She whispered. 'There is a frog sitting there. I am sure you don't want me to be served his dinner tonight!'

Their home was one of the most beautiful forests where everyone lived together. But it was also full of predators and scavengers. It seemed that everyone here was after everyone for food!

'It's the survival of the fittest my son.' Amma had once told him when he saw how the ferocious lion hunted down a deer tearing him into pieces, making blood ooze out of his fragile body. He chewed its flesh and then left it for the scavengers to have the rest. Leaving aside animals, there were plants that ate up insects when they entered their terrain. Jugni was very careful and kept herself away from those dreaded areas where carnivorous plants relished bugs.

Tonight, it wasn't one of the cool breezy nights. The temperature was higher than usual, and the forest was glowing with a peculiar kind of light from far.

'Jugni what kind of light is that?'

'A giant glow worm I guess... some cousin of mine.' Jugni said playfully, flapping her wings.

'No Jugni... It's not funny! See the sparks. The crackling sound... Can you hear that!' Gaj stood in attention. He had a strong sense of hearing. His parents had sensed something terrible was going to happen and had already warned him. The temperature in the woods was rising, and the heat was unbearable at times. The bushes had literally dried up. This made them have a tough time looking for food.

The hunting folks were still better off! They killed the weaker ones to fill their tummies, but the ones who depended on vegetation were simply starving.

'Listen carefully Jugni, I can hear them wailing.'

Sitting on Gaj's forehead, Jugni took a deep breath. The air was suffocating, unlike other days when it would fill her lungs with vigour and energy. Gaj could see the change in the skyline. It was gradually becoming hazy, getting covered with a sheet of thick smoke.

'Gaj, our forest is on fire!' Jugni shouted in horror as her eyes welled up with tears. 'The flames are coming towards this side. The wind is strong and it is feeding the fire.'

'But we are on this side of the pond! The fire will not come here.'

'Don't be silly. The forest is connected. We need to rush home and inform our families about the fire before it reaches here.'

While Gaj was still trying to comprehend what Jugni had said, he saw several animals running and hopping from the direction where the orange glow was flaring. The birds warbled in confusion. Tiny insects ran helter-skelter. Everyone looked horrified.

'Run Gaj, run from here…. There is fire in the woods!' Screamed Jugni. Gaj saw his kangaroo friend, who could hop for miles without taking any break. Her tan fur was covered with ash. Her skin was burned. Her little calf in the pouch looked nauseated with the smoke.

'Gaj there's not much time. Run… run fast!' Jugni screamed, petrified, as she saw flames shaping up like a monster. In no time, the fire reached them, devouring everything that came in its way.

Trees, the helpless victims, were crackling with flame, flaring up like matchsticks. They couldn't run around and thwart the dire situation. Birds that had made their abode on its branches had already deserted them. They cried in pain for help as flames engulfed the barks. But nobody came to rescue.

The peaceful night suddenly turned out to be the most terrifying one. Animals were running in the absolute pell-mell, causing a stampede. Many had bruised themselves getting trampled, while the ones trapped in fire gave out shrill cries as the flames consumed them.

Gaj tried to pick up speed too. But it seemed the fire moved much faster than him. Dry grass flared up with the wind effortlessly, and he was soon surrounded by the roaring blaze.

Gaj was flummoxed seeing all the animals howling and crying and running for life.

Like other animals, he, too, was scared of loud noise and fire. Living in serenity, he couldn't bear the loud noise of any kind. It was simply unendurable for him. It would hit his eardrums, causing immense trauma. So much so that Gaj and his family communicated with each other using extremely low frequency, which was hardly audible for many.

The smell of burned skin and plants was now filling up the air. Searing flame made the plants and animals gasp for breath. There was absolutely no escape. The fire was literally everywhere.

Amid the chaos, Gaj wanted to help others. But he did not know-how. He wanted to give shelter and protection to the traumatized animals. His tender heart wanted to do something for the habitats of the woods, but how… He looked around with confusion. Suddenly, an idea struck him. He turned back to go to the pond.

Airavata

'Gaj why are u going back?' Jugni screamed when she saw him turning around. As she tried to follow him, a whip of flame entangled her.

'Jugniii....'Gaj let out a loud trumpet in distress when he saw her being consumed by the flames.

He ran towards the pond without wasting any time. His feet burned as he ran over the smouldering grass. The sparks from the flame made the tiny hair on his back burn, emanating a foul odour. The puddle was heavily swathed with smoke now. The black and beautiful night was now consumed by the horrendous flames.

He drew some water from the pond with his trunk and squirted it over Jugni. But it was too late. The flames had charred her tiny body in no time. The monstrous fire came down with the water for a moment but roared up again, hurtling towards him.

Losing his best friend to the fire, Gaj now took this fight with the fire personally. *Come what may, I will not let the fire grow!*

He remembered what his father had told him: **survival of the fittest**. '*I will douse you, I am not going to give up so long as there is water in the pond.*' And he ran to and fro from one puddle to another, drawing water in his trunk, spraying it on the fire. The dancing flames scared him to the core, but he didn't give up. How he wished his family was around, for his little trunk could not hold enough water to put off the fire.

He went on relentlessly, sucking water and squirting it on the flames. The smell of burned skin was becoming pungent. His feet were hurting badly as they trampled the flaring ground. His eyes pained due to the acidic smoke, and his lungs were asphyxiated, but he did not give up.

The fire was the nemesis of the jungle from ancient times, but today he was bent upon fighting this enemy.

So long as there was energy in him, he would not give up. His father would be very proud of him, he thought as he dreamed of being crowned in the herd and applauded for saving the jungle. The jungle that was their abode for thousands of years. The jungle where he was born and played with his friends. The jungle where Jugni lived…

His tail had caught fire. His eyes were filled with tears as he thought of Jugni and her beautiful glowing tail, but *ouch*, his tail was hurting.

'Gaj… Gaaaaj…'

Amma and Baba were making their way through the fire and smoke. They half-burned themselves as they made their way towards the pond. They had heard his trumpet and followed the direction.

'Gaj… What are you doing here? You should have come to us when the fire started.'

'Baba, I was trying to put the fire off.' Gaj said, panting. 'Ss… see my taa…taa… tail… looks like Jugni's!' He said, holding a brave front, while a tear escaped from the corner of his eye. 'Jugni got burned Baba. I could not save her.' And he burst into tears.

'Gaj, you tried your best, boy! You are brave, but the fire is rife and can't be controlled. Let's hurry and move out of here!

Gaj's family had a beautiful trait… they never left behind any of their family members however grave the danger was!

***

A believer of one world family, Shristee loves to write songs of the soul. She had won copper medal for an All India Creative Writing competition while in school. She was also recognised for her contribution for English poetry in Youth festival of Lucknow Mahotsav. She had been a nominee for the Author of the Year-2019 at StoryMirror for her contribution towards English literature. Currently she is based out of Hyderabad and besides writing in her free time, works as Associate Editor with Chrysanthemum Chronicles.

Airavata
Musical Tale

Sreeja Mohandas

Once upon a time, long, long ago in the dense green forest of Uttampur, lived a herd of elephants. Now, these elephants were a sight to behold!

> Tall they were
>
> with skin like ebony.
>
> With long, curling tusks
>
> Of real ivory, nothing phoney.
>
> Great, big elephants and ones that were tinny,
>
> All types they were, slim, stocky, plump, and skinny.

My story begins here, my young friend,

So, for a few minutes, your ears do lend.

The elephants were very excited on that particular sunny day. Clouds that looked like popcorn played merrily in the sky, and the streams giggled as they fell over rocks on their way through the forest. The herd was expecting yet another brand new baby elephant!

Queen elephant waited for the announcement of the new baby in excitement. This meant that their herd would increase by one more member, and she prayed that the baby elephant would be as strong as the beautiful and powerful Mama elephant, Durga.

"It is a girl, your Majesty." trumpeted the happy messenger. "Both Mama and baby are doing fine."

Queen elephant sighed in relief as she accepted one of the nectar-like sweet mangoes that had come as a gift along with the news.

A baby girl was good for the herd.

Mama elephant, Durga looked at her pretty daughter in both joy and alarm. The little elephant was the prettiest one the herd had seen so far, with beautiful pearl grey skin and delicate eyes and ears. But what alarmed Mama Durga was that the baby elephant hadn't trumpeted so far. She had cleaned her and nursed her, but not a squeak had the little one made! She just lay looking at her with blue-grey, almond-shaped eyes without uttering a sound.

Mama Durga lifted the little one in her trunk and brought her closer to examine her. Just as she placed a kiss on the baby's head, the little one trumpeted out a perfect musical note. Mama listened in wonder. The baby trumpeted again. It was a song that lasted for a minute or two. The elephant aunts who had been standing close came up to Mama Durga looking very worried.

"Can't the baby trumpet then?" asked Aunt one.

"Her throat must be blocked, shake her a bit dear. It will clear out then." cooed Aunt two soothingly.

"Feed her again, quickly." panicked Aunt three. "Her voice sounds terrible. She must be hungry."

Mama elephant laughed aloud at their words. "She is just special, aunts. She is fine. You wait and see. I shall name this one Nakshatra, for a star she is and a star she will be. We shall call her Tara for short."

Tara grew up in the forest, a happy little creature, in the company of her playmates, who were surprisingly a monkey named Jamoon and a fawn named Shwetha. Sadly, the other little elephants did not play with her. They found her different, and her musical trumpeting scared them. The baby elephants stayed away from her as much as they could.

"You are not like us, Tara. We don't want to play with you."

This had made Tara very sad at first, and she had complained to her mother, but her mother always comforted her with the words, "You are special, Tara. They do not understand you. Give them time. They will be your friends one day. Also, you are lucky to have special friends like Jamoon and Shwetha." And so Tara continued playing with her non-elephant friends until that terrible day.

Airavata

It was that special day of the year when the Queen took the young elephants of the herd on a tour of her royal forest grounds. The Queen did this all by herself when she spoke to the young ones and decided who would be the future Queen among them. The tour always ended with a royal feast.

The elephant Mamas had been preparing for this grand event. They cleaned and sparkled their babies' trunks, ears, and toes and made flower garlands for their little necks. When the great Queen walked in to meet them, she was met by twelve little elephants, standing neatly in a row, trunks held high. Proud mamas huddled in the distance. Tara stood in great excitement amidst the others. Her friends Jamoon and Shwetha waved and cheered from a distance.

The tour began. The little elephants were having a lovely time watching new sights and listening to their clever Queen when it happened, quite suddenly. The Queen fell into a pit that had been half-hidden under large, fallen branches. She could have easily stepped out herself, but she had twisted her leg and, unable to move, had fainted with the pain.

The little elephants were terrified and confused at first. Then, all of them, including Tara, tried pulling the Queen out of the pit. It was impossible! She was too big, and they were too small. Also, this part of the forest was new to them, and they didn't know the way back to their mamas. They tried trumpeting aloud and calling out to their mamas, but the heavy rain that had begun drowned their voices out. They couldn't be heard. So after a while, they stopped crying and stood around the pit, shivering in the cold rain, looking miserable.

Seeing their sad faces, Tara dried her own tears and decided to give it one last try. Climbing up on a small rock, she held out her little trunk high and trumpeted out a song, loud and clear. The other little elephants looked on in wonder. When Tara finished the first one, the brave little elephant trumpeted yet another song. She was just as tired as her mates, but she just wouldn't stop. Now that the other little elephants had stopped their trumpeting, the notes of Tara's musical trumpeting rose high above the roar of the rain and flew right up to her Mama's flapping ears.

"That is Tara." said Mama Durga in alarm. "Our Queen must be in trouble, let us go find them." The mama elephants followed the sound of Tara's song and within minutes reached the hurt Queen and their weeping babies. Together, they pulled out the Queen from the pit and helped her back home, with a very tired Tara and the frightened yet happy little elephants staying close.

The Queen recovered in a few days and called for a grand celebration. The elephant mamas arrived with their babies for the feast. Tara's friends Jamoon and Shwetha were present too. Just before the feast began, the Queen called out to Mama Durga and asked her to bring Tara to her. A happy Tara went up to the Queen with her proud mother beside her. The Queen placed her great, big trunk on Tara's head and said loudly and clearly.

"Tara saved my life by bringing all of you to my rescue. This just goes to show that she is different for a reason. She is a born leader. I am thankful to her and I choose her as the next Queen."

The entire herd cheered in happiness, and the feast began. As Tara chomped on a delicious bunch of bananas, she smiled at her mother. Her mother had been right after all, for all the baby elephants were now her friends. They were proud of her and admired her musical trumpeting.

Being different was not so bad after all.

***

Sreeja Mohandas is a Writer and and a Poet. An English Language Trainer and a Social Counsellor by profession, she is also a Media person. She is a Voice Over Artist and is on the All India Radio panel as well.

Airavata Maharaj ki Jai!

Sonia Dogra

At the break of dawn, the Mishra clan stood at the Lakshman Jhula, waiting for two household members to join them. It was a morning in December of 1983, and the tingling sting of the cold air on his cheeks made Narendranath Mishra pull his scarf closer to his face. He was a well-built, thirty-five-year-old man with an air of confidence about him. On his shoulders, he carried Chhotu, the youngest chirag of the family who sat there, curiously inspecting the terrain like a mahout and shooting non-stop questions at his father. Next to the family patriarch stood the teenage twins, Babita and Kavita, with bags on their backs and frowns on their faces. They would have preferred a languorous day in bed with Rishi Kapoor songs playing in the background in place of the trek to Neelkanth temple. There was another person who agreed with them. Eleven-year-old Satish, the eldest of the three boys, all skin and bones and forever tired. Narendranath and his wife had tried every available home remedy to beef him up, but all in vain.

'I think we can start walking,' Narendranath addressed the children. 'It will take us a good time once the climb starts. Those two can catch up.' He shrugged his shoulders forcefully, throwing Chhotu up in the air, who giggled as he now settled on his baba's back, just like a sack of rice. The party then forged ahead, some with a zing and the others sluggishly behind them.

Back in room number 135 of Swargashram, which was a temporary winter retreat for the family, Kalavati Mishra hurriedly forced a multicoloured sweater down nine-year-old Anil's head.

'I think it's time you passed this on to Chhotu,' the boy garbled. 'It's rather tig..fftttm hhff mm…' he gasped for air.

'Chhotu has enough. It will do well for you this winter,' said Kalavati, pushing him towards the door. 'And now, we must hurry up.'

Anil was a fast runner, but today the family heirloom on his torso made him uncomfortable. Nonetheless, he held his mother's hand as the two flew past the Lakshman Jhula to be with the rest of the clan in no time.

'What's in there?' Satish was pulling at the string of Babita's bag when they caught up. The girl almost lost her balance.

'Don't you dare!' she snapped. 'You get to eat this only when you reach the top. By the way, stuffed puris and timur namak,' she said, walking off.

'Come on, I'm tired,' Satish called from behind.

'O chhori,' Kalavati's penetrating voice made everyone turn back. ``Give my boy a laddoo from the dabba,'' she said, walking towards the girls with significant steps.

The twins rolled their eyes in unison.

'I can have one too,' Anil followed his mother.

'Not at all!' She pulled him back.

Narendranath Mishra stood at the far end of the road. He had put Chhotu down and was waving vigorously to get his family's attention. 'We are wasting time,' he shouted. But the commotion around the laddoos refused to die down, which made him walk all the way back, Chhotu in tow right behind him.

Kalavati was a bundle of nerves by that time as Anil stood nibbling at not one but two laddoos simultaneously. Taking charge of the situation like the head of the family, Narendranath made them all sit down in the corner of the road flanked by a thick jungle of sal trees on both sides. He chose to appease his wife first with a bottle of water. Then he opened the steel dabba once again and handed over a piece of sweetmeat each to the girls and one to Chhotu. He sat down next to Kalavati and looked up. The sun wasn't visible as yet, but its faint light dappled the thick jungle.

Narendranath cleared his throat. 'At this rate we will not reach the temple before noon. We haven't even started climbing up yet,' he said. 'And don't you all want to enjoy the lush gardens up there? We will eat, play and pray. It's going to be a wonderful picnic!'

'Why did we have to walk all the way?' Satish asked. He was agitatedly prodding a bush with a twig.

'Because I wanted you to see this beautiful jungle road with its towering canopies. Looks like a fairy tale world of magic, doesn't it?'

'I remember coming for this trek while I was still a school girl,' Kalavati added. 'The hike is as arduous today as it was back then. Just the reason I wanted these girls to wear flip-flops but they must have their way.' She tightened her lips and sneered at the twins, who looked down at their not-so-high heels.

'Let them be,' Narendranath intervened.

'And what if we are chased by a group of monkeys or encounter those wild elephants on the way? How are they to run in their click clacks?' the irate mother retorted.

Anil, who had gobbled both laddoos by that time, looked at Kalavati with his eyes wide open. 'Monkeys and elephants! Is this a safari?' he asked.

'Sort of,' Narendranath said, lifting Chhotu in his arms and wiping off his sticky mouth while half a laddoo lay almost strangled in his fist. 'And now we must be off before Airavata Maharaj discovers us.' With that, he began to walk once again, with the train following him closely. Babita and Kavita were on either side of their mother, trying to convince her how comfortable their heels were and Satish dawdled behind them.

It was only nine in the morning, and it felt as if they had been walking for ages. A group of boys had already crossed them, and a couple going up on a Vespa had waved happily. Satish had wanted to squeeze between them in whatever space was available on the scooter, but Narendranath refused point-blank.

'Nothing doing. How will you ever build your stamina, boy?'

'Will we get to see the monkey baba?' Anil, who had kept pace with his father, wanted to know.

'Definitely. If not here, then certainly at the temple.'

'Will they attack us?'

'Not if you aren't eating anything.'

'And what if we are?'

'You just give it up and let them have it.'

'And what if I don't?' Satish joined in.

'Well,' chimed in Kalavati, 'then they will make sure they snatch it from you.'

Hearing this, Chhotu dusted the remaining ladoo off his hand.

'Don't worry,' Anil looked at him, 'monkeys don't like half-eaten, mashed ladoos,' he laughed. Chhotu scowled at him while the others too burst into laughter.

'And what about Airavata Maharaj? Does he like laddoos or puris?' Satish was curious now and had raced ahead of everyone. Kalavati was mighty pleased to see the boy marching right in front.

'Elephants love bananas, right baba?' Kavita leapt from behind, joining in the discussion.

Narendranath nodded. He was finding it difficult to talk while walking with Chhotu upon his shoulders once again. He wished to walk in silence. He remembered trekking up to Neelkanth several times as a boy and later as a young man, but it hadn't seemed so tough back then. A few minutes passed without a murmur. Narendranath turned around to see the others. Kalavati had removed her shawl and was already bathing in sweaty drops. The girls seemed to lament their decision about the heels, and Satish was again trailing far behind. The excitement he had managed to generate at the last stop had died down. Would they be able to complete the trek? Most importantly, would he be able to walk all the way up? What would his family think of him?

Narendranath was considering a second halt when the snapping of a twig made his ears stand up.

'Baba...' Anil tried to get his attention, but he held his finger to his lips, asking the boy to keep shut.

The others hurried to join Narendranath, a mix of fear and confusion visible on their faces. The orchestra of birdsongs that had occasionally been rising in the forest had ceased and in place of that arose the screeching noise of monkeys scurrying over treetops. It was only half-past ten, and the never-ending avenue seemed miles away from the first climb to Neelkanth. Had the family patriarch misjudged the trek?

'Baba,' Anil whispered, 'what is it?'

'Follow me,' said Narendranath.

The ménage scampered after him, halting only at the end of the road. Narendranath gestured to all of them to sit down. 'We might be getting lucky,' he said, putting down Chhotu. 'I sense a herd nearby. But I'm not sure how long before….' He gulped down a bottle of water. 'Maybe a few minutes or even a few hours. Will waiting right here make sense?'

He scanned the party, momentarily pausing to meet Kalavati's eyes. The latter stared at the man's face, beads of sweat adorning her brow. She shook her head.

'I think we must wait right here,' she stood up, brushing the dust off her hands. 'My girls can't seem to manage the click clack and Satish is ready to drop. We can hope for a safari here, right Anil?' she said, making a face at her husband.

So, it was decided. There was more adventure in waiting for a herd of elephants than climbing up the hill. The korai mat was spread in a bit of clearing right next to the road. The girls took off their sandals and wiggled their toes. Satish lay down right in the centre only to be nudged by Anil, who was quite capable of making a place for himself. That left Kalavati and Narendranath to find a spot each on the sodden leaves with Chhotu dozing off on his father's lap.

The next few hours were spent polishing off the stuffed puris and laddoos and an occasional fruit that had been thrown into the basket at the last moment. The bananas were saved diligently for Airavata Maharaj and his tribe. A hoot of monkeys or rustle of leaves was sometimes misconstrued as signs of an approaching herd, but as the day wore off, so did these sounds. The couple on the Vespa waved on their way back, and more and more people descended from the temple. It was then that Narendranath decided that they too must head back to Swargashram.

Empty dabbas made their way into the bags, and the party turned homeward. As they dragged their feet underneath the green and black canopy, Narendranath began the customary headcount. 'One, two, three, four, five, six….' He looked around and repeated. Someone was missing.

'Anil… where is Anil?' he shouted, and handing over Chhotu to Kalavati, he turned around to check on his little boy. There, a few metres away, stood Anil with his back to his father, and right ahead of him, a family of four majestic tuskers regally walked across the road.

The Mishras froze as Narendranath stood with a beatific smile on his face. The still Rishikesh jungle road suddenly began to echo with cries of "Airavata Maharaj ki jai!" as five young picnickers sealed their outing with a befitting end.

***

Sonia is a writer based in Delhi. She holds a personal record of submitting for anthologies and is unapologetic about badgering lit magazines with her submissions. A poet and romantic at heart, she is happy being a small fish in a big pond. Find her most active on her blog 'A Hundred Quills'

Renu in Haritham

Srivalli Rekha

The animals lived with their families and friends in the vast forest of Haritham. The rabbits hopped and scuttled around, nibbling grass. A deer darted through the trees, playing and searching for food. The monkeys swung from one branch to another, and the squirrels collected nuts.

Ants continued to build their anthills while the snakes tried to sneak in. Birds fly overhead, piling twigs and dry leaves to make a nest for their future babies. The old lion lived in a cave and came out only to hunt. However, he was a fair ruler, and his subjects were happy. Life was as good as ever in Haritham when a herd of elephants trampled through the forest opening.

They had arrived in search of food and water, and Haritham had both in abundance. The trees, shrubs, and bushes were lush with leaves, fruits, and berries, while the lake acted as a boundary on three sides, providing fresh water to the animals in all seasons.

Elephants spend almost eighteen hours a day searching and eating food. They can eat over one hundred and fifty kilos of food per day. However, food became scarce, and there was no rain for more than two years. It forced the herd to search for a new home. The young ones walked in the centre, surrounded by the older elephants.

After months and months of walking, the elephants reached Haritham and were delighted by the greenery they saw. The forest had so much food to fill their huge and hungry bellies.

"We can live here forever." The matriarch announced.

Others nodded in relief and excitement, swinging their trunks from one side to another. The calves leaned against their mothers, exhausted from the long trip they had made. The slightly older ones looked ready to explore the new forest and make friends. They all loved meeting other animals, talking to them, and helping the ones in trouble. Except for one young elephant called Renu whose favourite pastime was to bully others. He was a troublesome lad and had no intention of changing his ways.

"Don't do that, Renu!"

"Come back here!"

"Renu! Stop bothering that little rabbit."

On and on it went. They would reprimand Renu at least a dozen times a day. He would apologize, stay obedient for a while, and start his mischief again.

None of them could forget one incident when Renu stole two kits from a squirrel's litter and hid them in a bush. The poor squirrel was frantic, searching for her babies as Renu laughed. A porcupine found the kits whimpering in the bush and alerted others. One of the older elephants saw the commotion and went that way. He also noticed Renu sneaking away as he helped place the kits back on the tree. It was surprising how Renu could reach a branch that high to kidnap the kits. When asked, he said the kits were roaming around, so he hid them in a bush to save them from other animals.

The smaller animals refused to allow Renu into their territory again. Of course, that didn't stop the lad. He tried to trespass, but the food was already scarce by then, and he soon lost interest. Filling his tummy became a priority.

*****

As the herd was ready to enter Haritham, the matriarch turned to Renu and knocked him on the head with his trunk.

"Listen, rowdy fellow. If we get any complaints from the animals, we will send you away from here. We are peaceful animals and want to live with others, causing no nuisance. Do you understand?"

Renu looked up at the oldest female elephant with his wide eyes and nodded. "I will be good," he murmured.

"Look at the calves younger than you. No one acts like you do, Renu. Have you seen any of us troubling or hurting other animals?"

Renu shook his head, his wide ears flapping around his face. He thought they were all boring but didn't voice it aloud. He never understood why they were friendly to the animals when they were so powerful. What's wrong with having a little fun with the worthless animals?

"This is a matter of survival, Renu. You must be good or get kicked out of the herd."

"I won't do anything here," Renu murmured.

The matriarch didn't look convinced, but she said nothing. She then addressed the rest of her herd about being careful with smaller animals.

"Look where you walk and don't trudge any innocent animals. Once we meet the forest king, we'll try to scatter around instead of being together all the time."

The elephants blew their trunks in agreement, and they set off into Haritham. A helpful monkey gave directions to the old lion's cave, and the matriarch, along with two other elephants, went to meet the lion.

The meeting was successful as the lion permitted them to live in the forest. He warned the elephants to not hurt the other animals for the sake of it.

"Since you are vegetarians, you don't need to kill any animal to survive. But when you pull the branches from trees or dig the earth of salts and minerals, make sure you don't break the nests or damage the burrows."

The matriarch thanked the lion and promised to be careful. By the time the trio got back to the herd, Renu's mother was frantic.

"He vanished! I know he's up to no good. Save him, mother, please."

The matriarch let out a long sigh. The force of it shook the nearby shrubs, and a porcupine hurried away.

"Tell me what happened."

"We were standing still and waiting for you. The calves moved around a little, sniffing at the trees and bushes. They were learning the place, and we monitored them. I'm sure Renu was at my side, but when I turned, he wasn't there."

This was nothing new for the herd. Renu could slip away unnoticed, despite his size. Just when they started to search for him, one calf pointed at Renu, walking towards them.

"Where did you do?" The matriarch thundered.

"I was hungry… berries," Renu whispered. His trunk had pink and red stains on it, and the sweet scent of ripe fruit wafted from him.

"We are all hungry. Don't do this again." The matriarch warned him and told her herd about the lion's orders. The elephants nodded in relief and soon settled down into a routine.

*****

It had been three months since the elephants started living in the forest. The hiccups got more frequent in their lives, all thanks to one not-so-little elephant.

The animals could no longer bear Renu's antics. A few of them and the matriarch gathered near the old lion's cave.

"Talk." The old lion ordered.

"The young lad, Renu, is causing a lot of nuisances." The wise bear began.

"What did he do again?" The matriarch asked in a weary voice. She was tired of it all.

A fluffle of rabbits peaked from behind him in fright. The bear nudged them forward with his wide paw. "Tell her."

"Our littles were playing in the clearing when Renu arrived and blew a trunk full of dirt on them. He laughed and called them ugly when they protested. He said they looked like poo."

The matriarch resisted the urge to kick the lad, who, of course, wasn't at the scene, and asked the rabbits to continue.

"Yesterday Renu drowned the anthill by spraying water on it. The poor ants lost their home, and some of them got washed away in the water. A couple of days ago, he threatened to break a branch with a new nest, and the other day, he was pulling a monkey's tail as she howled in pain." The bear listed.

"What do you have to say, matriarch?" the old lion asked.

"I apologize on his behalf. We do our best to control him. Even the threat of sending him away doesn't work as he knows we can't really do that to a young one." The matriarch sighed.

She got an idea to put an end to the recurring mischief. "I feel helpless. Please teach Renu a lesson, and I promise that none of us will interfere. This is the only way to deal with him."

The rabbits looked at her in wonder. A couple of snakes that hung nearby hissed in approval.

"Are you sure, matriarch?" The bear asked.

"Yes. But please don't kill him. Just make him understand the importance of respecting others."

The lion nodded. "I agree. Come to me if you need any help."

The animals thanked him and went back to their respective jobs. The bear, rabbits, snakes, a monkey, three squirrels, and a colony of ants met in the evening and made a plan.

*****

Unaware of what had happened, Renu woke up the next morning with a plan to annoy the bear. He saw how the bear liked honey and thought it would be fun to break the honeysuckle on the bear's head. He stopped to observe a couple of his juniors on the way and snorted in disgust as they assisted badgers in widening their burrows.

"Woo hoo, fellas… want some h*elp*?" he sneered?

The badgers snarled. Renu chuckled as the calves glared at him.

"Go away."

"You are ordering me around? I can smack you with my trunk."

One calf rolled her eyes. "Yeah, and I'll tell the matriarch what you did."

"You are all pathetic," Renu grumbled and trudged away. He didn't need anybody to execute his plans, anyway. They were more of a hindrance, always stopping him and threatening to report to the matriarch.

Life in Haritham was fun, but he was getting bored by picking on only the weaker animals. That's why he upped the level and decided to take on the *wise* old bear instead. Let's see how clever he would be when the honeybees attacked, Renu thought and smirked.

He was munching on wild berries and shoots when he saw the ants building a new anthill. Renu knew he could do more than trouble the bear that way. After all, he had too much time on his hands. The other elephants, young and old, avoided him most of the time as he made it a point to protect his mother and the matriarch. That left him alone and to do as he pleased. Renu broke off a small branch, and he ambled towards the ants, chewing his food on the way.

"You teeny ants are at it again? What if I crush it with my foot? Say, say…" Renu laughed, lifting one solid foot in the air.

"Oh, please don't do that, Renu." The ant said, knowing the lad would stamp on it.

Renu laughed louder, swinging his trunk and flapping his ears. He raised his foot as high as he could and brought it down hard on the anthill.

"Oww!!"

He cried as long and sharp thorns pierced into his skin. The ants skittered away and watched Renu wail in pain. He couldn't put his foot on the ground as the small stem of thorns was lodged in his foot.

"I… I'll teach you…" he shouted and limped to the side. He didn't go far when the monkeys jumped onto his back and started tickling him. They pinched and poked using their nails.

Renu tried to dislodge them but ended up hurting his foot again. The thorns dug deeper inside.

"Noo… stop!" he cried.

The monkeys left him at last, but the snakes took their place. They hissed and wrapped themselves around Renu's neck and trunk, threatening to bite him, to scare him even further.

Renu fell to the ground and pleaded with them. "Leave me alone! Go away from me!"

As the snakes left, Renu breathed a sigh of relief. But his foot hurt, and he couldn't even get up again, no matter how hard he tried.

"Help! Help me, I say."

"Anybody here?"

No one answered his cries. A fluffle of rabbits walked past, ignoring Renu.

"Hey, you, help me. Why don't you listen to me?" He demanded in vain.

As the pain got worse and the day progressed into the evening, Renu realized that no animal cared for him. They took one look at his sad state and walked away. Some of them whispered amongst themselves loud enough for him to hear.

"Serves him right, you know. He would always keep hurting us. Now he'll know what it feels when he hurts us."

"Good for him. The poor ants were devastated when he destroyed their home."

"Very well. This lad deserves to suffer for ruining the bird's nest. They lost two eggs because of him."

And so the whispers continued. Renu understood he had to blame only himself for his current state. If he had listened to his mother and the matriarch, he wouldn't be in this position. The pain was unbearable, but there was no help. He wondered if he would have to stay that way forever. Even his family was ignoring him. Renu wondered if they were doing it on purpose. What if they really sent him away, Renu thought and cried again.

As the sunset behind the trees and the forest got dark, Renu knew that was it. They left him alone, knowing he was afraid of the night. They wanted him to be like them, helping others and being good. It was boring, but Renu saw how his actions ended up isolating him. His mother warned him of karma and how he'd have to face the consequences one day, but Renu laughed it away. He grasped the whole meaning of her words after being left to fend for himself when his foot hurt.

Renu decided he would at least try to change. He liked Haritham more than the previous place and didn't want to leave.

"I'm sorry! Help me, please! I will be good." He yelled, hoping the animals would come back. He wasn't sure how long he could bear the pain, the hunger pangs, and the blackness of the night, all at once.

"I promise. I'm sorry!" He shouted again and again until his voice got hoarse.

At last, Renu noticed a form walking towards him and got scared. He gulped and tried to move. He was already weak from not eating anything since the morning.

"It's me." The bear announced. He walked closer to Renu, examined the foot, and looked straight into the lad's eyes.

"You'll be good from now." It wasn't a question.

Renu blinked his tears and replied. "Yes, yes… I learned my lesson. Please help me."

The bear pulled out the thorny stem in one swift move. Renu shrieked in pain as the bear then pressed a few crushed leaves to the injured foot.

"Why do you trouble others, Renu?" The bear asked.

Renu hung his head in shame. "I… it makes me feel strong."

"But you are already strong. Look at your size. You'll grow bigger in the next few months. I noticed you don't bother the tigers or the cheetahs or any of the powerful animals. Is it because they will kill you?"

Renu nodded, realizing how bad it made him look. He was sure they wouldn't see through him. He underestimated them and paid the price.

"So you are a bully, and you know the matriarch won't send you away." the bear said.

"I'm sorry," Renu mumbled.

Why didn't your herd come when you were balling all day?"

Renu sniffled. "They got fed up with me?" The thought of it was terrifying, but he couldn't ignore it any longer.

"Yes, and no. They got fed up with your antics and felt you needed to see the truth of your actions and face the consequences on your own. They still love you, but the animals you hurt don't want you here. Many are afraid you will not change."

"I will change! I… love this place. Promise." Renu sobbed, curling his trunk into a coil.

"Alright. Your foot needs time to heal. Don't move for tonight. You'll feel better tomorrow morning." the bear patted Renu's injured foot.

"But it's dark here. I'm afraid of the night. Please, please, stay with me."

"Very well. Let me see what I can do about it."

The bear made an indistinct sound. Nothing happened for a few seconds. Then some animals stepped forward from behind the trees. They were the same ones Renu troubled during the past months.

Renu looked aghast and then squared his shoulders. He knew he had to apologize for his action, and that too face to face if he wanted another chance. If only he had listened earlier, he wouldn't have had to endure so much pain. "I'm sorry. Please forgive me."

The animals nodded. They didn't say a word but stayed back with Renu so that he wouldn't be alone through the night.

"You are all so good to me. I made many mistakes and didn't listen to my herd. From now onwards, I want to be your friend." Renu said.

"We are glad to know that you understood. We'll be your friends." A young deer replied.

The monkeys offered him a few fruits to eat. "You must be hungry. Eat this for now. I'll take you to a new tree tomorrow morning. It has tasty fruits in bright yellow color."

"Thank you."

*****

The animals gathered near the old lion's cave again after a couple of months. This time, however, Renu was with them and beaming with happiness. The lion praised him for saving an infant. The little monkey lost grip on her mother and fell from a top branch. Renu was nearby and rushed to grab the infant in his trunk before she could hit the ground.

"You were wonderful, Renu. I hope you've noticed how happy the forest is when you don't hurt your fellow animals." The lion said.

Renu nodded his gigantic head. "I do."

"You are stronger and loved by all. This feels better, doesn't it?"

Renu nodded. "Yes. I was wrong in thinking I had to show my strength only through bullying. It won't happen ever again."

"Oh, we are sure it won't. You are rather a sweet lad. Just needed a bit of fine-tuning, which our wise bear took care of."

The bear grinned and bowed. Renu looked at him with affection. He felt more comfortable talking to the old bear than his herd. It wasn't uncommon, the matriarch said with an indulgent smile.

"Go on, then. Enjoy the celebrations. I'm too old to join." The lion declared and went inside the cave.

The matriarch and the herd of elephants were relieved at the transformation in Renu. However, the calves were sceptical at first. Soon they played and accompanied him on the daily errands. He was even babysitting the young ones of his herd and of other animals, too. His mother was proud of the change in him and prayed it would last forever.

"Come, come, folks! Time to party!" The monkey announced, swinging from the branch.

The animals laughed and joined in the fun. They ate plenty of food and danced until the night.

The forest continued to flourish as the rains blessed them every year. The lake was flowing, and the trees were brimming with fruit. All the animals in Haritham lived in harmony for a long, long time.

* * *

An MBA graduate, Srivalli Rekha also has an MA in English Literature. She loves to write, blog, cook, take pictures, draw and craft silly things. Nature is her greatest inspiration. Books and music are her favorite companions. Her works have been a part of several anthologies (eBooks and paperback publications). Srivalli and her writer friends have founded The Hive Publishers, an indie publishing collective, at the end of 2019. She has self-published three works till date.

The Tug of War

Ramendra Kumar

"It's so boring," Hamza, the Hippo declared, trying to unsuccessfully suppress a yawn. Ringo, the rabbit, looked at Hippo's gaping mouth fascinated. He had always been quite sure that his entire family could walk through the opening at one go, and his entire clan could find refuge in the huge stomach in case of a calamity like a Tsunami.

"You are right, Hamza," added Lofty, the giraffe. "There is nothing to do in the jungle."

"Why don't we play a game?" suggested Chilka, the parrot, who had just gone on a two-week trip to the city to meet his twin, Pilka.

"What is a game? Is it something to eat," Hanu, the Hathi, the king of the jungle, asked. Hathi ate more than all the grass-eaters put together and yet remained perpetually hungry.

Ringo was sure there were half a dozen monsters in Hanu's belly. These creatures gobbled up everything unknown to Hanu, who was a relatively simple creature.

"A game is a kind of sport which human beings usually play for fun. Now Hanu Maharaj, before you ask what a sport is, let me explain." Chilka went on to elaborate on how various sports like cricket, football, hockey, table tennis, etc., were played.

He then looked around. "So did you understand what I mean by games and how these are played?"

Everyone kept quiet. Hanu lifted his trunk and kept staring at its tip. Hamza started searching for flies to beat up with his little tail, Lofty tried to search for non-existent shoots, and Ringo twitched his nose as if trying to sniff out the answer.

Chilka shook his head in exasperation and declared, "Okay guys let me tell you about a game that is simple and which we can all play."

The animals all nodded vigorously, Lofty with such enthusiasm that Ringo was scared his neck would snap.

"What is this game called?" asked Hamza.

"Tug of war."

"But we are peace loving creatures. Why should we fight a war?" Hanu declared.

"No, no Maharaj, it is not the kind of war you have in mind. Here the players are divided into two teams and made to stand in a straight line. In the case of humans they hold a rope and pull it from opposite sides. The team which is stronger pulls the other team to its side, thus winning the game."

"But how do we hold a rope?" asked Hamza.

"We don't, instead we will hold the tails and pull."

"What will the animals in the front hold?" asked Ringo.

"A brilliant question, Ringo! The teams will be led by two elephants. Hanuji can lead one team comprising all male animals while the queen, Mrs. Honey can lead the other team comprising all female animals. Mrs. and Mr. Hanu will lock their trunks and tug."

"So, what do you think of the idea?" Chilka asked, looking around.

"I think the idea is a great one. We can have lots of fun," declared Lofty, who was fond of a female giraffe called Sandy. 'It will be a perfect way to impress my Sandy'," he thought.

Chilka looked at Hanu for his reaction.

The elephant thought for some time and replied, "Let me consult Honey first," he lumbered away.

Hanu did not take a single decision without first checking with Honey, who was widely regarded as a brave and intelligent elephant.

An hour later, a declaration was made by the king: "The First Jungle Tug of War Contest would be held on the coming full moon night."

Preparations began in earnest. The teams had been formed, and practice sessions started under the guidance of Chilka and Pilka, who had been specially called from the town for the purpose.

Finally, it was the night of the contest, and the teams lined up. The birds were to play the role of cheerleaders and commentators - the art and craft of these two functions were taught to them by Pilka, who was an expert.

Hanu and Honey locked their trunks. Hanu's tail was held by Cheetu, the Cheeta, while Honey's tail was grasped by Bijlee, the leopard and so on. The last member of Hanu's team was Hamza, while Ruhi, the Rhino, was the final player of Honey's squad.

A line was drawn right in the middle, and the team which succeeded in pulling its opponent past that line would win. Chilka whistled, and a unique Tug of War on Planet Earth started.

Each side, egged on by the cheerleaders, pulled, puffed and panted. Sometimes Hanu's team would succeed in pulling Honey's team a few steps towards the line, and at other times the opposite would happen. But no team managed to make its adversary cross the line.

Airavata

The contest went on for two days and two nights. The animal babies started howling, the contestants themselves were ready to collapse with thirst and hunger, the cheerleaders had stopped cheering, and the commentators had retired. Still, no side was willing to give up.

Finally, Honey asked Hanu a question: "Hanu dear, in your madness to win over me have you forgotten what day it is?"

Hanu, who suffered from STML (Short Term Memory Loss), thought very hard and finally almost shouted in triumph, "It is our silver jubilee anniversary. 25 years ago we tied our trunks in this very jungle. Of course, I remember."

"So, what are you going to give me on this special occasion?"

"Anything you ask for, dear," Hanu gallantly replied.

"Anything? You promise?"

"Y..yes," Hanu answered, this time a bit guarded.

"Then allow me to win this contest."

"What! How can I?"

"You promised."

"But that's unfair!"

"All is fair in love and war, dear. And this is both the tug of love and the tug of war," Honey replied. She had spent some time in a circus and had picked up quite a little bit from her human master and mistress.

Hanu slackened his grip a bit, and Honey pulled with all her might. Hanu and his team tumbled forward and crossed the dividing line.

"Mrs. Honey and her team are the winners. They have triumphed over Mr. Hanu and his squad," declared Pilka.

The ladies did a victory dance while the gents sat in a line, their tails limp and their heads hanging down.

"Hey guys, come on, don't look so gloomy. It is our silver jubilee anniversary and I have decided to throw a grand party. We girls are going to organize a super feast for you in a jiffy," declared Honey and Hanu's eyes lit up. He raised his head and trumpeted, and started doing a little jig. The other animals, too, got up and joined their king.

Later after the feast, Hanu asked Honey, "What about my anniversary gift, Honey?"

"At the next 'Tug of War' contest I promise I'll 'allow' you to win," she declared and mumbled under her breath, 'Provided you remember my promise, Hanu dear'.

***

Ramendra Kumar (Ramen) is an award-winning writer and performance storyteller with 42 books. His writings have been translated into 30 languages and have found a place in several textbooks and anthologies, both within & outside the country. He has also been invited to prestigious international literary festivals.

A Pure Love Story

Meenu Sivaramakrishnan

Nestled amidst lush green forests and surrounded by majestic mountains was the village of Aanepuram. A small village where there lived about 20 families only. The people primarily made their living collecting wild yet tasty berries, sweet honey, firewood, etc., and selling them in the market while others reared cattle.

There was a small yet beautiful Lakshmi temple located at the edge of the village bordering the forest. The soft-natured Rangan was the priest who maintained the temple very well and performed the daily rituals for the Goddess sincerely. Everything was going as usual at Aanepuram until one day. It was 5.30 in the morning when Rangan entered the temple, as usual, to do the morning rituals when he was in for a surprise. Right at the entrance of the temple were a bunch of white flowers. They were so beautiful, with shades of yellow in the middle. The fragrance of the flowers was so heavenly, but Rangan did not know who had brought them.

"Hello… is anybody there? Who has got these flowers?" he called out loud as he looked around.

But it was just the sound of the mild breeze and chirping of birds that he heard in response. He loved the flowers and so took them in to make a lovely garland for the Goddess.

"Aha… so beautiful! May the Goddess bless that generous one!" said Rangan as he put the garland on the Goddess and whispered a silent prayer.

The day passed as usual, and Rangan too forgot about the flowers. But the next day, too, he found a similar bunch of the white flowers. In fact, this happened every day from then on, but Rangan wondered who brought the flowers and why would they not show their face. Every villager was asked, but no one had even seen those flowers before.

The summer season began, and Rukmini, Rangan's little daughter, got up early to fetch water from the village well every day. With the rising summer heat, it was one day when Rukmini got up at 5 am and walked towards the well. As she neared the temple, she heard a sudden rustling of leaves. Scared, she stopped there and quickly hid behind a tree and what she saw next surprised her totally! There came a medium-sized elephant carrying a bunch of white flowers in his trunk. As he reached the entrance, he placed the flowers down on the floor, lifted his trunk as if praying to the Goddess, then turned away and walked back into the forest.

Rukmini could not wait to tell her father, so she ran back home.

"Appa! Appa! I have to tell you this.", cried Rukmini as she stepped outside her house, still panting.

"Rukmini! Calm down. Why did you come running so fast?" asked Rangan as he was about to start towards the temple.

"I know who is keeping those flowers. I saw him today!" said the excited Rukmini.

"What? Who is it? "asked the curious Rangan.

"He is an elephant. I think a young one. He even prayed to the Goddess before going back into the forest."

"Rukmini, this is not a time for jokes. Did you really see? If so, tell me the truth.", said Rangan, getting a bit irritated.

"Appa! I am telling you the truth! He is an ELEPHANT! If you don't believe me, wait till tomorrow morning. I am sure he will come at the same time and you can see for yourself.", replied Rukmini

"Okay. We will do that.", said Rangan as he proceeded towards the temple.

The next day, Rangan and Rukmini went to the temple well before and hid behind the same tree. They waited patiently until finally, the sudden rustling of leaves was heard.

"Appa! He is coming", whispered Rukmini.

The same medium-sized elephant appeared the next moment, carrying a bunch of white flowers in his trunk. Just like the previous day, he placed the flowers on the floor, lifted his trunk in reverence to the Goddess and then walked back into the forest. Rangan could not believe his own eyes.

" My God! Is it like the son wants to adorn his mother with the beautiful fragrant flowers?"

"Unbelievable!" exclaimed Rangan.

Though it all seemed so magical, he knew the flowers were real, and he loved them too. Now, Rukmini loved the cute fat elephant. Given that the summer was getting hotter, she placed a huge tub outside the temple and filled it with water every night. The elephant drank from it every day after his temple visit.

Slowly she began to keep some food for him too. It could be big rice balls, a bunch of bananas or sometimes coconuts. Soon, she realised that bananas were his most favourite. Now she began to refer to him as "Gaja".

A couple of weeks passed by, and Rukmini was curious to find where Gaja lived and get the flower tree's location. So, the next day, she decided to follow Gaja as quietly as possible. Surprisingly, he hardly went a few kilometres into the forest and stopped near a patch of bamboo bushes. Rukmini hid behind a big tree some distance away and waited. He ate the bamboo leaves but stood there swinging his trunk now and then. Hours went by, and Rukmini decided to head back home. She followed him for the next two days too, but Gaja took her to the same place. But the third day, Rukmini was pleasantly surprised to find something which answered her many questions. She ran back home to tell her father.

"Appa! I have to tell you something about Gaja", she spoke excitedly.

"Rukmini, How many times have I told you not to follow him into the forest? It is very dangerous!" said Ranga with concern.

"No Appa. Gaja lives just outside our village and I don't think he will do any harm . But you will be stunned by what I am going to tell you.", said Rukmini

"What is it?" asked Ranga

" When I was waiting and watching Gaja from behind the tree as usual, a paper came flying down from one of the bamboo bushes with the breeze. And that was none other than the picture of our temple Goddess Lakshmi with two elephants on her two sides. Quickly Gaja picked it up and fixed it between the bamboo stalks."

"You were right, Appa. It looks like he considers her his mother and brings her the beautiful flowers.

Poor Gaja. I feel sad for him. Perhaps he has never seen his mother!" finished Rukmini.

"Oh! That is strange! But still we do not know whether it is true and he is an elephant from the wild. So, I want you to stop venturing into the forest again, Rukmini.", said Rangan.

"But Appa, I feel really sad for him. He is lonely. Maybe he wants to be loved and cared for. He needs a friend. Don't worry Appa. I have lived here ever since I was born. I will be fine.", she replied politely and walked back home.

While Rangan felt a bit sad for Gaja, he was concerned about his daughter's safety. But he knew she was a brave and smart girl. He looked at the Goddess, whispered a silent prayer and went about with his work.

The next day Rukmini did not hide behind the tree. She mustered her courage and went in front of him, holding the same tub that she kept outside the temple, with a bunch of his favourite bananas. Gaja, who was swinging his trunk all the while, stopped. There was no movement for a few moments except for the soft rustling of leaves due to the breeze. Rukmini could hear her own heart beating fast. She was alert to just flee in case Gaja charged at her. But the next moment, he began swinging his trunk again. Rukmini felt better. So, she went closer step by step. Now she picked up the bananas and stretched them towards Gaja. He again stopped swinging his trunk but this time lifted it to reach out to the bananas and put them into his mouth.

Rukmini smiled. She went closer to him and slowly touched his trunk, and even patted him.

"Gaja!" she said softly.

Pyoooooooong!

Gaja trumpeted mildly and then softly touched her head with his trunk. The bonding was instantaneous. Rukmini stroked him gently. Immediately Gaja wound his trunk around, bringing her closer to him but ensuring not to crush her. Then on, they become very close friends. Since Rukmini did not have any siblings or friends of her age, she came to Gaja every day, spent time and played with him. Gaja, too, lifted her with his trunk, placed her on his back and took her on short rides. In fact, as days went by, it seemed as if he could understand her language too. He followed and responded to everything that Rukmini said.

"Gaja, can you show me this flower tree? I just love them", said Rukmini showing the white flower.

"Pyoooooong..." he trumpeted and even nodded his head. He quickly lifted her onto his back and began walking a little into the forest.

Soon, the beautiful fragrance came wafting through the air, and Rukmini knew she was close to the tree. And there, some distance ahead was the medium-sized tree in which the flowers had grown in bunches too!

"Wow! This is indeed beautiful! Thank you Gaja for giving these flowers to the Goddess!", said Rukmini patting him softly.

"Pyooooooong!" responded Gaja. He was delighted too!

Slowly Rukmini introduced Gaja to her father and the people of the village too. Though initially hesitant, they soon realised he was a friendly elephant. They liked him too.

Airavata

Few years went by. The saplings of the white flower plants that they had planted had grown big and started giving them beautiful flowers. Some people began to sell the flowers in the market too.

Gaja had grown bigger and majestic. He began to live in the village just outside the temple. People who visited the temple dropped some food in the tub for Gaja, who touched their heads softly as if blessing them. But Gaja never ate unless Rukmini came, petted him and played with him.

Everything went well until one Autumn Season. It was in the morning when two jeeps carrying forest officials and a huge truck arrived at the temple.

" Who is the priest here?" called out one of the officers.

"Sir, My name is Rangan. I am the priest here.", said Rangan, wondering who these people are.

"Ok. Rangan, we are from the forest department. We have got the information that you have a wild elephant in the temple. Do you know how dangerous it is? Elephants have to be trained before they are used by people. ", said the officer so sternly.

"But Sir, Gaja was so young when we found him. My daughter has almost brought him up. He has grown up in this village and is a very friendly and nice elephant. He has not harmed us at all.", explained Rangan.

" He is an animal. You never know when he can turn wild. We know our job Rangan. Now, tell me where is he?" demanded the officer when Gaja came ambling carrying Rukmini on his back.

As Gaja dropped Rukmini down on the ground, the officer ordered his team,

" Boys… Now!" he shouted as darts came flying from the tranquiliser guns.

"No! GAJA…! "

"APPA… What is happening? Who are these people? " cried Rukmini in panic.

Within fifteen minutes, Gaja was sound asleep.

"Boys… Get him into the truck quickly… We just have 30 mins until he wakes up", instructed the officer as the others began to pick Gaja and load him into the truck.

By now, Rangan has updated his daughter with everything happening.

"Please Sir. Don't do this. Gaja is a very well-behaved and nice elephant. Our village people are not afraid of him. Please leave him Sir! PLEASE!" she pleaded, but the officer was in no mood to listen.

In fifteen minutes, they loaded him and drove away.

Rukmini was shattered. She was thinking about Gaja all the time, wondering where and how he was. She could not even sleep properly during the nights.

Meanwhile, Gaja was taken to an elephant training camp and put inside a Kraal (wooden enclosure). A mahout was appointed to train him. The usual ways were used to train Gaja, too, but he did not respond to any. Unlike any other captured elephant, Gaja did not display aggressive behaviour too. Neither did he react to harsh and loud vocal commands or showing of a stick, nor did he accept the food that was given. A week passed, yet Gaja refused to eat a single bite. Now the mahout noticed he was shedding tears too! He immediately informed the officers.

"Sir, I have trained many elephants till now but have never seen one which is neither aggressive nor responsive! Also, I have heard from my grandfather and father who were mahouts too, that elephants shed tears when they are in terrible sorrow but this is the first time I have seen one!" said the mahout looking at Gaja in wonder while also feeling sorry for him.

"Sir, I think he is missing the girl. He has not eaten anything for the last one week. We can't let him be like this Sir or he will die!" said the mahout.

"I don't believe in this drama. Let me try with someone more experienced than you.", said the officer and immediately put an older mahout in charge of training Gaja. But it just took one day for this mahout to confirm what the previous one had told about Gaja.

"Sir. You have to call the girl. He is just 10 years old and two more days like this will lead to his death for sure.", said the mahout firmly.

Finally, realising the urgency of the situation, the officer sent for Rukmini. Rukmini and Rangan arrived in the jeep. Jumping out of the jeep, Rukmini came running.

"Gaja... Gaja...", she called out.

Though Gaja was weak, he got up. Recognising the voice, he lifted his trunk and gave a mild yet strong trumpet.

Pyoooong!

'Please let me in", said Rukmini asking the officer to open the wooden enclosure. The minute Rukmini entered in, Gaja wound his trunk around, giving her a warm and loving embrace.

"Oh Gaja! I missed you so much!", said Rukmini, stroking him, and Gaja responded with a mild trumpet again.

"That is indeed pure love, I must accept!" said the officer.

"Yes Sir. Gaja means no harm. He feels loved and cared for by the girl. The village people too love him.", said the mahout.

"Hmmm… Girl, can you offer him food?" asked the officer.

Rukmini quickly got the tub with Gaja's favourite bananas and offered it to him. Immediately, Gaja took it, patted his body with the bunch and then ate it. For a moment, the officer felt as though he saw Gaja smile. Now, the officer realised that Gaja was well-behaved and friendly. So, Rukmini and Rangan stayed in the camp for two more days so that Rukmini could feed Gaja. His health improved, and he was now fit to be released.

"You may take him back. We won't trouble you again!" said the officer.

"Thank you so much Officer", said Rukmini and Rangan.

Gaja lifted Rukmini and Rangan onto his back as they rode back to their village. Life was back to normal at Aanepuram, and it was a happily ever after for Gaja back at the Lakshmi temple with Rukmini, Rangan and the village people.

Airavata

***

Meenu Sivaramakrishnan, a Performance Storyteller, Voice-Artist and Classical Music Teacher, believes stories are entertaining as well as enriching. In her humble attempt to revive the love for oral storytelling, she began her initiative called Katha Galatta - Unleash Ur Joy Thru' Stories. Meenu also has her podcast channel Kathapod through which she shares her favorite stories. She is a member of Bangalore Storytelling Society, Indian Storytelling Network and Federation of Asian Storytellers. She does interactive story sessions weaving musical elements as well as story based workshops for children and adults. Meenu also co-facilitates a course on "Art of Storytelling" for Management students at the Manipal Academy of Higher Education.

All in a Night's Time

Revathi Srinivasan

A loud bang startled one and all, and in an instant, rainbow-coloured showers poured from the sky. The crackling sounds kindled an interest in everyone's heart. The whole crowd looked up in unison. It looked like colourful sparkles splattered on a bed of dark navy blue sky. The sound of rhythmic beats filled the air as several *chenda* and *nagaswaram* artists played their instruments.

The village shone bright with festive lanterns and diyas. Every household displayed a *poo koolam* outside the door. The smell of bursting crackers mixed with sandalwood spread a sense of divinity in the air. Everyone seemed to be rejoicing and frolicking and why not? Today, their favourite deity Guruvayur-Appan or Lord Krishna would be brought out of the temple premises for the common man to worship.

Elderly couples sat across the side of the road with folded hands to get a glimpse of their God. Adults were busy with their chores and running around their young kids. But the ones super excited for the event were the children. Some girls wore colourful and some more traditional white *pattu pavadais* while the boys adorned *pattu veshtis* or bright kurtas.

Children leapt and hopped to get a better view. Their favourite event of the year was here. They were here to witness the majestic and royally decorated elephants. Yes, the deity will be brought out from the temple on the elephant's back.

Soon the conch was blown, the temple gates were opened wide, A parade of brightly dressed elephants stood swooshing their huge trunks. At the centre of the parade stood the leader of the clan, Yashoda. The temple deity was placed on her back as the mahout stood beside her.

Elders held their hands up in the air, shouting, "GuruvayoorAppa, Krishna"

Kids strained their necks to have a look at their favourite elephant-Yashoda who would tap her feet rhythmically with the music. Yashoda was called "The Dancing Gajamukhi". She would walk a little distance and then sway to the beats of the music. It was a treat to watch her.

Commotion broke out almost instantly when the gates were open. Loud whispers and pointed fingers drew towards the herd of elephants.

The kids shouted, "Look, Look," and ran near the elephants.

The security built a human chain to avoid any mishaps. Kids clapped in awe at the amazing sight.

Little Kanna crawled from beneath her mother, Yashoda and stood beside her. Yashoda had recently given birth to this little one, and this was his first public appearance. As the drums rolled, the elephants started their procession with gait. Trumpeting and swinging their trunks in the air. Everyone in the village seemed ecstatic and blessed at the same time.

"Amma, Wow! How amazing this place is!" exclaimed Kanna.

"Why didn't you let me come out of the temple? This is such a sparkly place. Amma, look, what are they, flying up?"

"Kanna, stay with me. Yes, the outside world is amazing yet dangerous. When your time comes, you will be allowed to go out," she paused, "And that flying thing, I have seen many children hold in their hands. It's filled with air, I guess it's called a balloon."

"And what is that? Are people eating from the colourful glasses," Kanna pointed with her trunk and moved a little away.

Yashoda pulled her back near her, "Kanna, please walk close to me. The crowd is increasing by the minute, bringing you along was such a bad idea."

"Amma, look who are they? They look so frightening."

"They are *Theyyam* dancers. Don't be afraid of them. They dress up loud so that their expressions are conveyed to the audience well."

Yashoda once again pulled her closer with her trunk, "Don't stray away. You are still very young."

But, Kanna was fascinated with the outside world. She was spellbound by the charm of the people, the decoratives, the tall neem trees around him. With every step she took, she felt that life inside the temple was very boring. It had very few people. Also, the elephants were placed at a safe distance away from all the hustle-bustle. If she is so bored, why should she stay there? What was the purpose? A number of questions ran in her mind.

"Amma, why do we stay in the temple? Why can't we roam about like the others?"

" We have a greater responsibility dear, we are the ones who carry the Lord on our backs. Since we have been doing this for ages, we have a great connection with the people in the village. They also feel safe around us. Also, we are very huge, which you can see, so it will pose a big danger if we start wandering on the streets as normal folks do."

"But, amma, I feel caged inside the temple. I want to run around and be adventurous."

"Your time will come, dear. Once you are old enough to lead a life of your own. I will give you full freedom. Now please concentrate on the procession."

Kanna wasn't completely convinced by her mother. The more she looked at her clan and the villagers around, the more she felt like breaking the shackles and running away. She made a sulking face and dragged along with her herd.

Buzz Buzz

"Aah! Go away, you fly," Kanna said as she walked, arching her big frame.

Buzz Buzz

"Will you…Wow! What is this?" Kanna was awestruck at the sight of the new tiny creature in front of her.

"Amma, look, what is that shining yellow creature?"

"Kanna, please let me concentrate. The mahout will get angry. What if the deity falls? Please keep quiet."

"Please, Amma, look."

Yashoda took a glance at it, "Oh, it's just a butterfly."

"Beautiful. What if it isn't just a creature but a fairy godmother?" Kanna stated, thrilled.

"Hey, but where are you flying away? Stop!"

The butterfly was in no mood to stop, it flapped its velvety wings, and off it flew.

"Wait, don't go. Please, wait," Kanna sprinted behind the butterfly.

"Kanna, Kanna. Don't go. Listen to me. It's dangerous," Yashoda shouted in vain.

She could not run behind her, because the mahout would not allow, and the other elephants too would object.

But Kanna strutted away. She banged into a few vending carts. People scattered seeing an elephant approaching them. They yelled and shouted as Kanna scuffled through the narrow festive path, breaking and damaging some goods.

Her focus was the butterfly alone. She smiled and danced as she marched behind the butterfly, completely unaware of the chaos she had created in the village. Suddenly the butterfly disappeared into the bushes.

"Oh, ho! Where did it go?" disappointed, she turned around.

The horror of the night had just begun. At least half a dozen dogs stood there staring at her. One by one, they started barking. The noise kept increasing, making Kanna nervous. She turned around and jolted into the bushes to run as fast as she could away from the dogs. It was dark, and she was in the middle of nowhere.

"Oh, what have I done?" she cursed herself, "Why didn't I listen to Amma?"

The only option she had was to either keep walking or stay put till dawn.

But poor Kanna was hungry already. She walked in search of food when at a distance she saw a field. She walked closer to realise that they were all sugar-canes.

"Wonderful!" Kanna exclaimed. She broke them one by one and relished the delicacy. Her joy was short-lived as she heard huge cries only to realise that a bunch of men were running towards her with huge sticks.

"Why do they want to hurt me? I am just eating, and I am just a kid."

Kanna had to immediately vacate the place and run for her life. She once again ran as fast as she could. Faraway, she saw bright light flashes dashing along.

"Maybe, it's my village. Oh, thank God. Finally, I can find my way to the temple," she beamed.

She approached the lights with utter confidence, only to be shattered once again. It was a highway, with big and small vehicles gushing in haste. She thought it best to not walk on the path. The racing vehicles scared her. So she sat under the shade of a huge tree and waited.

Squeak Squeak

Kanna jumped up, alarmed.

Squeak Squeak

She looked around but saw nothing.

Squeak Squeak

"Who is it? My night has already been horrible. Please show yourself."

"Move. You are on my way. *Squeak Squeak*"

"But, where are you? Why can't I see you?"

"Look down."

Kanna bent down to find a tiny little rat.

"Oh, you were here. Sorry, I didn't notice you."

"That's fine. Now please move."

"Okay, but why?"

"You are blocking the way to my house."
Kanna looked around, she could not find any house.

The rat slapped his forehead, "Oh, don't look at places around your eyes, bend down and see."

Kanna bent down to look and found a small hole beside the tree.

"Oh, this is your house. Sorry."

"It's fine. So what's your story?"

"My story?" Kanna was immediately transported to the events of the evening and recited them one by one to the rat.

"That's really sad, But…"

Meoww Meoww

"Oh no, she is here again," the rat stood terrorised.

"Who is here?" Kanna looked puzzled.

"It's Billi, the cat. She comes here at this time searching for food. Generally, I run away into my house before she arrives. But, today, I completely forgot about her while talking to you."

"She comes for food? So, why are you running?"

"Oh, silly elephant! Rats are a cat's food. Don't you know that?"

"Awww, is it?" Kanna made a weird face.

Meoww Meoww

"It's a lucky day," Billi walked closer, "No unwanted drama, no running around. Do you understand, my dear little friend? Just one pounce and I will fill my tummy today."

Billi slithered like a snake towards the poor rat.

The rat was petrified, and it looked up at Kanna.

Kanna could not just stand and watch, she had to do something.

First, she tried to intervene, "Look, Billi, don't trouble him. Go away."

Billed meowed, "You stay out of this."

Billi sprang up in the air to have a perfect landing on the rat but was caught mid-air.

Kanna entangled her by her trunk and flung Billi high up in the air. Bili landed on a nearby thorny bush and ran away immediately.

"Thank you so much, little elephant."

"I didn't like Billi's attitude. Moreover, who eats rats?" Kanna winked at the rat.

The rat smiled, "I know the way to the village. I can take you there first thing in the morning."

Kanna was elated and she heaved a sigh of relief.

"I just want to go back to my mother. She had warned me that I should be careful and stay with her till I get a little older. I should have listened to her. I belittled her job as a temple elephant. But, now I realise that every job has its own set of responsibilities. I am sure she could not come after me because she was bound by her duties."

"My friend, it's never too late to realise your mistakes. So chill, we will meet your mother at dawn."

At daybreak, both the new friends walked towards the village. As they neared, they saw a couple of men and women running towards them.

"Oh, no. Not again. I think we should run away," Kanna said.

The rat hopped on Kanna's back to examine the approaching crowd.

"They don't carry any sticks or harmful things. Let's keep walking. Look, the village is very near."

Kanna thought it best to take the chance and continued walking. Soon, Kanna could hear people's eager voices.

"Look, look, our Kanna is back."

At that instance, Kanna felt safe and wanted. She walked into the village as dozens of people came towards her to pat her trunk. Some kissed her. Kids clapped and danced with joy. A few women offered her fruits to eat. At a distance, she saw the temple entrance and her mother standing at the gate.

Kanna ran towards her and hugged her. Yashoda caressed her little one.

"Sorry, Amma. I will never leave you. I will listen to whatever you say."

"Kanna, I was confident you will find your way back home. So, did you have your adventure, all in a night's time?" Yashoda trumpeted, and they both had a hearty laugh.

The mahout smiled at the mother-daughter duo and exclaimed, "I think Kanna feels caged inside the temple. I should make arrangements for regular trips to the village."

Chenda - a cylindrical percussion instrument originating in the state of Kerala.

Nagaswaram - a double-reed wind instrument from South India) artists played their instruments.

Poo koolam -flower decoration in a rangoli.

Pattu pavadais -traditional south Indian dress made of silk for girls.

pattu veshtis -traditional south Indian dress made of silk for boys

***

Revathi Srinivasan is a classical dance teacher by profession. Writing stories and tiny tales is her passion, she has been actively participating at many writing portals. A die-hard fan of Indian movies coupled with perennial love for dance and music drags her into dramatic writing emphasizing human emotions. One of her short stories has been published in the anthology Tea with a drop of honey.

The Little Zola

Preeti S. Manaktala

In the dense rainforest of Sinharaja in Sri Lanka lived a little calf Zola with his mama elephant Ela and papa elephant Zoe. Little Zola was always happy and excited to dance around the trees, playing with the falling leaves. He would often suck sand in his little trunk and then sneeze continuously, making his mama and papa very anxious. He was naughty and carefree. His favourite prank was to run round and round the trees and trouble his mom when it was bathing time or bedtime.

This family of three was happy and excited about a new soon-to-arrive member- a baby sibling for little Zola. Almost daily, the trio would go to the river in the jungle for their bath. Zola would walk right in between his parents during this two km walk, and on days he felt very lazy, he would just tag blithely behind. He would pretend to be tired on such languorous days and then collapse to the ground, refusing to walk, till he was nudged and poked again by his mother to resume his walk till the river.

Ela walked through those familiar trails every day.

With little Zola and her man in tow.

These harmless, friendly pachyderms

Swayed leisurely in their gait.

As they moved around in search of food and water

to nurse and to nurture

The unborn calf within.

Enclosed within the veils of her warm womb,

hidden away from this barbaric world

A life beckoned inside, unharmed.

Oblivion to the mean world outside..

One day papa elephant couldn't accompany them to the river as he was called for the monthly elephant meeting by the herd, so he had to join the parade.

Hence, mama elephant, along with Zola, headed to the river for a good scrubbing bath. Little Zola was reluctant again today for his bath. Just like every other day, he was scared and sceptical to step inside the cold water.

Mama elephant decided to ignore his tantrums today and went straight to the river, leaving him behind. Filling her trunk with water, she started washing her own back as the little one nervously marched left and right, unable to decide whether he must step inside the water or just stay dry. Filling her trunk again, this time she splashed and sprayed some water on Zola, making him squeal in excitement and run around in circles. Eventually, once completely wet, he trod with his reluctant tiny steps into the river to join his mother. The mother and the baby played along, splashing and cuddling in the water. She lovingly scrubbed his back, and they both made their happy cheers echo in the woods.

It was late afternoon now, and it was time for food. She heard her stomach grumble and growl with hunger. The little one growing inside her needed some food. She started poking Zola to come out from the river, and he now apparently was in no mood to leave the stream.

But finally, after some nudging and poking, they both started their walk back home when they spotted three young boys perched upon a tree on the left side of the patchy road, laughing and throwing stones and sticks at each other. Ela gently overtook Zola now and came to his left side so that he could be on the safe side away from these unruly boys. The boys seemed to be galvanized by the huge elephant passing in front of them, stopping their deviltry for a while to look at her in awe, wondering why her stomach was so bulging and rounded. Suddenly, one of the boys spotted Zola, walking meekly and scared beside his mother.

They started making scary sounds to intimidate the little pachyderm. Ela could sense the danger and the wrong vibes and started marching faster, making her calf involuntarily run to match up to her speed. Small stones targeted at Zola started bouncing off Ela's back as she covered her calf. She let out a loud screeching trumpet showing her annoyance and anger towards the unruly boys and also, as an attempt, SOS call for the other elephants in the vicinity to come for her help. Seeing her anger, the boys panicked and nervously fled the scene leaving the surroundings and their heartbeats calm and peaceful again.

Ela was very hungry now and felt weak but kept walking. They soon arrive at the pond, which was a landmark that their home was near. The pond was surrounded by many fruit trees and bushes, so Ela decided to scout for some fruits for lunch. As she approached the pond, she saw the three boys again, this time with a pineapple in their hand, heading towards them. They walked gently towards Ela and Zola and slowly placed the fruit down on the road keeping a safe distance from her. Yearning for some food, Ela came closer to the pineapple but with her eyes glued on the boys, who in turn started retracing their steps back and fled from the scene again. Ela scanned the fruit for a while, sniffing it through her trunk, then offered it to Zola, who clearly wasn't interested in the fruits, and moved his head left and right in rejection. In no mood to pamper him, she took the little pineapple straight to her mouth.

Little did she know that the boys had planted a live cracker inside the fruit, which immediately exploded inside her mouth, leaving her bleeding profusely. Her jaw broke due to the blast inside her mouth, and she ran hysterically, shrieking, shouting in pain towards the pond. Zola couldn't understand what had just happened as he saw his mother miserably crying. He helplessly paced around her, not knowing what to do while the boys, proud of their deadly prank, laughed and celebrated in the distance.

Ela lowered herself in the pond to sink her burning mouth inside the water as little Zola sobbed, standing beside her. After a few minutes of trembling and howling in pain, she froze and stopped moving. There was dead silence all around. Oblivious to her death, little Zola sat beside her and continued stroking her with his little trunk, hoping to ease her pain and hoping that soon his mom would get up and they both shall walk back home.

The budding life inside her couldn't survive

Airavata

They both left

For a new world may be better than this one

They both left

this cruel, ruthless, selfish world.

And it's multifaceted manipulative morons.

The yet to be born life-left, Oblivion to the fact how

his mother was put to sleep forever,

her end came disguised in a fruit.

Yes, they both left.

For a new world may be better than this one

Sans cruel beings.

Little Zola still wonders why his mom couldn't get up again, why she didn't respond to his voice and cries that day? Why and where did the men take her away in a huge truck? Would she come back? Apparently, Zola has now stopped dancing around the trees or playing with the falling leaves. He has given up all his mischief and tantrums hoping that his mom will soon be back. He now lives scared, very scared of humans, and cries inconsolably if he sees one…

<u>Disclaimer:</u> *This story is based on an actual incident that took place in 2020 in Kerala's Silent Valley Forest, when a pregnant elephant was given a pineapple filled with powerful crackers that exploded in her mouth, taking her life…*

Moral: Every life matters. As we have families and share with them a deep bond, likewise animals too have families and feelings of love, longing, hurt, and pain. Let's pledge to be sensitive humans- as truly every life does matter.

***

Preeti S. Manaktala resides in Bangalore, India. She is currently serving as in-house Poetry Editor for a reputed publication house and online journal. She is a published author, poet, blogger and a contributing writer to various online sites. She has won many accolades and recognition for her poetry contribution to various online contests. She calls herself a writer in progress and believes that life is a melange of learnings.

Her Latest books – Indian Summer In Verses- A Poetry Anthology.

Macabre Takes – A Thriller Anthology.

Yaanai kutty and Mooshak

Chandra Sundeep

Mellow golden streaks formed beautiful patterns on the kitchen floor. It was still the wee hours. Most of the Junglepuram residents were still huddled under their sheets. But not Mrs. Trumpeetha, or Amma to her beloved son Yaanai Kutty. She believed in waking up with the sun, and making the most of the day.

A tangy, spicy aroma wafted throughout the house. Amma was busy stirring the contents lest they stick in the pot. She continued stirring while reciting her morning hymns at the same time.

"Amma!" Little Kutty came thumping into the kitchen.

"Amma, I am scared!" he trumpeted while blowing tears through his nostrils.

The panic-stricken mother almost dropped the ladle in alarm. "What happened? A bad dream?"

"No. Not a dream. A m-m-monster…" he wailed.

"Monster? Where?"

"There !" Kutty wailed, pointing towards the garden.

Amma looked outside, fearing the worst. What if he was right! She grabbed the rolling pin from the drawer and stood near the large French window—watching for signs of danger.

But to her surprise, everything looked fine. The dew drops sparkled like pearls on the verdant green grass. Pink and red rose buds were swaying in the soft morning breeze.

Mrs and Mr Caw Caw waved to her as they left their nest in search of worms. The matriarch of the grasshopper family, Mrs. Tidda, was practicing Tai-Chi. Her neighbor Miss. Hiran, the neighbourhood doe, was busy stretching. Her teacher, Mr. Woof, was in the downward dog pose. Mr. and Mrs. Moo Moo were out on their morning run, supplying milk to all their customers.

Nothing seemed out of the ordinary.

"Who? What? Where?"

"Ammaaaa! There," he pointed towards the mango tree. The branches were drooping under the weight of big juicy mangoes. A family of koels was busy enjoying their morning juice.

"Them? Darling, you have known them since forever. Koel aunt has always sung melodious lullabies to you."

"No ! Not them!" Kutty cried. "Look there. Under the tree." He hid behind Amma as the grass stalks danced on their own. Only his trunk appeared from behind, still pointing towards the tree.

"Ah! That! It is just a little -"

"It's not little. Why don't you believe me?!" Kutty screamed his guts out, not letting Amma complete her sentence.

Amma said, "Come on then. Let's go to the garden and check"

"No!" little Kutty stomped his feet and let out fountains of tears.

"Why?"

"I am scared. That's where the scary monster lives. He has sharp teeth, long ears, and big round eyes." Kutty stood on his feet and opened his arms wide. "This big!"

"Hmm… ears bigger than yours?" Amma smiled, ruffling the soft hair at the top of his head.

"Yes!" he flapped his fan ears furiously.

"And eyes bigger than yours too?" She blinked in mock disbelief.

"Yes Amma. Not only big, they are scary too!" he nodded.

"I know it sounds scary. I understand, but what do we do? Should we face the monster or stay inside?" She asked, and waited for an answer. But when only silence greeted her, she pretended to ignore him and turned her attention to the pot.

Mmm… she took a deep breath, inhaling the mesmerizing aroma. Her stomach grumbled in response. But she knew she had to solve Kutty's problem before thinking of breakfast.

"Amma?" a meek whisper filled the silence.

"Yes, Kutty?"

"Will you be angry if I want to stay inside?"

Amma's heart melted at the sight of her child trembling in fear. He looks so fragile. *I have to help him face his fears. He needs to learn - running away never helps.*

"Not at all. We can stay inside."

She lifted him up and made him sit on the kitchen counter. "But what happens when you want to go to the park? Or play with your friends Lionel, Goatum, Butternath or Wolfie?"

"They can come here. We can play at home."

"But you can't play so many games inside. No football. No cycling. No swinging. Will your friends be fine with it?"

He shrugged in response and became silent again.

"And what about you? Are you fine with not going out? And never playing outdoor games ever again?" She filled a glass of water and handed it to him. "And tomorrow is Monday. How will you go to school?"

Kutty sipped on the water, lost in thoughts.

"Won't your teacher miss you? You won't be able to show her your volcano project."

Kutty let out a helpless groan. "Amma, what if the monster attacks us? Who will save us? Appa is not here either!"

"Why fear when Amma is here!" Amma flexed her muscles and beamed. "So, you want to go and check?"

She silently recited her prayers, hoping Kutty would agree.

"Can I take my bat?"

"Bat?"

"Yes Amma. To beat the monster." He glanced at the monster's home once again.

Amma's cheeks rose as she smiled, "alright. Go get it. I am waiting."

She arranged the plates and bowls on the dining table while Kutty ran to his room.

"I am here!" Kutty trumpeted a war cry. With the bat in his hand, he seemed to have found courage to defeat the monster.

"Let's go," Amma said.

But the moment they stepped onto the grass, Kutty's courage vanished into thin air. He shuddered and clasped Amma's hands. His heart thundered louder than clouds rumbling on a rainy day. He felt tiny little butterflies flutter in his stomach. The bat slipped from his hand and landed with a loud thud.

His tiny soft hair stood up, and countless mini bumps erupted all over his body. His thick rough skin looked even more rough. "A-a-amma. Let's go back inside," he whimpered.

"It's nothing, Kutty. We have come till here, a few steps more." She clasped his hand and led the scared little child forward.

"Hello! Anybody home?" Amma knelt down on the grass near the scary hole.

Kutty hissed, "what are you doing Amma?"

He got ready to sprint as he heard the little door creak open.

"Aaah!" Kutty screamed.

"Aaah!" the monster shrieked back inside and banged the door shut.

"Kutty wait!" Amma grabbed him by his arm.

She tapped on the door and said, "Hello… I am Mrs. Trumpeetha. I wanted to welcome you into the neighbourhood."

She waited patiently with a smile on her face, while a river of sweat flowed down Kuttys' back.

In no time, the door opened, and a sweet voice answered. "Hello, I am Mrs. Mousaline. It's so kind of you to welcome us. We just moved in last night!"

Kutty's jaw dropped in amazement.

The voice continued, "I am sorry for my son's behavior. He is still adjusting, and fears strangers."

"Oh! Not at all! We understand," Amma said. "Don't we, Kutty?" she asked.

Kutty eyed the tiny mouse standing next to his mother. "H-h-hello." He spoke softly.

"Hi, I am Mooshak." The little mouse offered his tiny hand.

"I am Kutty. So, you are not a-" he hesitated before completing his question, "monster?"

"Do I look like one to you?" Mooshak glared and soon burst out into laughter.

Kutty's cheeks turned red with shame and anger. "Why did you shriek when you saw me?"

The little mouse squeaked, "I thought you were a monster."

The boys rolled on the floor laughing. And their mothers couldn't have been happier.

"Kutty, why don't you bring your ball. You both can play together!"

"Yippee!" the kids squeaked and jumped.

Kutty ran towards his room, but stopped midway and ran back towards his mother. "I love you Amma." he hugged her.

"Catch me if you can!" he shouted to little Mooshak and scampered through the grass.

Mrs. Trumpeetha and Mrs. Mousalina seemed relieved. Their children not only had learnt to face their fears but also made new friends.

***

Chandra Sundeep is a writer and poet whose short stories, articles and poems have appeared in various anthologies, journals and online platforms.

Little Gobu

Yatin Tawde

It was a sunny morning. The butterflies fluttered around from one flower to the next. One butterfly settled between the eyes of Little Gobu, the elephant kid. Gobu tried to watch its wings open and close. But soon he gave up. Squinting his eyes made him dizzy. Gobu waved his trunk before his eyes. The butterfly flew away to join his friends on the flowers. Gobu scampered behind the butterflies, sometimes to his right and sometimes to his left, waving his small trunk to disturb them.

Just then he heard his mother call him. "Govardhaaan.."

Gobu got excited. Leaving the butterflies alone, he trotted towards his mother, his head bouncing in rhythm. 'There she is', he thought. Then he saw that she was surrounded by his many aunts. 'Oh no', he thought, 'now I will be slobbered with kisses by all my aunts. Why can't they leave me alone with my Mom'?

That way he liked his father more, as he left him alone to bond around the woods. In fact, his father stayed away from the herd for long periods. Little Gobu was also proud of his regal mom, as she always strode ahead of the herd with his aunts following close behind her. And he? Well, he loved to walk between his mother's legs, feeling the warmth of her body.

"Mummy, mummy, mummy...", he cried out as he reached her.

"Govardhan, now we will be going to *Ketakivan*. Stay with the herd. Don't be naughty. Don't run behind the birds and butterflies. Understood?"Mummy instructed in a grave tone.

"Don't be naughty Gobuuu...", trumpeted the aunties in unison.

Gobu just flapped his ears to drown out their voices. 'Grown-ups...', he thought, irritated.

"And remember Govardhan. While going to *Ketakivan*, we will pass through a huge, black expanse of hard ground. It will be very hot to walk on it. We will walk through the nearby pond so that our feet will be cold before we step on the hot ground. But once we start crossing, we will have to run so that we are on the other side faster. Ok, Govardhan?" His mother wanted to make sure that he had understood. Little Gobu just nodded, his head bobbing up and down.

"And that is not all, fast, roaring animals race across the hard ground. Most of them are small but some are large. If they hit us, they can cause us injuries. And you are so small, you can get seriously injured, so it is important that you stay between me and your aunties." Mom was giving him a good lecture. Gobu thought his Mom was being extra cautionary.

She continued, "And let me tell you, these fast animals scream violently as they go. Many elephants have froze in fright hearing them scream. Please ignore that noise and you will be good. Ok, Govardhan?", she asked. Again getting a nod from him.

And so their journey started. Little Gobu stayed with his mom as they walked. If he fell behind, his aunts protected him. They put their trunks protectively on his head making him run to catch up with his mother. 'Oh! gross', he thought, whenever he felt the wet trunk of one of his aunts on his head. 'Why doesn't my mom stay alone? Why does she have to move with all these old, irritating aunties?'

"What? Did you say something Govardhan?", asked his mother as she led the group.

"No, nothing, Mom. I didn't say anything, Mom.", he replied timidly. 'Oh my God, can she read my thoughts?', he panicked.

And so their journey continued. Afterall he was just a child and soon he started wandering here and there again, sometimes running behind a rabbit and sometimes behind a bird. But his aunts were always nearby, to push him towards his mother.

As soon as they reached the pond, little Gobu ran towards it, forgetting all his mother's warnings.

"Govardhan. Be careful.", she cried out. But Gobu was in no mood to listen. He frolicked in the water to his heart's content. He filled up his trunk with water and sprayed it on his irritating aunts. 'Take that, you old girls', he thought to himself but his aunts just laughed gleefully.

Little Gobu saw some ducks and followed them in delight, his trunk waving from side to side. But they were very nimble and he could never catch them.

"Come Govardhan. We cannot stay here forever. Come out fast", his mother cried out from a distance. Poor Little Gobu reluctantly emerged from the pond, water dripping from his body and joined the herd.

"Now, I hope you remember all that I had told you before we started. We will now cross the black expanse where strange animals race across, screaming wildly. Be careful, ok?" Mother wanted to make sure that Govardhan remembered everything.

Soon, the herd reached the fringes of the black ground. Little Gobu watched in fascination as shiny animals sped across the ground, making all sorts of horrifying noises. These animals did not stop for them to cross, they raced across, as if their lives depended on zooming ahead.

His mother watched everything in full concentration. "Now!", she shouted as soon as there was some respite from those screaming animals. The herd started moving fast, but a huge animal approached them at great speed. The herd still pushed ahead.

But hey! Where was Govardhan? Well, as soon as the huge animal approached making a cacophony, poor Gobu froze in fright. He just moved backwards to avoid being gobbled up by the huge animal. To his relief, it didn't stop even to look at him and just sped away. When he came back to his senses, he realized that his mom and all his aunts were on the other side. Tears started flowing from his eyes.

"Mommy!", he cried out in desperation.

"Govardhan. My Govardhan.", cried out his Mom.

"Gobuuu...", all his aunts cried out..

Little Govardhan was shaking with fright. He could see his mother and his aunts but couldn't join them. The shiny animals continued to speed across, oblivious of all the drama unfolding.

Suddenly he saw one of his aunts coming back on the black ground and stopping. Seeing her there, some of the shiny animals slowed down, but tried to go past his aunt. He was relieved to see that his aunt was not injured. Then another two aunts followed and they also stood and stopped on the black ground. Now the shiny animals came to a standstill but they continued making shrieking noises. His aunts were unmoved by their ruckus and some more joined them together trumpeting in unison.

Little Gobu got excited. They were coming back for him! The next few moments passed in a jiffy. In no time his mother was beside him prodding him forward to cross the black ground. As he passed his aunts, they touched his head with their trunks, trumpeting in delight. Soon they had crossed the black ground and were on the other side.

Little Gobu was happy. Even the shiny animals seemed to be happy seeing this as small hands emerged and waved at them as they raced past again. Soon the herd entered *Ketakivan* on the other side of the black ground.

Little Gobu's aunts say that he has changed. Now, whenever one of his aunts slobbers him with kisses, he doesn't run away. He returns the kisses in delight. He has understood that the herd's strength lies in numbers. And his aunts and the herd is his strength. He shudders to think what would have happened if his mom and he were alone on that fateful day.

Glossary : *Ketakivan* – a forest

Black ground – a highway

***

Yatindra has published his own e-book, 'Reflections of a blogger' and his stories have been a part of Anthologies like, 'Hawk's Nest', 'Route 13: Highway to Hell' and 'Blood runs Cold'.

The Elephant and the Snail

C. V. Lakshmi

It had just rained. The grass looked like a new green carpet, fresh and bright. Toto, the baby elephant was very happy. He loved the smell of the rain on the earth. He raised up his small trunk and sniffed.

"Ah, lovely!" he said to himself.

Just then, he thought he heard a small voice---very faint. In fact, he was not even sure he had heard it. So he kept very quiet and still. Yes, there it was again. A faint voice was saying,

"What is lovely?"

Toto looked all around. He could not see anyone. The voice came again, soft and whispery.

"Look near your left front foot. But don't move, please!"

Toto looked down, and saw a small pink creature. It had a soft body and no legs. Out of its head, there grew two long feelers. At the end of the feelers were its eyes. There was a round, spiral shell on its back.

"Was it you who spoke just now?" Toto asked the snail.

"Of course!" said the snail, "Do you see anybody else around?"

Toto shook his head. "Who are you?" he asked curiously.

"I am a snail," said the tiny creature in its tiny voice. Toto put out his trunk to touch it. Oh look! Where was the snail? He could not see it anywhere now, though he looked this way and that. All he could see was the shell.

"What happened? Snail, where are you?" he called.

"I am here, inside my shell!"

Toto was surprised. "Really? How come?"

"Well I don't like to be touched. So I went into my shell."

"Okay, I won't touch you again, do come out!"

The snail came out. Toto said, "Do you go into your shell all the time?"

"Yes," said the snail. "It is my house, you know. So if I feel I am in danger, I just go in!"

"That's cool!" said Toto, thinking what a big house **he** would need to carry on his back, for himself!

Toto wanted to know his new friend's name. The snail said, "My name is Helio."

"Hello?" said Toto doubtfully.

"No, Helio," said the snail, laughing very softly. "You must listen carefully, my dear elephant! After all, you do have such huge ears."

"Ah yes, now I have got it," Toto said quickly, in case Helio made more fun of him. "My name is Toto, by the way."

He wondered aloud why he had never seen a snail before.

"Well, Toto," said Helio, "A lot of us are around, but we take care to not be seen. There are many animals who would like to eat us, you see!"

"Oh, but you can always hide in your shell then," Toto said joyfully. He did not like the idea of his friend being in danger of getting eaten.

"Yes, that helps, but when the humans come hunting for us, we have a tough time. They do not give up so easily. Also, they have ways of getting us out of our shells…" said another snail. While Toto and Helio were talking, they were joined by some more snails, the friends and family of Helio. The new snail's name was Spiro. What he had just said sent a chill down the baby elephant's spine.

"Oh, that's scary," said Toto, trembling.

No sooner had he said this, they all heard some humans approaching. What bad luck!

"Quick, hide!" trumpeted Toto. However, he had also seen that snails move very, very slowly. At any other time, it would be funny, saying, "Quick" to a snail, but now was not the time for fun.

"Where can we? There is only grass here. The humans know where to look for us. Even if we go into any hole in the ground, they are sure to dig us up. Anyway, there is no time!"

Then Toto got an idea. Without waiting to ask, he began scooping up the snails with his trunk and putting them on his back. The surprised snails immediately went into their shells. This made it easier for Toto, because then it was like picking up pebbles. One or two snails began to cry, thinking Toto was eating them, but Helio and Spiro trusted Toto. Before long, the snails were safely on Toto's back, just behind his head. They would be out of sight even if anybody looked directly at the elephant.

All at once, the humans arrived. They were villagers who lived outside the forest, and came in search of some herbs, roots, and yes, snails! They ignored the elephant: he was just a baby. Anyway, they were only interested in collecting snails. They hunted about for quite some time, but in vain.

Airavata

Toto moved back and forth, trumpeting at them, until at last, the villagers gave up. They were afraid too, that the baby elephant's noise would bring the bigger elephants out. They certainly did not want that! Big angry elephants could flatten their fields in no time! Cursing and grumbling, the humans left.

Toto heaved a big sigh of relief. Then, very faintly, he felt soft tickles on his neck and back, where he had put the snails. "Whatever are you doing?" he laughed. Spiro, Helio and the others were wandering around on his back. Helio said, "You can bring us down. Thank you so much, Toto! I think we are safe now."

Toto carefully lifted the snails down again and they began to look for shelter. Now, in all the excitement of making new friends and then hiding them from the humans, Toto did not notice that he had come quite far into the forest. Now he looked around and saw that he did not know where he was! He became sad. He was a little scared. What if he could not get out of this place? His tail drooped. His trunk became limp.

Helio saw him looking sad and asked, "What's the matter?"

"Er, I am lost, I think," said Toto in a very small voice. "How will I get home?"

"Do you know where your home is?" said the snail, a little worried too.

"It is on the edge of the forest, to the east, where the sun rises," said Toto.

"Oh, then, there is no problem!" said Helio joyfully. "We were on that side of the forest this morning. I can show you the way back!"

"Er, really?" Toto was doubtful. It would take the whole day and maybe even more, to follow the snail. After all, snails did move so slowly! It did not seem like a good idea!

"Don't worry," said the snail, "I won't try and lead you back out of the forest; it will take too long. But, can you see this silvery line?" He pointed to a thin, shiny line coming out from its tail.

"Yes," said Toto. "What about it?"

"Well, it is my trail. As I go along, I leave a sticky trail, which shines in the sun. Many of us came that way. So our trails can be seen together. All that you have to do is just go along our trails, and you will come to the edge of the forest!" the snail said.

"Oh, that is so easy! Here I go! Thank you Helio!" said Toto, and hurried off along the snail's trail.

In no time at all, Toto reached the edge of the forest, and quickly found his mother and the rest of his family. They all sat around him and soon he was telling them about the day he had had, and his new friends, the helpful snails.

From then on, Toto was very careful to watch where he was going, in case he trod on any small creatures. He would also look for those shimmering trails, to find his friends. Sometimes the trail he followed led to other snails, so he made friends with them all.

Toto, Helio, Spiro and all the others have great fun playing together, laughing and teasing each other. Who would have thought such big and small creatures could become such good friends?

***

Lakshmi has been writing articles and short stories for the magazines Eve's Weekly, Femina, Woman's Era and Good Housekeeping. She had a column in Today(afternoon paper of India Today group). A book of children's stories, "Bahadur the Tiger" has been published by Pauline Publications, Mumbai. Some of her stories are available on Readomania Premium. Her Readomania page is https://www.readomania.com/profile

She has also written articles for Women's Web.

When an Elephant Comes To School

Sreeparna Sen

Okay. Don't panic. Everything is going to be alright. They are your classmates. They are not bad. They are just uncomfortable because they have never seen an elephant in their class before.

Jerry, the young elephant, tried to confront his fears as he brushed his tuskers in the morning. It was another school day after the weekend and his first week in the new school was not very encouraging.

"Jerry, be quick. You will miss the bus otherwise." Jerry's mother, Mrs Trumpet yelled from outside.

The mention of the bus ran down a shiver across his spine. The gang would be there!

But, he could not possibly lock himself inside the washroom for the rest of his life. So without an option, he got ready and reached the breakfast table.

"Look dear, I have prepared your favourite banana pancake. And I have also packed some for your tiffin."

Jerry did not utter a word. Somehow holding back his tears he tried to take a few bites.

Mrs Trumpet knew her son was sad. "Don't fret my golden boy. I know you miss your old home. You miss your school, you miss your friends. Please give yourself some time. You will make more friends in the new school. And you will have a lot of fun."

Jerry could not control himself anymore. He pushed away the plate and stormed out of the door without even bidding his mother a proper goodbye. The breakfast remained on the table, untouched.

***

Life had been tough for Jerry since his family moved to the cosmopolitan city of Vivaria, miles away from their quaint town of elephants, Tuskerville. Jerry's father Mr Trumpet was a police officer and was recently transferred to the city. So he brought along his small family, wife Fanny and son, Jerry.

Vivaria is a mammal metropolis where all animals, from the massive predators to the tiniest shrews lived and thrived. Elephants usually loved leading a secluded life. So in the vibrant city, the number of mighty elephants were comparatively less. But, these days with aggressive urbanization more and more elephants had started to move out for jobs and business. Jerry's family was one such path breaker.

However, growing up amidst the peaceful savannah of the suburb, Jerry felt like a fish out of water in the racket of the city. Moreover, the kids at schools made his life more difficult.

The bus arrived soon. Bracing his bag tightly around his trunk, Jerry took diffident steps towards the furthest corner.

He took a seat beside the window and looked outside. Everything about the new city awed him, but it was difficult to see much with tears filling up the brims of his eyes. He remembered his happy days in Tuskerville and all his sadness turned into anger. Why did Papa have to come to this city? Nothing would have happened if only they could have stayed back.

However, Jerry's chain of thoughts broke when the bus screeched to a halt at the next stoppage and the dreaded group started onboarding. Along came the fashionista gazelle Chinkara, followed by the swift cheetah Sheryl and the smooth blackbuck Becky.

Jerry's heart pounded fast, praying for a boon of invisibility. But his prayers weren't answered. The trio boarded the bus, busy chatting among themselves. They were about to take a seat when Becky spotted a trembling Jerry on the last seat.

"Hey, let's address the elephant in the room, oops in the bus, first. Isn't that our fluffy new friend?"

Chinkara and Sheryl were quick to join him.

"No wonder the bus looked so tired today. The poor engine had to drag this heavyweight after all."

With each passing remark, Jerry shrank a little more. They passed a few more nasty comments and took their seats. When the bus reached the gate of the school, Jerry was almost convinced he should go back. This school wasn't the place he wanted to be in. But somehow dragged his feet to descend from the bus.

The lanky giraffe Grace was waiting for the moment. He used his long legs to topple the little elephant as soon as he tried to get down. With a large thud, Jerry fell to the ground.

For the next several moments, everything became blurry around. When he looked up finally, he saw the trio was laughing at a distance and was now joined by Grace. Jerry could not control his tears anymore.

"Are you hurt?" A meek voice inquired. It was a tiny rabbit.

"Hi, I am Miffy. Can you get up? Or should I help?

Jerry looked at the mere wisp of the rabbit and could not control his smile. A bunny offering help to an elephant! But, without being rude he nodded a simple no. Then, he got up with much trouble.

"Don't worry. They bully every newbie. You saw the gazelle Chinkara. She is the daughter of one of the board members. She broke my friend Cooper's noise when he was pushed a little too hard."

Jerry looked around to find Cooper. A sheepish fawn stood beside the bunny. He extended his trunk as a gesture to make friendship. Suddenly the day started to look brighter.

***

A month had passed for Jerry in the new school. The bullying had not stopped but facing the bullies with friends had calmed his nerves. He still did miss his friends in Tuskerville, yet looked forward to creating new memories with Miffy and Cooper. Mrs Trumpet was also happy with the change and promised to arrange a slumber party for his new friends. Jerry even decided to request his papa for a small cot to accommodate Miffy.

After a few weeks, the much-awaited day of the sleepover arrived. Jerry was very excited to host his new friends at home.

"Jerry, I forgot to order the ice cream. Why don't you take your friends to the ice cream parlour next block and buy some ice cream?"

The children went out in a cheerful mood. The trouble started as they left the ice cream parlour and reached the corner of the road. Busy in frolicking amongst themselves Jerry did not notice that he almost bumped into Chinkara. Though she was not hurt yet made a big deal about it.

"Do you know why we don't see elephants around this place much? Because they aren't civilised enough to live here." Becky made a taunt.

"Hey, he did not see, okay. You can't speak to my friend like this?"

Miffy jumped on the bandwagon. The bullies did not take that well. Soon Grace pinned Miffy to the sidewall and hissed, "Oh, the fat ass has appointed a bodyguard. And such a fearsome one. So cute bunny, you want us to apologise?"

"Hey leave my friend, " Cooper kept aside his gawkiness and tried to intervene.

"Oh, look even the dumb has suddenly grown a tongue," Sheryl smirked and grabbed him by his neck.

"You are hurting me. Leave me," Cooper struggled to free himself from the grasp.

Jerry could not decide what to do. His mother had always warned him against using his strength to fight other classmates. But, this was a different situation.

He tried to confront Sheryl who violently dismissed him. And in the process hit a motorcycle parked sideways. It was perhaps not balanced properly and it knocked over Chinkara who fell inside the drain with the heavy bike on her.
Grace left Miffy and tried to pull the fallen gazelle, but failed. The bike was too weighty for the kids. Chinkara was badly hurt and started to scream. Unfortunately, the street was empty and there were no other animals to help the children.

"Should we run, Miffy?" Cooper inquired. Sheryl had released him.

"We can't leave Jerry."

And then they saw the most fascinating scene. The young calf had wrapped the handle of the motorcycle and with much pressure was trying to remove it. Sheryl and Grace held one side of the bike and Jerry pulled the other side. Together after some time, the young ones were able to free Chinkara, who was now crying profusely because of the injuries.

***

The slumber party was a big hit, though the friends lost their ice cream bucket. They discussed their little adventure the whole night. Mrs Trumpet was so proud that his son had helped his foes too.

Chinkara suffered a limb injury and was not able to attend school for many days to come. As for the others, when they realised the real strength of Jerry, they did not dare to tease him anymore. No, Jerry and his little group were not friends with the bullies but they learnt to live cordially.

As for bullying, Jerry had decided to be the shield against any such miscreants. He now knew - that strength is not what you show off but, what you are built with and can be always channelled in good ways.

***

Sreeparna Sen is a Computer Engineer, working in a Bank and finds her solace in writing. She has authored the book Tales of Wizardencil and is a part of 10 anthologies including an international project Until Dawn. To name a few of other published anthologies are Hawk's Nest, Tea with a drop of Honey, Blood Runs Cold, Route 13 – Highway to Hell, Love in Trying Times and Sharing Lipstick. Sreeparna frequently writes in her blog Wizardencil By Sreeparna Sen and manages a Facebook page with the same name, where you can find stories written both in English and Bengali.

Imaginations Run Wild

Gowri Bhargav

"Students! Now that I have taught you everything about elephants, take out your notebooks, draw the picture of an elephant and write a few facts about it." said Ms. Chitra to all the students of class 3.

Ms. Chitra was their science teacher.

All the students took out their classwork. They began recollecting the facts that they had learnt a few minutes ago and completed the task in a few minutes. But Sundari had hardly been paying attention. She was busy daydreaming. She seemed to be lost in a realm of her own.

"SUNDARI! Haven't you finished the task yet? Finish up quickly. I have warned you several times to pay attention." Ms. Chitra's voice bellowed in the air.

"Sorry, ma'am! I will do it right away," said Sundari, sounding apologetic.

She had no clue what she was supposed to do but she heard a few of her friends uttering the word "Elephant".

"Hmm! I guess we are supposed to draw an elephant and write a few points about it," she said to herself and began doodling seriously as though she had a mission to accomplish.

"Maaaam…I finished," yelled Sundari at the top of her voice.

The teacher came hurriedly to collect her notebook. As she flipped her pages to take a look at what she had done, she was taken aback.

"Sundari! This is utter rubbish. What have you done?" asked Ms. Chitra, furiously.

"But ma'am! This is what came to my mind. Doesn't it look good?"

"Look good? Silly girl. First of all, this is not an art class. And even if it was, no one would draw something like this. Your elephant is white, has five heads, and seems to be floating amidst the clouds."

"This picture flashed in my mind so I drew it, ma'am. My elephant can fly amidst the clouds."

"Enough Sundari. Your imagination is running too wild. At this rate, you will fail badly in all the subjects. Your future is doomed. I have been very patient with you since the beginning of the academic year. But you don't seem to show any signs of improvement. I will inform the principal. Your parents will be asked to come tomorrow. Now go back to your seat."

Sundari went back to her seat feeling dejected. The other students began giggling, looking at her notebook. Sundari was very quiet for the rest of the day. She neither ate her lunch nor did she talk with any of her classmates. Even on the bus, when all the children were singing and making jokes she had a grim face.

After coming home, she quickly rushed to her room, took her science notebook from her school bag. She tore the page on which she had drawn her elephant, crumpled and threw it, and burst out crying.

Sundari's mom Meena, was perplexed. Sundari would usually come home and narrate all the happenings to her animatedly. But something seemed terribly wrong with her today. She wondered what possibly could have gone wrong.

"Sundari…! What happened my dear?" she questioned, entering her room.

"I don't like school. My teacher thinks I'm not good. She said my drawing looked funny. My friends made fun of me. She said you and Appa would be asked to meet the principal," said Sundari in between her sobs.

"What did you draw dear? Let me have a look."

Sundari pointed at the crumpled paper that was lying on the floor.

Meena picked up the crumpled paper. She unwrapped it to see what her daughter had drawn. She was quite surprised.

"Amazing. Remarkable. How did you manage to draw this?" she asked.

Sundari wondered if her mom was joking.

"Amma! Stop making fun of me."

"Sundari! You have no idea what you have drawn. This is Airavata- the divine elephant that belongs to Lord Indra."

"Really? I didn't know that. I just drew whatever I imagined."

"Don't be concerned about what others say. I'm sure you will be a great artist one day."

Sundari was still not convinced about what her mother said. She presumed that it was just to cheer her up.

That night after having dinner she went to bed. A thousand thoughts bombarded her mind. Sundari didn't know when she fell asleep. She could suddenly hear a loud trumpet. Sundari woke up with a start. As she gazed outside her window, she saw a white elephant similar to the one she had drawn, floating in the air.

"Am I dreaming? This can't be real," she exclaimed.

"No Sundari. You are not dreaming. I am Airavata, the same elephant that you have drawn. I have come all the way from heaven," said the elephant.

"Why have you come to meet ME?"

"You see, once you drew my picture, my messengers informed me about it. I have magical powers. I was eager to meet the girl who had drawn me."

"That's awesome. So what next?"

"Hop onto my back. We can fly amidst the clouds. I will take you to a world of fantasy where you can have a lot of fun."

Sundari hopped onto his back. They zoomed across the sky and traveled to the land of fantasy. She could not believe what she saw. There were horses that could fly, unicorns, colored cows, birds that could talk, waterfalls that flowed from bottom to top. She was seeing things that her mind had always imagined all these days.

Finally, after the wonderful ride, Airavata dropped her back at home.

"Aah! Do you have to go? It was so much fun," said Sundari.

"There are so many children like you who need me. I have to tell them that it is perfectly alright to draw flying elephants, dancing horses and talking cows. Whenever you need me, all you have to do is draw my picture and whisper my name thrice. And I will appear in a jiffy. But don't tell anyone about me," said Airavata.

"Thank you very much. I feel so much better now. Don't worry! You have my word. I will not tell anyone.Not even to my favorite teddy."

"And remember Sundari. Always spread your wings of imagination. You have tremendous potential to excel. The world needs people like you who think outside the box" said Airavata before bidding her goodbye.

The next day Sundari woke up feeling very happy. She ran to her mom and hugged her.

"Amma! Can you please enroll me in art classes? I want to become an artist," she urged.

"Hmmm! You seem to be very happy, unlike yesterday evening. Did you have a wonderful dream?"

Sundari just chuckled. She didn't want to reveal the secret.

"Ok, Sundari! Get ready for school", said her mom.

"Amma! What if the principal calls you to complain about me?"

"Don't worry! I'll handle it. She will be able to understand that some children are just different and they have vivid imagination. As for your teacher, I already spoke to her about you yesterday night. Everything is settled. Just go to school and have fun. And…"

"And what?"

"Try paying attention to what your teachers say whenever you are bored of imagining things," said her mom and burst out laughing.

Sundari could not control her laughter either.

***

Gowri is a certified storyteller, an avid reader and an aspiring writer who enjoys weaving words into stories, articles, poems.She has won several online contests conducted by literary groups. Her works have been published in various online portals, literary magazines and anthologies.

In Pursuit of Peace and Harmony

Preethi Warrier

"*Hati Aamar Bondhu*!" Mimi excitedly chimed in, as her ten-year-old classmates chanted in unison.

The young volunteers from the elephant NGO cheered and clapped, these little sessions with children of tea plantation workers were always fun.

"Can an elephant read sign boards? Does he know you live close to his forest?" A young man intoned.

"Nooooooo!!" Shouted the children enthusiastically.

"An elephant doesn't harm you on purpose. It chases you only when it senses danger. So, should we tease him or pelt him with stones? Should we anger him?"

"Nooooo !!" Screamed the children again.

"Great." Replied the NGO volunteers. "So, what do we do if we see a lone elephant or a herd in the plantations?"

"Inform the forest officials!" Mimi answered the loudest.

"*Shabash* Mimi." Her answer was met with loud applause.

Mimi proudly looked around, absorbing the admiration of her teachers and classmates.

But Nandu sat at a far corner, acting oblivious to all the chatter around him. Neither did he participate in the gathering, nor did he respond to anything that was being called out. He looked out of the window all along, with a brooding expression on his young face.

Mimi understood why Nandu behaved in such a peculiar manner, in fact the whole class did. That was perhaps why all of them, even the teachers, let him be.

"Nandu, wait. Walk slowly." Mimi tried catching up with Nandu on their way back home.

"You think I can laugh and make merry like you, when these people tell us elephants are our friends? They are not. My mother had never harmed anyone, why did that tusker chase and trample her? *Baba* stopped going to work since then, I am at the mercy of my uncle's family. Given a chance, I will hurt all elephants on earth, and punish every one of those creatures." Nandu walked faster, with heavy steps.

The estate owner's bungalow stood menacingly on the side of the road, the children would stop for a while and marvel at the sight, the orchards, the cobbled pathway, and of course, the rich man's collection of mighty elephants. The pachyderms flapping their ears, walking around graciously, devouring tons of jaggery and bananas, captivated every little one. They were his pride, the display of his immense wealth and power.

But as Nandu and Mimi passed by the mansion that day, there seemed to be an unusually large crowd gathered near the walls. The duo pushed their way to the front out of curiosity and they stood rooted to the spot.

Far removed from the other elephants, lay two little calves, tiny, hugging each other, not letting go. Mimi's eyes looked for the mother, she had seen calves before, snuggling their mothers and hanging on to their tails. But this was different. They were not only cute, but perfect replicas.

"*Dada*!" she called out to the mahout. "Where is their mother?"

"She's dead. And you know what, they are miracle babies, healthy identical twins, both male. They'll fetch a lot when they grow up." The mahout replied with a twinkle in his eyes.

"But then who will feed and nurture them?" Poor Mimi was still anxious.

The mahout triumphantly flashed two huge milk bottles, and as the children gasped in amazement, he placed the feeding bottles in the calves' mouths. The hungry baby elephants sucked from the bottle, as the crowd cheered at this spectacle.

Mimi walked away and it was Nandu's turn to catch up.

"Serves them right, one of them separated me from my mother, now they are separated from theirs." Nandu scoffed.

Mimi turned back in anger, "You talk so harsh Nandu, I don't want to be friends with you anymore."

The next morning, Mimi woke up to the loud clamor of men and women discussing something heatedly. She heard her parents too.

"Such a massacre. He has brought down the makeshift shops, destroyed the thatched huts, and plucked off all our bananas."

"This can't be a herd, they don't enter residential localities, they stick to the fields and plantations. This is definitely a single elephant's doing."

"But lone tuskers usually hide in the jungles, attacking when they are threatened. This looks like he was really angry."

Rubbing her sleepy eyes, Mimi stepped out of her shanty and far ahead, she could see the marketplace almost shattered. Fortunately, her house was built of brick and mortar, all weren't that lucky. Some huts and barns made of hay had been destroyed too.

"Let's keep watch tonight, atop the tree at the village entrance. If he visits again, we'll have him captured." Mimi heard them all agree.

Dusk fell, and even before they got their dinner ready, the villagers were caught off-guard. The rogue elephant was on the streets, plundering everything in sight. It shook the trees, growling in anger. The villagers ran helter-skelter, looking for refuge. As the elephant banged on the walls of their homes, people threw rocks and whatever they could lay their hands on. The elephant trumpeted loud, before retreating to the plantations on the hillock. It's growls still echoed in the background.

"It's not a tusker, it's a female." Someone muttered, when the mayhem calmed down, "They generally behave like this when they lose their little ones."

"But look at the devastation she has caused. We'll approach the forest officials first thing in the morning." Many villagers resonated.

"The forest department will only let her loose deeper into the jungle. What if she returns? There's only one permanent solution to this problem - let the plantation owner and his mahouts capture and tame her in their estate. The man is rich, he gets away with procuring elephants, by hook or crook. Why should we care." This somehow seemed to be the most agreeable solution and everyone nodded in affirmation.

Mimi dreaded the thought of an elephant being captured, the entire procedure sent chills down her spine. They would dig a deep pit and the poor animal would innocently fall into the trap, hurting itself badly in the fall. Tight rope nooses would be tied all around its neck and legs. Other mighty domesticated elephants would pull the captured one from the front and some others would push it from the back. The mahouts would poke at it with sharp objects if it turned violent.

The injured elephant would struggle to free itself, in turn tightening its noose, and finally after many hours of torture, it would finally give up and follow the elephant troupe. Mimi had witnessed this once, she couldn't bear to imagine it again, the wounds, the desperate cries to break free…

She had also seen the wild elephants in the estate being beaten to submission. Her father had once mentioned that they were even starved for days, to get them to obey.

"*Baba*, let us inform my NGO *Dada* and *Didi*, they have instructed us to let them or the forest officials know. They say it's illegal to capture wild elephants." Mimi pleaded.

"Mimi." Her father stroked her head, "It's the elephant's fate, we can't handle everything, right *beta*. Moreover, the elephant will be happy and well fed at the estate, she will learn, just like all others. So don't worry."

Mimi couldn't sleep all night, were the twins actually orphans? Was it just sheer coincidence that this elephant attacked the village just a day after the twins were brought in?

She had to tell someone, something wasn't right. The sky was beginning to turn orange, the sun would rise soon. It was still dark outside and her parents were fast asleep. So, she gently opened the door and snuck out.

"Nandu, wake up." She whispered, nudging Nandu from his open window.

"What?" Nandu was taken aback, "Mimi, what are you doing here?"

"Shhh… you are taking your cycle, and we are going to NGO *Dada's* house."

"It's far away, at the other end of the village, I can't pedal for so long. And why?" Nandu grumbled.

Mimi shared her concern with him.

"Good riddance, let her be captured. And how can you be so sure the twins are hers?"

"How cruel can you be, Nandu? It's been three years since you lost your mother, and you are still upset and bitter. So, don't you understand how those babies would feel? Do you want them to hate mankind forever? Elephants have a great memory, the mother elephant will never forgive us, what if she escapes and attacks us all again? Please Nandu, we have been taught in school, elephants are our friends, they are just animals, please help me help them. For the sake of our friendship." Mimi was in tears.

Something in her voice set Nandu thinking. Without a word, he quietly rose from bed and together on a deserted street, they cycled down to their *Dada's* quarters.

***

The elephant twins did turn out to be snatched from their mother and not orphaned as the mahout had claimed. The birth of twins was rare among elephants, and the babies were male, which meant they could fetch a fortune for their tusks too. But they were born in the jungle, their mother had fiercely protected them and violently sent the captors packing. So, the landlord and his men had shot a sedative dart on the mother elephant and artfully abducted the calves. A case was filed against the miscreants and the babies were rescued.

The whole village had gathered to witness the touching scene, when the forest officials got the babies reunited with their mother. The elephant felt her children with her trunk, as though showering them with kisses. She warmly embraced the two and the babies trotted around the mother in excitement. With a loud trumpet, the elephant slowly disappeared into the jungle with her babies in tow.

That evening, Mimi and Nandu sat together along a brook, splashing water with their feet.

"Thank you Nandu, none of this would have been possible without you. I know you too are very happy, so, do you still hold a grudge?" Mimi gently prodded.

"I still haven't forgiven that elephant, but then, he was in musth and he didn't know what he was doing. I understand that now. I feel happy I did something kind and that you are my best friend." Nandu held Mimi's hands.

Together, they gazed at the setting sun, as sounds of the forest engulfed them. Though unknowingly, they had set an example and laid the foundation for a peaceful man and animal co-existence in their community.

***

Preethi Warrier has completed her Masters in Electronics Engineering and is an Assistant Professor. She is one among the winners of the TOI Write India Campaign Season-1, for the famous author Anita Nair.Her work can be found in anthologies like Arising From The Dust, Born Too Soon, She- The Warrior, Travel Diaries, Secret Diary, A Kaleidoscope of Asia, Sharing Lipstick and Shattered. She is a regular blogger with Momspresso, Womens' Web, LetsMakeStoriesDino, Chrysanthemum Chronicles, Beyond the Box, Induswoman Online, Juggernaut Books, Story Mirror, Pratilipi and Sharing Stories. She enjoys writing 100 word stories and has garnered appreciation on many platforms. She also won Second Prize at Asian Literary Society's Gitesh-Biva Memorial Awards-2020. Preethi resides in Mumbai with her husband and son.

The Albino Princess

Narayani V Manapadam

Once upon a time, there lived a group of mighty elephants in a dense forest in Thekkady, Kerala. The king was called Gajendra. He ruled over his tiny kingdom with kindness and love. He had an imposing frame. His massive white tusks shone in the rays of the midday sun. The sound of his trumpeting could be heard in faraway places. Every wild animal was scared of him. None of them had the courage to cross his path. But Gajendra was like a coconut.

He looked tough from the outside. However he was a soft-hearted husband. After a hectic day in the jungle, he loved to be with his queen Gajeshwari. He whispered sweet tales in her ears. Her eyes crinkled with joy, and she giggled nonstop when he cracked jokes about naughty monkeys. Finally, they went to sleep in a happy frame of mind.

[The arrival of the princess]

The joyous moment arrived a year after the grand wedding of Gajendra and Gajeshwari. The elephants waited with bated breath for the good news. An hour later, Gajeshwari was blessed with a bony female calf. A pleased Gajendra distributed free sugarcanes to all his subjects.

"My Queen! Have you thought of a name for our daughter?" asked Gajendra, his long trunk softly caressing her forehead.

Gajeshwari looked lovingly at her calf, who was trying to stand up, but kept on falling to the ground. "Airavati! She will be called Airavati!"

A tiny drop of tear rolled down the king's eye. "I hope she will be accepted by our subjects! She doesn't look like any of us. She looks so… white!"

Gajeshwari snuggled up to her husband. "She is divine. She is God's gift. The Lord of the Devas has a white elephant, who is considered divine. Why should you worry?"

"My dearest queen! We cannot compare ourselves with Gods. We are mere animals, after all."

"Your Majesty! I tell you, our Airavati will make us proud. Just wait and watch!"

[The antics of Princess Airavati]

The cute baby elephant Airavati kept her parents on their toes. Impatient to explore the strange looking world around her, she would spread her four legs apart and try to heave herself up. In the beginning, her attempts were not successful. She would slip and land on her back. Her mother would then prod her gently with her trunk, and she would roll over. Slowly, she started to totter and take hesitant steps. The sight of his daughter walking for the first time made Gajendra smile. Gajeshwari was a good mother, and would forever be alert for any sign of an enemy. She need not have bothered. Their subjects stood at a respective distance, grazing on the lush green grass. Sometimes they would pluck juicy fruits from the trees, and tuck them into their huge mouths. They did wonder about the strange colour of Airavati. She was not like them. She was not grey. She had been born white, but as the days went by, her skin had given way to a light shade of pink. That didn't stop the king and the queen from showering their affection on the goofy little princess. The members of the herd continued to be loyal to their kingdom.

Three months passed by. Airavati was growing up fast. One morning, while sprinkling water over herself, she asked her mother, "*Amma*! Why do I look different from you and *achchan*?"

Gajeshwari swayed her trunk playfully. "Nature has made you different. It's our duty to accept whatever our *amma* offers us!"

Airavati peered at her mother. "But you are my *amma*!"

The queen of the elephants laughed. "I am your *amma*! But there is a mother above me. Above all of us. She is called Nature!"

"Can I meet her?" asked Airavati innocently, her ears flapping.

Gajeshwari smiled. "Nature is around us, my child. In the water you drink. In the milk you drink from me. In the leaves which *achchan* eats. In the sun which shines over us. In the moon which lulls us to sleep. She is everywhere, Airavati."

"Is she also there in the flies which torment me, *amma*?" she asked in a rueful tone. Her tiny tail flipped from side to side.

"Yes, my sweetie pie!" Gajeshwari kissed her daughter, and drew her closer towards her bosom.

Airavati burped, and giggled loudly.

[Airavati learns an important lesson]

Fat tears trickled down little Airavati's eyes. She looked at her reflection in the clear river. Her mother was busy drinking water. Suddenly, the princess turned back, and rolled over the mud. Seven times. Eight times. Nine times. Ten times.

"What are you doing?" Gajeshwari asked in a loud voice.

Airavati stopped. "*Amma*! I want to be like you. Like my uncles and aunties. Like my *acchan*! See! My belly has become grey. Like you. I will repeat it until my whole body turns normal!"

The queen rushed to her calf. "Stop it, my child!"

"Wait, *amma*! I am not done."

An angry Gajeshwari stomped back to the river, and returned in a moment. She sprayed a huge jet of water over her daughter. The greyish mud slid off her body, like dew drops from a soft leaf, and Airavati was back to being pink.

The princess looked at her mother. "*Amma*! What did you do? Now I can never be like you!" she sniffled.

Gajeshwari hugged Airavati. "Hush! Hush, my baby! You are special. That's why our mother, Nature, has made you like this. I have told you this so many times. You don't listen to your mother!"

"I am sorry, *amma*! I won't disobey you anymore. I promise you!" Airavati whispered softly.

Her mother kissed her, and they ran towards the river to take a bath. Again.

[All's well that end well]

The herd of elephants gathered at the riverside. It was a special occasion for the clan. The official coronation of their princess was to take place. They stood next to one another, forming a straight line. Gajendra and Gajeshwari appeared, nodding at their faithful subjects, and thanking them for their constant support. They stopped once they reached the centre. They turned back. Airavati, the three-year-old albino elephant stepped on to the stage of her life in a graceful manner. The bumbling calf was nowhere to be seen. In its place was a confident adult elephant. She had come to terms with the reality that she would never be like the others. With acceptance came self-esteem. There was no stopping Airavati. She would prove her worth.

Gajendra plucked out some grass and placed it carefully on her daughter's forehead. Airavati bowed her head in front of her parents. The members of the herd trumpeted and swayed their heads once. The verdict was clear. They had accepted Airavati as their future queen.

The princess took the holy oath at the riverbank. "Folks! I hereby swear upon our mother, Nature, that I will rule over my kingdom in a fair and just manner. I assure you that none of you will be treated differently because you're different."

The majestic pachyderms bent their heavy bodies slightly, as a mark of respect for their queen. The heavens opened up, blessing their beloved Airavati. The forest was in safe hands.

***

Narayani is an aspiring writer trapped in the boring world of MS Excel. She's a crazy cat lady, a badge she proudly flaunts. She maintains a blog where she writes about random stuff.

Gappu's Homeward Journey

Aditi Lahiry

It was a pleasant morning in the jungle of Bandipur. The deer family had just finished taking a stroll. They were just about to enter inside that part of the jungle, where the oldest Banyan tree stood. It had given shelter to many animals and birds for years. Bhumi, the black bear, was also approaching the Banyan tree. He had consumed so much honey that he was hardly able to keep his balance while walking. He rolled over on the ground. The monkeys began to chatter, and birds chirped. Everyone was assembling near the tree because Mahabali, the herd leader of elephants who used to hold meetings in the forest, had invited all the animals for an urgent meeting.

" Why could Mahabali , 'The Great Storyteller' call all of us at this hour?" asked Bhumi. " I can hardly keep my eyes open. I had a good amount of honey collected from the huge bee hive , near the grey cave last night and I went to slumber quite late. That is the reason, I feel so lethargic and dull today," Bhumi continued to explain.

" That's ok Bhumi Anna, Mahabali chikappa always comes up early in the morning and shares wonderful stories. I love listening to his stories, " said Hiranya, the deer. Soon, Kami, the dark-faced langur, appeared with her son Chotu. Garuda, the Brahminy Kite, brought the news that Mahabali Chikappa was moving with a gait and moving along with a very old Elephant.

As soon as Mahabali arrived near the tree, along with the old elephant, who appeared too new to this forest, all the listeners gathered around him. They were too eager to listen to the stories.

Chotu freed himself from his mother's clutches and began to play with the too old elephant. He jumped on his back and tried to pull his tail, but Kami pulled her back and asked her to sit and listen to the story.

Mahabali instructed everyone to sit down and then said, " Today, I have asked all of you to assemble at this hour to tell you about Gappu, our new member in the forest. As you all can see, he is very old and he has just begun to enjoy his life of freedom in our forest. "

All the animals listened to Mahabali with rapt attention. They wanted to know who this old elephant was? Bhumi was the first to speak. "Ah! Well, it looks like this new member has not much energy left. Did he belong to this forest? Has he arrived from somewhere else? Will he be able to live happily? We are all eager to listen to the story of his life, please."

"Dear all, in order to begin the story of Gappu's life, let's go back to the time when he was born," Mahabali thus started narrating the story. " Gappu was born in the forests of Jalpaiguri, in North Bengal. Like other baby elephants, he loved to roll in the mud, splash the mud all over his body and enjoy life thoroughly in the wilderness. That is how he used to happily enjoy his life until one fateful day while he was enjoying himself in the muddy water in the core area of the forest, and all of a sudden, everything turned dark in front of his eyes. "

He continued, "When he woke up the following day, he was not in the forest, and there was no sign of his mother or, for that matter, the entire herd of elephants. His foot was tied to a thick iron shackle, and the shackle was tied to a strong pole. He began to weep and wail and called out to his mother. But only a strange-looking creature walked in front of him. He patted Gappu and gave him a bunch of bananas, which he ate up feeling extremely hungry.

As he looked around, he found some other elephants too. One which had enormous ears, just like a fan. He spoke to Gappu and said, " Hi Gappu , I am Jumbo . I have come from Africa. You are in the Circus now. That strange looking creature , who just fed you is Raju . He will soon start training you to perform tricks in the Circus show. Be very careful when he teaches you. Every time you commit an error he will hit you with a cane ."

Gappu listened with rapt attention, and from that moment on, Gappu and Jumbo became best friends. Raju began to train them to perform various tricks like jumping on the rings, small stools and juggling with colourful balls. After six months of training, he was ready to perform. Whenever he performed well, Raju gave him a special treat of jaggery, pineapple, and papayas. Yet, on days when he was down and could not perform well, Raju used to hit him with a cane. Sometimes, when he hit hard, Gappu and Jumbo's wounds would bleed too.

During one show, when the circus tent was too crowded, a trapeze artist, named Melina, decided to sit on Gappu's back and enter the stage, when all of a sudden some ants entered inside Gappu's trunk and the very next moment what everyone saw and felt was a loud

" Ha ... chhooooo", and with that, Melina fell on the ground. She was covered with dirt, and the audience began to laugh loudly. Gappu went wild with the sound, and before Raju could control him, he started running all over the stage and then ran down to all the visitors.

Seeing him run, Jumbo followed, Baloo, the black bear, followed him, and Rani and Raja, the monkeys, followed. They created such chaos that day that all the shows were cancelled. Meanwhile, Gappu and Jumbo fled away from the circus and wandered in the outskirts of Mysore.

That was when one of the mahouts of the Mysore Palace spotted them and brought them to the palace. They were both beautifully decorated and trained for the upcoming Dussehra festival. They carried the golden chariot of the goddess all around the city during the evening. A long procession followed them. After the grand celebration got over, they were taken back to the palace. They were now trained to give children and foreign tourists a ride on an everyday basis.

Soon Gappu began to enjoy this life, but deep in his heart, he longed for freedom and wished to run to the forest. They stayed in the palace and enjoyed this life for almost thirty-five years until one day when a young boy riding on Jumbo pricked him with a pin. Jumbo dropped the boy immediately and began to run. He ran towards the other side of the palace, where construction work was going on and stepped on the bed of nails, which made him bleed. " He was injured so badly that both his hind legs had to be amputated . As I watched this ghory incident, I was shocked. They took Jumbo away and he never returned after this incident. I kept waiting for him for many days.", Gappu, the old elephant, now spoke.

"One day, when they took me for a walk near the forest, a strange man with thick and curled moustaches fired at us. My mahout left me and ran away. That man caught me and took me deep inside the forest. He used to make me collect a lot of wooden logs which had a unique fragrance. I had seen the priests in the Mysore Palace burning some sticks which had a similar fragrance. Even during the Dussehra festival, the chariot that was led with the procession had the same fragrance.

This man was the cruelest and once even cut off my long tusks. It was indeed painful. He used to cause terror in the entire region, and the police were searching for him. Last week, they caught him, and I was released in the forest. ", Gappu the elderly elephant, explained with terror in his eyes.

Mahabali, the great storyteller, then explained that now Gappu had finally arrived home, and for the first time in his entire life, he felt free to enjoy his life in the natural forest.

All the animals who had assembled there decided to take turns to take care of old Gappu and help him enjoy the last days of his life in the free and natural ambiance. "The lush green forest of Bandipur , would help you heal better. We will bring food for you everyday , " Bhumi said.

The forest of Bandipur is where Gappu's home was. His life was full of adventures, but everywhere he went, he missed freedom. In his last days, he was lucky to get a taste of freedom. He guided other animals to stay and taste freedom. The young elephants learnt great lessons from him. " Always stay close to your herd , while you bathe in the river", he was advising Rushu and Doni, two young elephants again, as he watched them approaching the river. They were trying to stay away from the herd.

***

Aditi is an English and French Language trainer and passionate about writing short stories, poems and story telling too.

Airavata goes to the Lake

Harshita Nanda

The sun peeked over the mountains heralding the arrival of a new day. The soft breeze made the leaves of the palm tree dance and sway. The birds chirped merrily, welcoming the new morning as they busily flitted around. As the sun rose higher, it fell on the brick walls of the elephant enclosure at the edge of the forest. This enclosure was the home of elephants who belonged to the temple. The elephants took part in the rituals for religious festivals. At the moment, though, the enclosure was empty save for one very irritated baby elephant, who was making a mess by scattering straw everywhere. The baby elephant's name was Airavata.

Airavata being the youngest was loved and pampered by all. Today, however, Airavata was sulking as all the other elephants had been taken to the temple. The foreheads of the elephants had been decorated with colours, and their backs were covered with silks. They all looked very grand and regal. Airavata had wanted to go with them, but his mother, Amma, told him he was too small. "Too small huh," he thought, flapping his big ears. "I am a month old now. I am BIG! Amma does not understand how bored I get alone in the enclosure".

Suddenly he saw Goraiya sweep in. Goraiya, the sparrow, was his best friend in the whole world. Goraiya used to tell him stories about the big forest. Goraiya had also told him about the lake in the middle of the forest. A lake that Airavat really, really wanted to see. Airavat couldn't imagine how much fun it would be in the lake. He could play all day long in it, and the water would never get over like it did in the water trough of the enclosure. But how could he, Airavat thought, when he was not even allowed to go out.

"Why the sulky face"? Goraiya asked, perching on the wall. "I am bored! All I do is wander around this small enclosure. I want to see the forest and the lake", Airavata whined. Goraiya felt sad for Airavat. Goraiya could fly wherever she wanted to. There were no locks and gates to keep her inside a small area. And she really did not like seeing Airavat so sad. He was, after all, her best friend.

She thought and thought very hard, and suddenly, she had an idea. Hopping excitedly, she said, "I know just the fellow who can help you! This job can be done only by Badri the monkey"! Badri was mischievous, but he always knew how to crack the problem."Be ready tomorrow", she called out to Airavat before she extended her wings and flew off.

The following day, after Amma and the other elephants, were taken to the temple, Goraiya flew into the enclosure. "Psst, Psst", she whispered to Airavat, "go to the gate". Puzzled, Airavata went to the gate, where he saw Badri sitting on the wall. The human, who made sure no elephant escaped the enclosure, was sleeping on a chair. Badri gave a cheery wave to Airavata. Hopping down, Badri plucked the cap from the human's head, startling him awake. Seeing Badri holding his hat, the human shouted at Badri shaking his fists. Badri, grinning, leapt and jumped into the enclosure, taunting the human. The human was now angry at Badri. He opened the gate of the enclosure rushing in with his stick raised to hit Badri. "NOW!" shouted Goraiya to Airavat. Airavata quickly slipped through the gate and entered the forest. Airavata ran as fast as his legs would go, trampling through the bushes in the jungle, following Goraiya as she flew ahead. He felt a rush of adrenaline at the freedom to run freely! Up ahead, he could see a clearing and something gleaming beyond. "What is that"? He asked excitedly. Badri, who by then had joined them, grinned and replied, "That my friend is the lake"! Hearing this, Airavata ran even faster and, with a big whoop, jumped into the lake. Goraiya and Badri soon joined him, and all three had a rollicking time splashing each other.

Airavata felt happy playing with his friends until his stomach gave a big rumble. Goraiya laughed and said, "come on, let's get you something to eat". As they were stepping out from the lake, they heard the dreaded roar of the motor engine. "Oh No!" said Muniya, distressed, "The humans have found you!" Badri, sensing danger, quickly hid in the trees along with Goraiya. Airavat was left all alone in the clearing, shivering with cold and fear.

Three jeeps filled with humans roared into the clearing, coming to a stop where Airavat was standing. The first human to get down was the one who used to take amma to the temple. Airavata's heart was now beating very fast. Airavat wondered if he would be hit by the iron stick he had sometimes seen in the human's hand. But the human just patted his head softly. Another human now climbed down from the jeep. He seemed to be an important one, as all the others bowed to him. He had a long red mark on his forehead. He, too, patted Airavata's forehead and held out a banana for Airavata. Airavat was quite hungry, so he took the banana. But as soon as Airavata ate the banana, the world spun around him, and he fell down.

After a few hours, Airavat blinked his eyes open slowly. He was lying on the ground. He tried to get up, but his head and neck throbbed. Goraiya hopped close to him. "Are you ok"? she asked, " I was so worried!". "What happened"? Airavat asked, surprised to see himself still in the clearing. Goraiya shook her head, " I don't know. After you fell, all the humans surrounded you. We couldn't see anything, and then they just left". Airavata and Goraiya were puzzled. Why did the humans not punish Airavata for running away and take him back to the enclosure?

Goraiya flitted about Airavata, encouraging him to stand when they heard the sound of elephants trumpeting. Airavat and Goraiya were surprised to see all the temple elephants sauntering into the clearing. "Amma!!" shouted Airavata, spotting his mother, and ran towards her. Hugging Airavat tightly, Amma said, "Naughty boy! Do you know how worried I was"!

"Sorry Amma, I won't run away again", Airavat said in a small voice. "I sure hope not. Where will you run from here? We all are now going to be living in this forest"! amma said, laughing. "Really amma? But how?" asked Airavata. "Who knows what the humans think? They took out all of us from the enclosure and left us at the edge of the forest. We knew you would be at the lake, so we all came here. Now, do you want to play with water or not? Amma said.

Airavata nodded happily, and both of them laughed as they raced each other to get into the water where the other elephants were already playing!

***

Harshita Nanda is a lover of the written word, her forte has been writing microfiction. She has recently published her first book "Xanadu" this Story "Airavata Goes To The Jungle" was written for a daughter of a friend who asked her why she doesn't write stories for children.

The Memorable Birthday

Ramya Viswanathan

"Happy Birthday to you!"

"Happy Birthday to you!"

"Happy Birthday dear Veena"

"Happy Birthday to you!"

The voices grew loud, spreading cheers in the air. A big round of applause then ensued.

"Don't forget to make a wish before blowing off the candle, Veena", Nithya, her friend, reminded Veena.

Ten-year-old Veen nodded in acceptance. Closing her eyes for a few seconds, she wanted to wish many things for the moment. But one preceded all. Something she deeply longed for. Wishing it, she then blew the candle. She fed the first piece to her parents, and then her friends surrounded her with gifts.

After the long evening, Veena was all set to open her gifts that now occupied a part of her bedroom.

"I know, it is the weekend. Still, open the presents soon and retire to bed before midnight, alright dear?" her mother said.

"No bedtime story Ma?" Veena asked.

"Your papa is already tired. He shall read you tomorrow, Veena. Once again Happy Birthday darling," saying so Veena's mother left the room.

Birthdays are always exciting for Veena. New dress, chocolates, cake cutting with friends, a memorable day that she would await each year.

Reading the name on the cover, Veena began to open her presents. Most of them were storybooks, as her friends knew how she loved fairy tales and magical stories. Some beautiful teddy bears also were added to the existing bunch, which had crossed a dozen already.

Keeping them aside, she stretched herself, pulling her blanket as her eyes showed signs of tiredness. Soon she was fast asleep. The clock struck midnight when she felt someone waking her up. With blurry eyes, she saw someone or rather something standing. First, she thought it was her teddy bear. But it wasn't this huge. Rubbing her eyes well, she sat up and looked at it. Her eyes now widened to see an elephant standing on two legs. As she watched even more keener, the elephant had a spectacle on its trunk and a cute blue bow tie in its neck.

"Happy Birthday Veena, By the way, I am Timothy and you can call me Timmy." The elephant spoke.

Still surprised, Veena was unable to speak. Finally, gathering some courage, she said, "Am I dreaming, or are you real?"

"Every girl I meet has this doubt! Sigh! Veena dear, you are not dreaming and I am real. The purpose of my visit is to fulfill your wish when you blew the candle before cutting your birthday cake." Timmy smiled.

Veena recollected her wish. She wanted to visit the magical land that she heard in the bedtime stories her dad used to read from when she was two years old.

"So am I going to the magical land?" Veena exclaimed.

Timmy grinned as a whooshing wind blew and took them away.

The next moment, Veena was in a different place. She felt the pleasant smell of flowers. It was like she was standing in beautifully painted scenery. She looked around for a while, and then Timmy interrupted.

"Shall we begin our tour, dear?"

"Oh yes. Before that, may I know why and how my wish was granted?" Veena was curious.

"There is an evaluation process that reviews the wishes of every kid during their birthday. Let me check yours," saying, so Timmy opened his iPad.

After browsing for a while, he replied.

"So Veena, when your friends made fun of you that a fairyland or a magical space never existed, you put your foot down and fought, saying that it did exist, and you would visit there someday. You believed in us, my dear. Then the following are the other reasons.

- You fought for your friend when the elder students tried to bully her
- Always shared your food with the unfortunate people you see on the roadside.
- Obeyed your parents, and you had been a very good girl

So are we clear now?"

Veena was so delighted to hear about herself.

"Yes, Timmy! Let's go," now she was onboard.

They walked through the lovely greenery path. The chirping of the cute purple birds, the multi-coloured roses made Veena instantly fall in love with them.

"We have reached our first stop," Timmy said.

Veena looked at the place. A magnificent palace stood before her. They entered the gates and walked through a while when she noticed her. She looked beautiful in her lovely gown. But something seemed different. She was holding a sword and was fighting against a man. Veena looked closer at her, and then something caught her eyes; the sparkling shoes, she found her.

"It is Cinderella! But why is she fighting with her Prince?" Veena questioned.

Adjusting his bow tie, Timmy answered.

"Actually, she isn't fighting but learning to fight and the Prince is teaching her the skill."

"But why? They were supposed to live happily ever after." Veena was still puzzled.

"Oh, the reason is every woman needs to protect herself and not depend upon others. That way even though Cinderella is the Queen, she must know how to safeguard herself and her people."

Veena was totally taken aback. She imagined Cinderella dancing with him all day, but the reality was different.

With some thoughts hovering in her mind, Veena and Timmy continued their journey.

Their next stop was the most exciting part for Veena, the fairy city. There were hundreds of small, pretty creatures flying around. Veena felt her barbie dolls turned into butterflies. All of them had a tiny wand and were dressed in flowing gowns. All seemed very busy, which astonished Veena.

"Timmy, what are the fairies doing?"

"They are working!"

"What! Why? They have their magical wands. One swish and their needs would be done." Veena's idea of the fairies opened from her mind.

"Oh dear! I do have to agree that they possess the magic wand but they never use it unnecessarily. Work is a part of their lifestyle like how your parents go to the office. In a similar way, they do a lot here. Some can stitch beautiful clothes, while some can make pretty cute jewelry. As you can see, the string of beads that is holding my spectacles were made by one of them."

Veena then looked at Timmy closer. Yes! It was glittering, the beads that made up the string of his glasses. In his grey shade, they looked even prettier. She went near one of the fairies who were busy scraping some bits of a mushroom.

Reading her mind, Timmy spoke, "She is a talented interior designer. Just remodeling one of the oldest houses. You know with her magical touch it would soon take over a fresh look."

By then, a cute little fairy came to Veena and gave her a pink bracelet. It had fairy figurines all over.

"Thank You" Veena was overwhelmed with joy. The fairy waved her goodbye and went back to her house, a stout green mushroom.

With yet another string of thoughts creeping into Veena's mind, they reached their following location. A sudden fragrance wafted into her as she breathed in deep.

"Roses!" she exclaimed.

Yes, it was a beautiful garden of roses with vibrant colours. Pink, yellow, red, orange and weirdly even green roses bloomed and blushed in the gentle winds. She felt like floating on a soft, fluffy colourful cloud.

"Where are we?"

"Why don't you take a guess, my dear? Let me give you a clue. What would you do when one of your teeth falls?" Timmy asked with a naughty twinkle in his eyes.

"I would keep it under my pillow that night so that the tooth fairy would come and take it, leaving behind a candy for me." Veena quickly answered, like reciting a poem from her kindergarten days.

"Yes! We are going to meet her," opening his arms wide in the air, Timmy replied.

With radiant eyes, in a glittering long gown walked in the Tooth Fairy. She waved at Veena and welcomed them to her flower garden.

"Wow! The roses are so beautiful," Veena spoke, forgetting to blink.

"This one is yours," saying so, the Tooth Fairy pointed a pink one at Veena.

"How is that?"

"Whenever a kid believes in me and hides their fallen tooth under the pillow, then I visit them, leaving a candy behind, as you know. I bring the tooth to my garden here and plant it. The next day it blooms into a beautiful rose," she spoke in such a soft voice that made Veena wonder if she sang.

Now the pink rose felt some kind of connection to Veena. Caressing its petals softly, she blew a kiss to it and waved the Fairy goodbye.

Their final destination was the mischievous anthill. Veena has already read that the ants are hard workers at any given time of the year. To her surprise, she saw a crowd peeping into an ant who seemed like he stood in the middle of making something.

"Timmy!"

"Hush dear. Let us watch them from a distance."

"Oh, what is happening?"

"The most mischievous ant in the entire lot luckily made it to the Wizardry course by clearing the entrance exam. Of all these years except him, none had been able to step into the magical course. He was naughty but I should admit, he was intellectual as well. So after graduation, he has finally started his course here, and to prove himself, he is busy making the healing potion. It involves permanent relief for the others from their constant backache that emerges out of carrying heavy loads, day and night. The most important thing here is, he never gave up, even when people mocked him. He tried hard and achieved his dream." After the long speech, Timmy walked to the pond to gulp down some water. A few drops sprinkled over his glasses, which he neatly wiped off, and came back to Veena. She was as well immersed along with the others, noticing how the potion came.

After immensely stirring the pot, the colour changed from purple to green, and all cheered over. Veena was excited as well, and she gave the ant a huge round of applause. The ant who succeeded in his mission bowed before the rest to show his gratitude. He had become the hero of the day, and it thrilled Veena to watch them celebrate their happiness.

Their tour had come to an end, and worried lines were seen all over her face.

"Will you bring me here again for my next birthday?" her eyes pleaded.

"Our fairy Godmother decides upon that and I promise to recommend your name again," giving her a warm hug, Timmy clasped her hands tight to drop her home.

"Thank You Timmy", she kissed his forehead. Timmy also felt heavy whenever he would bid farewell to the kids. That was the part where his heart always sank.

In a moment, Veena was on her bed under the blanket, and she slept thinking of her journey.

The next morning, she narrated the entire incident to her parents.

"She had a wonderful dream?" her parents whispered to each other.

Veena then looked at her wrist. The bracelet with the fairy figurines shone brightly. Now, she waited for her next birthday. Would it be magical?

***

Ramya V is an IT professional who delves into the world of books. A voracious reader who believes the pen is mightier to bring about a change. She dedicates her time to writing stories and poems in English and Tamil. She picks her pen to write when she stumbles upon any social incident that she feels needs attention. Writing fiction inspired from real life incidents, tops her list. In 2018, she also won the event – 'Which quote of Mahatma Gandhi changed your heart' hosted by Gandhi World Foundation. Apart from bagging quite some anthologies as a co-author, her works are regularly published on online sites such as Women's Web and Women's Web Tamil. She is also a recipient of the Literoma Author Achiever Award 2021.

True Friendship Never Ends

Zenobia Merchant

There was a hushed silence that befell the jungle. All the animals went about their daily chores with no greetings or camaraderie. Animosity left a stale smell in the air.

Jumbo, the elephant, walked past the stream carrying a trunkload of logs. His head hung low. He carried on with his chores almost mechanically. After unloading his last lot of the day, he retired to his home at the far end of the forest. Entering his home, he made himself dinner, which was eaten in stark silence. He washed the vessels and laid them to dry and retired for the night. He looked at the frame on his bedside and kissed his friend's goodnight.

The next morning began like any other day for Jumbo. He was on his 6th trip when he heard a whimper. He went towards the direction of the sound only to find his friend Fluffy the rabbit stuck in a wire mesh.

"Fluffy, are you hurt? Did the mesh cut through you?" Jumbo inquired.

"I'm ok Jumbo. Could you please ask Simba to come and help me? Am sure you wouldn't want to associate with us anymore." Fluffy cried, writhing in pain.

Fluffy's words felt like a knife piercing through his heart. The events which he was trying to forget came flashing in front of him...

Fluffy, Simba the lion, and Jumbo were the thickest friends in the jungle. Their friendship amazed everyone and made them wonder how the three who were so different from each other yet bonded so well.

Fluffy was the heart of the trio, always into some antics, jumping and hopping around, keeping the other two on their toes. Simba and Jumbo were the lazy ones who liked to lie by the lake and rest.

Eva the snake was extremely jealous of this trio and somehow wanted to break the bond between them.

One day, when Jumbo was too tired to be with his friends, he caught a wink by the river bank and was surprised to see Eva next to him.

"Ah! You are alone. Where are your friends? Guess they left you alone and finally took off. Guess the rumours were true?", Eva hissed at Jumbo.

Jumbo was clueless. "What rumour are you talking about?"

"Fluffy and Simba both consider you dull and a slowpoke. Because of your heavy body, you don't enjoy experimenting with them and tire easily. Fluffy and Simba are lithe and nimble and like to be on the move and prefer each other than being with you."

"This can't be true. My friends would never say something like this about me. You must be mistaken, Eva," replied a visibly shaken Jumbo.

"Is it? Then why don't you go to the playground and see for yourself how they are cherishing their time spent, without you."

Jumbo marched towards the play area and was shocked to see the sight that beheld him. Fluffy and Simba were chasing each other and didn't seem to miss him at all. He remembered Eva's words and thought them to be true. Hurt and dejected, he walked away from there.

"Hey Simba, wasn't it Jumbo who just left? Why do you think he came back? Eva had already passed on his message that he didn't want to be disturbed."

"Fluffy, you know how Jumbo is. He must've come over to say bye and walked away, seeing us in play. He's so caring he wouldn't have disturbed us," Simba answered, taking Jumbo's side.

Just then Eva slithered- "Guess the rumours are true then. Jumbo walked past you two without saying a word. He's been talking to the others about how bored he gets with your childish games and finds your company boring. He is on the lookout for more mature and interesting friends."

Fluffy and Simba couldn't believe their ears. Eva's words hurt them and both thought them to be true since Jumbo went by without acknowledging them. They both distanced themselves from Jumbo so that he could make friends of his own liking.

Jumbo felt restless and decided to have a chat with his friends the next day. He would take part and be more physically active with them if that's what they wanted. Their friendship meant the world to him.

He packed Fluffy and Simba's favourite treats and reached their favourite spot. Both were sitting quietly by the river and were shocked to see Jumbo there. When Jumbo offered them the goodies, Fluffy thanked him and asked why was he there and did he find himself the friends that he was looking for?

Simba also added that Jumbo was right and that their childish games must've been boring for Jumbo. The exchange shocked jumbo and he replied that it was vice versa and that they were bored of his company and lethargy and so wanted him to quit the group. Just then, Eva came around and added to Jumbo's wound by agreeing with him that all that he had heard the other two say was the truth.

Eva dragged Jumbo from there where he was not needed and tried introducing him to new friends, but Jumbo missed Fluffy and Simba and distanced himself from everyone. It had been 6 months since the incident, and neither of the friends tried to break the ice. Eva kept hovering around Jumbo and didn't let the trio meet or talk out their differences.

When Jumbo saw Fluffy in pain, he couldn't care less. "Fluffy, I know you don't like me and would rather prefer Simba to help you, but I still consider you both as my best friends and I cannot see you in agony. Let me help you from this mesh and then we can part ways again and become strangers."

Fluffy was shocked to hear Jumbo's words and realised Jumbo's true intent and love. He started crying with relief and told him all that Eva had told them. Both friends realise the mischief created by Eva to break their friendship and how they let this mistrust creep into their strong bond, and almost destroy their friendship.

They went looking for Simba and cleared all the misunderstanding and confusion and hugged just like old times and promised to speak to each other first, before believing any third person.

They vowed to make their friendship even stronger and not let anything or anyone come between them.

Moral:- Don't let misunderstanding destroy a relationship. Always talk it out openly and sort differences face to face.

***

Zenobia Merchant is a Writer/Poet/Blogger/Content Writer by Passion and a Math Tutor by Profession.

She has written Poems and Jingles since her school days and loves to read varied genres, fiction being the food for her mind. Passionate about murder mysteries and psychological thrillers, 'Gone Girl', 'The Fountain Head' and 'The Alchemist' feature amongst her favourites. She has written content for various online platforms and her work has been a part of many anthologies.

Rathi and Damayanti

Sivaranjini Anandan

Airavata

In the days of royal kings and ethnic queens in India, temples were the symbol of rich architecture, art, and culture. Elephants were part of such huge empires. They were part of the army during wars, a means of travel for the royal family, they were a symbol of treasures, royalty and good luck for the emperor.

Elephants are not just giants, but they have the biggest brains of all the animals on the earth, So they never forget a thing stored in their memory. They communicate with their herd with 70 varieties of calls. Their trunks are as strong as the hope that dwells in a brave human soul yet sensitive as the rose flower too.They are great swimmers and use their trunks like snorkels. Elephants are similar to human beings when it comes to love for their family. They grow within a big inclusive joint family with sisters, aunts, and cousins.

Once upon a time there was a beautiful elephant, greenish-grey in colour, glowing like white gold. Its feet were strong as the banyan tree that withstood the stormy wind and mouth as red as shining red carpet at the entrance in the palace. Its eye was sparkling like a mixture of blue, red, and purple colours that glitter being part of the soap bubble that floats in the air.

Because it appeared magnanimous and magnificent, she was named Rathi. And was the favourite elephant of every member of the royal family, including the royal princess Damayanthi.

She carried the princess on her back from being a little girl to the day she was a beautiful bride. Life was as smooth as taking the most travelled path every day for the splendid royal elephant. Tasty food, love and care was always part of its royal treatment. Life can never be better and breezy, it thought to itself.

Like all of us, there were hard days in her life as well. She met with an accident and injured her legs. The elephant could not travel like before or get attention from the royal family or the royal treatment that was given earlier. Her world changed drastically. The river was the only place he could slowly walk to with its damaged leg. "Now that is life too." she murmured in a melancholy tone to its own reflection in the river.

But, there was something as strong as his trunk. It was the love of his mother.

"Things can never be the same mom. Why is it like this?"

The mother with love and wisdom in her eyes replied, "You know, dear, it is not what others think of you that can make your life better, but what you think and believe about yourself and your own abilities that can help you, believe in yourself and your inner glow and emerge as the unbeatable version of yourself."

"The Airavata, our heavenly ancestor, also known as the elephant of the clouds, is a white elephant with ten tusks and five trunks born out of the churning of the ocean and carried lord Indira. He had the magical powers to fly and, I am sure, one day, you will be able to fly too." She said comforting Rathi.

"You are too funny mom, here I am unable to walk properly and you are giving me false hopes!"

Rathi almost lost interest in life. It was darkness all around for the poor thing.

"Had I been safer while rolling the wooden rollers working for the palace renovation, I would not have hurt my legs that led to this injury." she would ruminate aloud.

The elephant was not able to forget the painful days of its life. For it flashed on his mind now and then. For some time she brooded over her past mistakes and regretted not being cautious. But all this thinking only led to despair.

After many days of reflection and contemplation Rathi decided to accept his flaws and even win over them. She disclosed to her mother about the hope that fills her heart every time she sees her, and her undeterring belief that she could fly, fills her with positivity.

The Jumbo often stood in front of the God of good beginnings Ganesha whenever she felt the hope in her heart getting drenched in the river of her self-doubt and prayed.

"I thought, since your face is the same as mine, you will listen to my prayer."

"I cannot live like before nor do I carry the royal family on my back and walk miles like I did before ,but when I see the love my mother's love for me, an invisible wand of magic touches me and forces me to believe that I will be back even stronger than before."

"I do not know if I can ever fly. But, if this came true, I can't wait to see the happiness on my mothers face." Rathi prayed with bowed head in front of the idol near the river bank.

The next day, the elephant wandered and isolated herself. It was the festive season and, Damayanthi, the princess, visited her parents. During her stay she was told about Rathi and her plight. She was saddened to know about her favorite pet, childhood friend and well-wisher.She went looking for her.

Airavata

"Oh Rathi! What happened to the legs that carried me miles? How have you been?"

Her eyes welled up with tears as she hugged her strong trunk.

Rathi tried to console her and whipped her tears away. Since then everyday she made it a point to visit the garden to check on Rahti.

One morning she went collecting flowers by the riverside on her own without her royal servants. She liked visiting this place often as she saw the reflection of her husband for the very first time in the river waters when he visited her kingdom even before their marriage.

This was her favourite destination.

She would often sit there near the water and the lotus leaves and enjoy the scent and view of the nearby garden.

While she was performing her daily ritual of collecting flowers that day to decorate the Ganapathi idol she unexpectedly slipped in the river. Frightened and scared she started shouting for help. Rathi heard Damayanthi's voice for help, she swiftly reached the river to rescue the princess and helped her get out of the deep waters.

Damayanti was still trembling in fear but was speechless with immense gratitude in her eyes.

"You came with wounded legs to save me. You have shown the world that love lies within every being. I feel blessed to find that selfless love in your tender heart. I may be the Queen of my kingdom but for you, I am still your same little princess" Damayanthi cried as she hugged Rathi.

On their return home, Rathi was blessed by the elephant God with the power to fly. She transformed into Airavatha and flew with the princess on her back. When the mother elephant saw people garlanding and applauding Rathi, her happiness had no bounds.

"I always knew, dear, that you will fly. I am so proud of you. And yes, you were and always will be my Airavatha, who brought the rain of happiness for this kingdom."

"Mom, I do not know what made me forget all my pain but whenever I see your eyes shining with happiness and pride and positivity ,I get the power to overcome all the hurdles of life."

Eventually, the elephants made a run towards each other, screaming and trumpeting the whole time. When the mother-daughter duo met, they formed a loud, rumbling mass of flapping ears, clicked tusks, and entwined trunks and filled the air with a symphony of the trumpets, rumble screams, and roars.

It was Ganesh Chaturthi, so there was bliss and happiness all around. And, the princess was all set to return to back her inlaws. Rathi was once again respected, loved, and worshipped for the occasion as the news of her saving the princess spread all over the kingdom.

Rathi was back on her feet and was ready to carry the princess back home. It made a loud happy roar as she knelt before the princess to climb on her back.

***

Sivaranjini is a teacher by passion. She is a blogger and an ebook author with an engineering degree in food technology and masters in administration. She loves to blog about the world of food technology. She explores new horizons of food technology writing with her blog.

She also blogs about self-improvement, wherein she writes inspirational stories and talks about the power of appreciating the simple yet beautiful things of life. She also has two stories in two anthology (eBooks) to her name.

25 Days Around the World

Priyanka Chatterjee (Golpodidi)

Mount-K, a week before Biswakarma Puja

"Maa! This year I want to stay in Kolkata a little longer! And this time, can I be on my own, pleaseeeeeee?", asked Gansu.

Durga raised her eyebrows.

"Every year I have to tag along with you, Lax, Sarso and KK; and that too for just a 4 days stay we have to travel for 7 days. Not worth it! This year can I leave a little earlier please to explore Kolkata with my friends? But promise – on the way back here from Kolkata, I would join you four. Also Saptami,

Astami, Nabami, Dashami, these four days— I won't move an inch away from you. Pakka promise!"

Durga didn't seem happy with all that pleading. Gansu didn't sound convincing at all.

"Maa, I have to anyway visit Kolkata during Biswakarma Puja along with other friends from our herd. Even though I am physically not entirely like them, our hearts connect. I have turned 10 this year. I need to go with them more for moral support, you know that! All that I am asking is after Biswakarma Puja, instead of coming back and going again on Saptami, I want to extend my stay for a month. 7 days travel each way is hectic, Maa. Can I please stay back with others? I promise I will never venture alone. Wherever I go, we will go together as a herd. Now that should be a deal, Maa!"

Durga still kept nodding her head from left to right, at regular intervals, as Gansu spoke without stopping. But gradually the pace of her nodding became slower and slower and finally it stopped. Seeing that, Gansu smiled from-ear-to-ear.

"Thank you, Maa. You are the best Maa in the world. I will be your good boy I promise. See you, Lax, Sarso and KK in another month's time. I can't wait to share my adventure stories with you four."

Durga hugged Gansu for she had never stayed without him - not even for a single day. And now her 10-yr-old son would be on his own for a month. Would he be able to manage? He can't control his hunger, what if he over-eats? What if he falls sick? But on the contrary, this experience will also make Gansu tougher.

A faint smile appeared on Durga's face - Why not! Gansu is quite mature, intelligent, kind and powerful, compared to his age. "Go, Gansu and come back with lots of stories to tell.",said Durga.

Gansu aka Ganesha, her half-elephant half-human son left for the Earth, precisely Kolkata.

Kolkata, 16th September, on Biswakarma Puja eve

Thump! Gansu and his elephant friends land on Earth. It was time to get inside the clay idols, before Puja starts. Thankfully the elephant herd has reached on time. Lord Biswakarma has not dialled the rider service yet. Before they could relax for sometime, there came the call. Lord Biswakarma is ready with his metal axe. Gansu and friends fetched him and arrived in no time; Biswakarma sat on the back of the elephant and soon they reached the Puja Pandal. Tomorrow is going to be a long day. After 7 days of tiring travel from Mount-K, Gansu finally fell asleep lying cozily under Biswakarma's Dhoti.

Kolkata, 17th September, Biswakarma Puja

Morning, Kolkata. All set for the day. Morning rituals began. The priest has arrived. Gansu loved the Agarbatti aroma in the room, but what attracted him more was the smell of the food. The fruits that are kept for Prasad as well as the Bhog that is being cooked in the vicinity. All the craftsmen – the blacksmiths, the potters, the factory-workers, the engineers in the neighborhood are making merry since their hard work during the entire year gets recognised on this one single day. They can eat as much Mutton and Rice as they want, today. They can play music and dance to the fast numbers as long as they want to today. Nobody would complain, nobody would ask for the volume of work completed today. Biswakarma Puja was their day. Gansu also was intermittently moving to those tunes and secretly grabbing his bites from Puja Prasad and Bhog kept in front of the Biswakarma idol. It was a long day but the day after is going to be even longer as Gansu's month-long adventure begins tomorrow.

Kolkata, 18th September, the day after Biswakarma Puja

With the first rays of the Sun, Gansu woke up with a start. Whispered in elephant language and the sound ripples reached all other Vahanas of all the idols around. They bid Lord Biswakarma adieu. He would be good even without them on his way back as humans would immerse him in the Ganges river and the way in through the sacred water is fairly easy.

Now the elephant herd was free from their duties and everyone wished for happy times where they could dance, sing, make merry and travel through Kolkata and beyond.

Kolkata, 20th September, two days after Biswakarma Puja

Gansu and friends were walking down the alley when they heard a shrill. As they rushed in that direction, they paused for a moment in awe. One plastic-thatched hut in the slums was on fire and there was a baby crawling inside, crying maybe for her mom. Nobody around was coming forward to lend a helping hand. Gansu looked at his friends. They stepped backwards too and dwindled their trunks in disapproval.

Gansu remembered his mother's words "Never move alone without your herd." 'But Maa, I don't have a choice here! Someone is dying' he thought.

Gansu walked in as fast as he could. The heat of the fire made his face turn red. The flames made his skin feel almost burnt. Should he go back? But he couldn't turn back as Gansu looked into the baby's eyes. She had already stretched her arms to her saviour. Gansu had to move inside!

While everyone in the elephant herd had lost hope for Gansu- there he was! Coming outside the hut with the baby bundled in his trunk. Gansu safely put the baby on the ground and joined back his herd.

Thereon, everyone stopped talking to him. They won't take the blame when there would be a show cause motion on Mount-K. They had NO to Gansu a million times but he didn't listen. How could he do it! How could he risk his own lives! They were confident that Durga would definitely teach her a good lesson.

Kolkata, 11th October, Durga Puja Saptami

Gansu was very tensed, what would Maa say when they meet today. He had his intentions right and he didn't mean to disobey Maa. But he didn't have much choice except moving away from the herd and to attend to what was important. Gansu informed Maa everything in the presence of Lax, Sarso and KK. Even though Gansu's brother and sisters disapproved of his adventures, Durga didn't scold him at all. Next four days passed in a jiffy. Many human children this year found the Ganesha idol in the Durga Puja Pandal winking at them, smiling and secretly waving at them. The one month rendezvous of Gansu came to an end with Dashami as the entire family travelled back to Mount-K.

Mount-K Award Ceremony Day

Few months have passed since Durga and her sons and daughters came back from Earth. Today once again there's reason enough to be happy as today was Mount-K Award Ceremony Day. Everybody reached there prim and proper. Nobody knew who was the lucky fella to get the award this year. All gods, goddesses, their consorts, Vahanas, associates waited with bated breaths.The envelope was opened by the master of ceremonies-

"This year's award goes to…" Gansu closed his eyes and wished if he would have not gone beyond his own limits, while helping others. Maa asked him to be safe and always stay with the herd. But his call of duty made him do those things. Anyway, this is not the last year of awards. There would be another time. But wait, what! The emcee said-

"This year's Mount-K Award goes to our beloved Gansu for showcasing exceptional leadership skills and inspiring others."

The entire elephant herd cheered.

"Three cheers for Gansu, hip hip hooray!"

***

Priyanka Chatterjee aka 'Golpodidi' is an International Story Consultant, an Award-winning Storyteller, a Process Drama Coach, a Design Thinker, an MBA (Gold Medalist), an alumna of International Institute of Storytelling, Emerson College, UK. She's the Artistic Director, Arts4Change International; Director, Storytelling Education and Arts India Council (SEAIC).

With 15+ years of experience in Fortune 500 MNCs & leading Indian Media House, she founded 'Wild Strawberry' - an Art Exploration Organisation. Till date, 'Wild Strawberry' is tasted by more than 2.5 Lakh children and 50000 adults as Chatterjee has traveled the world with her Story bag. She believes- "The power to change your life lies in changing your story."

Jumborina and Rose Fairy

Vijeta Harishankar

Long ago, somewhere far away in the blue sky, beyond those white clouds, was the world of Fairies.

And what do you think the Fairy Land looked like?

Well, if you were to see it by yourself, I'm sure you would have called it the prettiest thing ever witnessed by you.

It had a different charm to itself. The sky there was pink while the water ran violet. The tree trunks were blue with the leaves glittering like pure gold, and the stones and pebbles were all emeralds, rubies and diamonds.

Hmm... I can already feel the sparkle in your eyes.

The ground there was unlike the one we have on our planet. It was special. It was like a trampoline. Nobody ever walked or ran in fairyland. All they did was bounce happily like a ball, else rolled or cartwheeled merrily to reach a place.

The fairyland enjoyed one season which was everlasting, that was the season of bliss and peace, and those who dwelled there were all as tiny as a little bird. The tallest of the creatures grew just about a foot tall. Though the land allowed the critters to enjoy their freedom, it did have few rules to sustain the season of mirth and harmony.

Won't you be interested to know what it was?

It was the austere usage of the Magic words; Please, Thank You, and Sorry.

Ah! Such a Wise practice, isn't it?

There was no room for people to sulk or to remain sad with long faces. And even if they ever had one, the offender was wise and nice enough to rectify the folly by uttering those magic words.

In this land of bliss and magic lived a tiny, chubby, and naughty Jumborina. She was an active baby elephant who lived with her parents, somewhere deep in the fairyland woods. Jumborina was three years old when her parents decided to put her in a nearby school.

Though initially, she resented going to school, standing in the queue with one hand distance, reciting those nursery rhymes, and listening to her teacher, she soon began enjoying it as the place helped her make new friends. She had made a special friend too, Tina, the cub with whom she shared her tiffin box during recess.

After eating their breakfast, they played on the slides and swings in the school's soft play area. Somedays, their teacher encouraged them to play tag, hopscotch, and even hide and seek. During these times, the entire class went hopping about and had loads of fun.

After school had gotten over, she went back to her home all hopping and bouncing with joy, hand in hand with her best friend, Tina.

And don't you wish to know how small they both were?

Psst! to give you an idea, they were just the size of the tiniest ball you have in your play zone!

Tina's house came before Jumborina's. Once she bid her adieu, she preferred taking a bit longer route to her own house.

This particular path had lots of trees that stood tall on the sidewalk. Also, the route was filled with sparkling pebbles, which Jumborina enjoyed collecting. She had a brilliant collection of such dazzling stones, which she had carefully kept inside the rainbow-coloured bag stitched by her mother.

Just before she took a turn towards her house was a beautiful violet lake. It was home to a variety of fishes and turtles. Jumborina would take a slight deviation from her path and spend some time throwing a few pebbles into the water. She enjoyed watching the ripples that those stones created when they hit the water body. She would later return home all happy, waiting for the next morning.

One day as she approached the path that led to the lake, she found an amusing sight. She saw a cute little fairy girl taking off her wings and placing them on a golden-hued rock near the lake. She thereafter dipped her right big toe and churned the violet water as though she was examining the temperature. All the while, Jumborina observed her hiding behind a huge tree. The fairy later went merrily swimming to the other side of the lake.

The wings that lay temporarily abandoned caught the attention of little Jumborina.

' Oh! How I wish I too had such a lovely pair of wings to fly!' She sighed at the thought of it and later went her way.

The following day and the day after it... and again, Jumborina found the fairy girl almost at the same time, coming for a swim and leaving behind her wings, only to come out after a long gap to take her belongings and eventually flying away to an unknown destination.

Those wings by now had caught the fancy of the baby elephant. The more she tried to keep her gaze away from them, the more challenging it became for her to handle her desire to try them on.

' Rina my child, how much ever you like someone else's belongings, you'll stay away from it, alright! And if you still can't get over your temptation to touch it, you'll do so only after seeking permission.' Her mother's voice ricocheted inside her mind.

Though an obedient child, this time, Jumborina decided to overlook her mother's advice and go with the flow of her temptation. Without her awareness, she went bouncing towards the wings, and in no time, she had them wearing and attempting to fly.

Boing she went up and *boing* she came down. She tried once again and came down...**Boing.**

She later got petrified,' What if the fairy comes out and finds her wings missing from the place?'

She promptly placed them back with a determination to try them again the next day.

At home and in school, she was tempted to share it with her mother and Tina. But then she decided otherwise.

The following day on her way back home, she took the longer route and stood behind the big tree all over again. She waited with bated breath for the fairy girl to get into the water. Once that happened, she gingerly bounced towards the wings, and *Boing Boing*, she went again.

Boing up Boing down and *Boing Boing* she went up-down like a spring.

Trrrr....she heard a sound and Oh my! She found herself hanging by the tree branch. The world had turned topsy turvy in a snap. She looked up and realised the tattered wings, at that point, were the only saving grace, safeguarding her from an impending fall. She attempted to wriggle her legs, but they were stuck deep inside the hole of the tree trunk. With all her might, she pulled them out only to land face down...Thud!

'Aww...' she cried bitterly, over her bruised face and limbs. Somehow, with great effort, she pushed herself to go near the lake. She was rinsing her face and limbs when she heard the gurgling sound coming from the lake. She knew it was the fairy girl coming back to take her wings.

Jumborina sat biting her nails feverishly.

' How do I face her now?'

' Oh golly, Why didn't I listen to mommy's advice?' She cursed herself all the more.

'Oh, God! Oh, God! Where do I hide my face?'

Saying this, she dunked herself in the lake water. If her lungs had cooperated, she had plans to stay there forever, but unfortunately, they resisted after some time, and she had to come out, panting and puffing for breath.

' Waaah! Boohoohoo.' She found the fairy girl crying.

' My wings, what happened to them? Who did this? Now how do I go back to mamma?'

The fairy girl wailed inconsolably.

Meanwhile, Jumborina gently bounced and went near her. The sad fairy was still to acknowledge her presence when Jumborina initiated the conversation with a guilt-ridden heart.

' Don't cry, we can mend this,' said Jumborina hesitantly.

' What do you mean, we can mend this? It takes a fortnight to grow a new pair of wings. I can't stay here for so long, all alone, away from home, away from my mom,' Fairy girl said worryingly.

' And who are you, by the way?' She eventually asked Jumborina the question she had dreaded the most.

' I... I... I'm Jumborina and I'm to be blamed for your tragedy.' She confessed.

' Whaaat...How dare you? How could you?'

Jumborina was shivering from head to toe when she remembered the magic words. She quickly used them to her rescue.

' I'm sorry, please forgive me! Please!' She pleaded. Once she uttered those magic words, she knew she could handle things in a better way.

' My ...my mom is good at stitching.
I'm sure she will know how to mend this.'

' Is it? Please take me to her. My mom doesn't know I'm here. How I wish I had not kept this a secret. ' The fairy girl brooded.

' What is your name? If I may ask you?' Asked Jumborina.

' My name is Rose and I'm from Lullaby island. I came here for a swim. I enjoy coming here, occasionally.'

' I know, I have been observing you,' informed Jumborina.

' You have been spying on me? Since when?' quizzed Rose.

' There is no time for such an explanation, please allow me to take you to my mom, she'll help us. And I sincerely apologise for my folly.'

The two reached Jumborina's house and were welcomed by her mother. They soon told her about everything that had happened.

' Hmm...Rina, that's why I always tell you to stay away from other people's belongings.' Mommy elephant had not finished when Rose eagerly handed over her tattered wings to her, 'Could you mend this for me? Please! My Mommy doesn't know I'm here and I have to get back home on time.'

' My...My ... what is left for me to mend them... nothing! It's trash. I can't do anything about it,' sighed Mommy elephant and sat down fluttering her eyes in dismay.

' Waat?... then how do I get home? It takes a good two weeks to grow a new pair.' cried Rose fairy.

' Jumborina, look what have you done to her?' Mommy elephant got annoyed.

' Any other way, we can help you, dearie?' Mommy asked with all concern.

Rose scratched her head in desperation before an unexpected smile crossed her lips.

' Aunty, could you make temporary wings for me using bird's feathers?'

' Of course darling, but who would help us?' Mommy elephant began pondering.

' Mommy, who else but our neighbour, Macaw aunty. She is kind-hearted. I'm sure she will be fine to lend a few,' suggested Jumborina excitedly.

' Take me to her right away, please,' said Rose anxiously.

They were soon at Macaw aunty's door, knocking, waiting impatiently for her to open.

'Rina dear, Long time… no see… What brings you here my child?' Asked Macaw aunty tenderly.

' Aunty, could you please help us with a few feathers. Please don't say No, this is my friend Rose and that'll help her go back home.'

Saying this, Jumborina narrated the entire incident to her.

' Of course, I will but under one condition.'

' What?' the two girls asked in chorus.

' Well, I have to go shopping a bit. Would you mind babysitting my sweet little chick for an hour? I'll be back soon.'

The baby was sleeping peacefully. The two smiled at Mrs. Macaw, a silent way of conveying a Yes.

After all, what trouble could a sleeping baby give?

It had to be a cakewalk, thought the duo.

'Certainly aunty,' they said enthusiastically.

No sooner did the mother leave the house than the chick got up. Initially, it smiled and looked playful. Taking it as a positive sign, Jumborina and Rose began to baby talk with the chick.

For a moment, things looked perfect. But soon, the scenario changed, and the chick started to miss its mother. It all commenced with a silent grumble that in no time turned into a loud wail.

'Waaah...waah...waah ...,' went the baby, showing no sign to stop. Jumborina and Rose pressed their respective ears shut and stood at one end of the house. The chick began to flutter its wings and was about to fly away, searching for its mother, when the two went bouncing towards it and held it firmly. The baby, displeased with their touch and firm grip, started to wail even louder. When mommy Elephant heard the chick's cries, she panicked and decided to visit Mrs Macaw's place.

Mrs Macaw, on the other hand, came back at lightning speed, her wings losing their strength under the weight of shopping bags. She almost got a panic attack on seeing her chick in the doorway about to take its first flight.

'My baby! Mommy is back,' saying that she hugged the chick, and the house fell into immediate silence.

Meanwhile, Mommy Elephant entered the house glaring at Jumborina.

'Mumma, I swear, we tried our best to keep the baby happy but the baby wouldn't listen. Please believe us,' said she, now almost in tears.

'Hey, Rina, don't cry dear, take these feathers and help your friend reach her mom. I'm sure you both now realise the strength of mother's love,' said Mrs. Macaw as she handed over a bunch of feathers to the girls.

The three thanked her and left for home. Mommy Elephant stitched a fresh pair of wings in no time for Rose.

She couldn't believe her eyes, 'Thank You, aunty, these look much prettier than the ones I had.'

She wore them on and flew away happily to her home. On the way back, she promised to herself never to hide anything from her dear mom.

Jumborina, on the other hand, felt exhausted. She had had an eventful day filled with a lot of learning. She kissed her mommy and promised she would never loiter around and come home straight after school. Also, she was determined never to touch anyone's things without seeking their permission. Subsequently, she learned to remain content with what she had and never eye for someone else's belongings.

***

Vijeta Harishankar is a budding writer and an avid blogger whose articles get featured on the top blogging sites of the country, like Women's web and Momspresso. She enjoys writing short stories, poetries and articles related to social and current issues.

Airavata

CA Pooja Kabra

The sculptors were tired. Sweat glistened on their faces. But they were content. All Ganesha idols had been meticulously completed. Smiling and vibrant faces of different forms of Ganesha adorned the pandal. The next day, it was Ganesha Chaturthi. The hard work they had put in all these months will finally be paid off. The lights were switched off, and all of them left with hopes in their heart.

When taciturn silence ruled the city in the middle of the night, the pandal was lit up as if a million stars had entered there to party and shine. All the Ganesha's had come to life. It was their final night in the pandal, and they wanted to celebrate their last day together. The Krishna-Ganesha holding the flute started playing it.

"Gannu, when Krishna plays it, everyone is mesmerised. But, yours is hurting the ears. You need to take lessons from him.Once, when you leave the Earth, I will enrol you in " Krishna Flute Classes". By next year , you will be perfectly trained", said Maa Parvati.

Gannu had no choice. His mother's words need to be followed; otherwise, what will the World think of him, he wondered.

Chotu mouse came up to him and said, "You get heavy in these ten days. Control your diet this time. Just sugar free sweets are allowed. No laddoos and modaks for you this time otherwise it gets so much difficult for me to carry you. You just eat and poor me has to suffer", said Chotu.

Airavata

"Don't worry Gannu. Enrol for my Zumba classes and we will do weight training on trees. This year we will do pilate classes too and you will be back in shape before Diwali", said Miss Jasmine monkey.

Poor Gannu. This was the festival time. How will he control it, he thought.

The party started. Peacocks danced, cuckoo's sang. Krishna, Brahma all got gifts for Ganesha. Maa Saraswati gifted her a pen while Maa Annapurna got a big motichoor birthday cake for him. It was Ganesha's birthday, and everyone was having a gala time.

But the Airavata elephant was sitting silently in the corner. Tears flowed silently from his eyes.

Gannu went near him. "What happened Airavata? You look sad. Every time you are the first to wish, but today you didn't do that, " asked Gannu.

Airavata kept quiet. Everyone gathered around him. The most chirpy and enthusiastic person in their gang was depressed, and they could not leave him alone.

"What happened Airavata? Speak something. Your silence is killing me", said Gannu.

" Your father is a murderer. And you too. Because of you, my mother got killed", replied the angry Airavata. His eyes were fiery red, with tears and grief.

Airavata

There was pin-drop silence in the hall. No one had expected this from Airavata. He was Gannu's best friend. Dancing and singing together, they faced every storm.

Gannu was hurt deeply. His eyes welled up with tears. He looked at his father helplessly. Shiva hugged his son. Then he went near Airavata and tried to hug him, but he stepped back.

"Airavata , I know you are angry with me. But listen....."

" I don't want to listen to anything. You killed my mother. I became an orphan because of you. Everyone out here has a mother who loves him, scolds him when wrong, and prepares their favourite dishes but I don't have any. Sometimes I even want to hug my mother, listen to bedtime stories and lullabies, lie down in her lap.But you snatched all those wonderful moments from me. You are a killer and I will not forgive you", replied Airavata.

Everyone was bewildered. How should they handle this tricky situation?

Maa Parvati came forward, and she hugged Airavata. After a brief pause, she said, "Airavata, in anger you are repeating the same mistake which Lord Shiva did. He beheaded his son and you are killing your friendship relation. I know Shiva ordered for the head of a mother who slept with her face opposite to her child. Your mother was the unlucky one", said Parvati

"But Lord Shiva could have attached your son's head to the deceased body by his power and magic", said the grieving Airavata.

"Some things are not in the hands of God also. Even we have our own limitations", replied Parvati.

"It also taught that whether awake or asleep, a mother should not turn her back to the duties she is complied to do".

Silence dominated the hall when Maa Parvati spoke.

"And you were never orphaned, my child. We all were present there to take care of you. Airavata, can you tell me any animal who is worshipped like you?" asked Pavati.

Airavata nodded his head.

"Every animal out here is a vehicle to carry God but your mother got the power to become the face of my child. The whole World worships her, prays for removal of difficulties, every auspicious occasion is marked by her presence", said Parvati.

Airavata looked at his friend Gannu. He got a new perspective and now he could feel his mother around. He went and hugged Gannu. The words had calmed down his anger.

Tears poured from everyone's eyes. Airavata touched Lord Shiva's and Maa Parvati's feet and pleaded with them to forgive him for his misbehaviour. Both of them blessed Airavata and hugged him.

Airavata went to his friend Gannu and said sorry. Gannu hugged him tightly. The entire audience clapped and jumped with joy. Both the friends cut the cake together.

" Ganpati Bappa Mourya"., the entire pandal reverberated with its sound.

The moon smiled in the sky, and the stars twinkled at this beautiful rendezvous. All the malice and misunderstanding in hearts had finally got resolved.

This Ganesha Chaturthi had marked new beginnings.

The Sun started colouring the sky in tangerine hues. All the idols hugged each other, bid goodbye, and promised to meet each other soon in heaven.

***

CA Pooja Kabra Professionally a Chartered Accountant and an artist and blogger by passion. For her , life is a white canvas which she paints sometimes with words and sometimes with colours. She shares her work on Facebook by the name of Ca Pooja Kabra.

Sumukha's Saga

Radha Murali

Airavata

As the temple bell rang at a distance with a melodious dingdong chime, it was time for me to stretch my chubby four legs and wake up to another fun-filled day at Keshavapura village.

The rising sun rays fell on the ground like golden beams, and the rooster cock a doodle doo with all its might. With mud pots on the head, many young ladies dressed in colourful clothes walked towards the common water tap to collect water for their home needs.

While waiting for their turn to fill the water, Girija, a young girl blessed with a mellifluous voice, sang a song with a cheerful tune about the yellow Magnolia champaca flowers and mango trees that grew abundantly in Keshavapura. The ladies clapped and sang along with a smile on their faces. With the anklets making a clunking sound, they returned to their homes singing with water-filled pots on their heads.

Oh! Before I continue with my saga and before it slips from my memory, let me introduce myself. I am a four-year-old Sumukha fondly called Sumu by Mahadevan, my tall largehearted mahout who lives with his family in a tiny yet cozy hut, on the banks of Avighna river.

Seventy-five-year-old Bheema daddu, the eldest family member, loved to sit at the entrance of the home and chat with all the passers by. He would ask with concern, "Kapila, has your leg pain become better? "Pramoda, did you finish building the shed for the Gowri cow?" The neighbours and village dwellers would answer Bheema daddu's questions patiently and move on for their work.

Frail yet energetic seventy-year-old Uma dadi was a favourite of all the ladies of Keshavpura as she taught them how to make tasty, tangy seasonal pickles and crispy savouries during festivals. Any wedding, any event, no menus were finalized without Uma dadi's final nod. The village cook himself would ask, "dadi, should I make gram flour ladoos or roasted, fried gram laddoos for Bhupati's engagement ceremony?

My mahout's wife, Kapila amma, always adorned herself with a big bindi and champaca flowers on her neatly combed bun. I beamed with contentment when she took her time off at night after her busy work in the kitchen to sing a lullaby for me and six-month-old Skanda, whom she would swing in the cloth cradle made with Uma dadi's sari. Listening to her soothing voice, I would curl myself to sleep in a shed covered with soft green grass made especially for me by my Mahadevan mahout.

SidhiPriya, or Sidhu as she was fondly called, was the chirpy seven-year-old daughter with two ribboned plaits, and she was the apple of everyone's eye. Her continuous chatter and infectious smile made us listen to her and feel lighthearted. She would question," Bhima daadu, why do you have such a bushy moustache ? "May I comb it " Uma dadi , why has your hair become silvery grey? Can I paint it black again so that your hair looks like mine, Kapila amma?" The grandparents would give a gentle smile and enjoy her constant babble.

And what do I say about my dear, dear mahout? When Mahadevan Bapu referred to me as his seventh family member among his relatives and friends, my heart swelled with fondness and pride. I would twitch my curly trunk and fan my ears to welcome him when I would see him walking towards me first thing in the morning to clean the shed, refill the drinking water and feed fresh food with his loving, caring hands.

As he would sweep the floor, he would share his chalked-out route plan of the day to visit the neighbouring town to earn some money by entertaining people with simple tricks performed by us. I would listen to him keenly and approve the plan by nodding my trunk and performing a jiggly dance.

After Mahadevan mahout finished his morning chores and left Sidhu in Saraswati Pathshala, a village school, in his old worn-out cycle, we two began our walk towards Santhpur town where a fair was being held. It was an excellent opportunity to entertain the audience and earn some money for my mahout.

The walk was long, but my Mahadevan Mahout kept talking to me about his dreams and played a melodious tune on his flute to keep the journey going. Some passerby gave us a ripe bunch of bananas and freshly cropped sugarcane to munch.

The fair was filled with people of different ages, and we had fun performing bat ball games, balancing a wheel on my head, saluting with my two folded legs, and throwing a colourful paper garland with a perfect aim on a bottle.

Airavata

The crowd cheered, clapped, and filled the steel plate kept in front of me with jingling coins and rupee notes.

After tying me to a rope hooked to a pole, my mahout went around the fair buying colourful glass bangles for Kapila ma, a blue knitted muffler for Bheema dadu, a handmade puppet for his Sidhu, a cloth purse for Uma dadi to keep her medicines and a colourful rattler for Skanda to play with.

As I stood alone in the fair waiting for Mahadevan mahout, a group of children came suddenly and burst crackers near me. I stood still with fear and started making a trumpeting noise hoping my master would hear me and come to my rescue. Tears rolled from my eyes, and I yearned to go back to Keshavpur to be among my family members.

As the children began to laugh heartily at my expense, my mahout sensed danger, and he came rushing towards me with protected arms to engulf and soothe me with his kind words. The children ran away, and my mahout and I soon headed back towards Keshavpur.

As Avighna river approached, I knew it was my favourite part of the day to get into the tempting cool water for my bath. As the mahout cleaned me with a brush to remove the muddy stains on my body, I splashed and sprayed water like a hosepipe on my Mahadevan mahout.

I felt so important when I suddenly spotted a flock of tourists who were visiting Keshavpur, watching me with awe from a close distance while I was playing in the water. The final icing on the cake was the photo session when the tourists requested my mahout to take them to his abode and allow them to click a family picture with me in the centre. As my beaming family posed for them, they, in turn, gave a crisp five hundred rupee note as a kind gesture and departed towards their lodging.

My joy knew no bounds when the Mahout came to feed me my dinner that night and tied a brass bell around my neck. It was his gift for me bought from the fair. I nodded my head and made a jangling noise to thank my master for such a pleasant surprise.

As the family retired for the night, Sidhu, as usual, came promptly to share her school tale. As she began to narrate how some of her friends Kaveesha,

Poorvaja, and Shipra were caught by the headmaster for playing pranks while the teacher, Bhalachandra sir, was teaching them about the kings riding on elephants during battle, my eyes twinkled brighter. I imagined myself to be adorned with a silk robe, a dazzling caparison on my forehead, a pearl necklace adorning my neck, and a brave king of Keshavpur sitting on my back.

Sidhu's prattle continued. It sounded like music to my ears, and I went into a deep slumber in no time.

As the temple bell would ring the next dawn again, my yet another fun-filled day would soon begin... will I go to another town, will I take the temple deity on parade, will I carry a bridegroom on my back to reach the wedding venue, only my Madhavan mahout knows the plan.

And as far as I am concerned, I am ready to begin my day by humming a cheerful song.

I am Sumukha known as Sumu

I live happily with my family and little Sidhu

Do visit me when you come to Keshavpur

My village is not far from town Santhpur

I may be only three feet tall

But I am surely adored by all

If you don't find me in my shed

I am bound to be spotted in the Avighna river bed.

***

Radha Murali is a primary level teacher by profession and a Reading host with My Chapter One Gym , she enjoys working immensely with young minds. Playing and being with small children gives her abundant energy and teaches her to have a positive and open outlook towards life. Listening to music and going for long walks helps her to kick start her day with spirit and reading books with a hot cup of tea makes her day complete.

Love beyond...

Ramya Iyer

Oru ooru le (in a village), in Tamil Nadu, in South India, in a beautiful house, lived Mani, a playful warm eight year old boy with his big beautiful family - his Amma Appa with his five brothers, his Chithi and Chitappa (uncle and aunty), their five sons and his darling Paati, grandmother.

In this village, there was a beautiful Vinayaga koil (Ganesha temple) by the banks of the river Kaveri. And in this temple, there lived a lovely temple elephant. She was adopted by the temple when she was very young. She was very playful and everyone adored her. And Ambi, her caregiver looked after her with a lot of love.

"Mani, konjum poo kondu wa, (please bring flowers)"

"Mani, konjum Raju ve kutindu va, (can you fetch Raju for me)"

"Mani, andhe kadailendu , ka kilo vazha pazham konda, indha kaasu, michey kaas le mitaai

vangiko, (can you buy some bananas and buy some mitaai for yourself with the remaining money)"

Along with being the person that his family relied upon for many such jobs, he was also reached out by everyone in the village. Young and old adored little Mani too.

Yes, on the note of adoration, the temple elephant was adored by all and Mani and the elephant adored each other too. Every time Mani met her at the temple, he would gently stroke her. She would sprinkle tiny flowers fallen from the parijatha tree on Mani. Mani loved how he would smell of fresh flowers. Mani lovingly named her... well! There is a cute anecdote behind her name...

One evening, when Mani was returning after running an errand for a neighbour, not very far from the temple he saw something huge shining near the temple.

"Oh, has the Nila, the moon come down to visit us?", he wondered.

And as he curiously approached to have a closer look only to realize that it was her - the temple elephant, his friend. He stood next to her and said, "Everyone calls you koil yaanai- temple elephant but from today, I will call you Nila ! You are my Nila ! You are our Nila."

And that name stuck with everyone and going forward everyone started calling her Nila.

On many occasions Mani would sing to Nila

"Nila odi wa, (Nila come running to me)" a song that his mother would sing to him while putting

him to sleep. Nila loved it!

In the mornings, at the temple, one could listen to the cool and calm Kaveri river flowing, the chirping of the birds and Nila's greeting trumpeting. Ambi took very good care of her. The temple devotees would pray to Lord Vinayaga whose idol was adorned with flowers and arugampul (Durva in Sanskrit, Bermuda grass in English) garlands. They would then meet Nila on their way out of the temple and then proceed to face the day.

After the morning's worship, Nila and Ambi would set out. Their first stop would be the river where Ambi would give Nila a bath. And this would be the time Mani would come with a pot to fill water from the river. He would come running to the river, so as not to miss Nila and Ambi. Nila would be waiting for her friend. She loved splashing water on herself, but she found it more amusing to splash water on Mani.

Swoooooooshhhhhh. It was one of her favourite things to do while having a bath.

"Nila… pannadhey, (don't do that, Nila)", Mani would plead, of course not wanting Nila to listen. He loved every bit of this, just like Nila. They had a secret language too, it seemed as if Mani and Nila understood so much about each other. It was a love beyond words, boundaries that they shared. Ambi would smilingly observe these adorable children.

Every day, Mani would forget why in the first place he had come to the river. And also, this is not the only time he can fill water, but Nila wouldn't be here all day. After his playtime with Nila he would fill water and run back home to finish other errands before getting ready for pallikudam (school).

Mani's favourite day of the week was Sunday. Because, on Sundays, "jaali jaali, fun, fun", he would join Nila and Ambi on a stroll in the village. "When will Sunday come, when will Sunday come, when will Sunday come?" he would keep asking.

Yes, on Sundays, after Nila's bath, they would begin their stroll. Everyone knew them and greeted them with love. Along the way, they would meet Thaayi, an old paati (grandmother) who sold flowers and hand-woven garlands. She would have many different flowers such as semparuthi (hibiscus), thamarai(lotus), malligai (jasmine) and roja (rose). Thaayi would gently pinch Mani's pink cheeks, as he smiled and gave her a hug.

Thaayi would stroke Nila's trunk and garland him with one of her special creations, which she would keep ready every morning. Nila would nod in response and Ambi would smile at this exchange. Mani helped Thaayi sort the freshly collected flowers. She would have a treat ready, a mitaai for Mani too, which would make him jump in excitement.

"Nee romba samathu pulay, (you are a lovely boy)." she would say

"Neenum paati, (you too)." Mani would respond. They would break into laughter and just be with

each other for a few minutes.

"Pilayarappa kaapathu! (Lord Ganesha save us all)." Thaayi would then say as she bid farewell. They

would next meet Tamarai, a young eight-year old girl, who was the village fruit seller Gopalan's

daughter. Tamarai would help her Appa with their fruit cart, when she was not at school. The fruit cart

was just outside their home. An aromatic kaapi (coffee) smell would waft through the air.

"Mani, indhaa verkadalai urundai, (here take some groundnut ladoo/candy)", Tamarai would offer

Mani.

"Nila, indhaa vazhapazham (here, take some bananas)", Tamarai would say, and gently feed Nila some bananas. Tamarai would remember to keep the bananas attached to their stem, the way Nila liked. And the friends would sit to feast on the scrumptious feast.

Chandramma would step out of the house with two tumblers of steaming kaapi. Gopalan would offer one to Ambi. They would drink their coffee by the cart while watching Tamarai and Mani jumping in glee as Nila instantly devoured the bananas. Once the older men finished their kaapi, Tamarai would give Nila a hug though she was so tiny that she just about reached Nila's knees.

Nila, Mani and Ambi would set out on their path, yet again. They would now meet Ambi's friend, the village taiyalkaran (tailor) at his shop. His name was Selva. Selva would have news of the entire village and would share it with Ambi.

"Ambi, did you hear, Abdul's son is going to town for a job."

"Ambi, you know, Meenakshi amma's grand-daughter's marriage is fixed. I've got a big order for blouses and shirts for the wedding kootam (party)"

"Ambi, I heard that this year, our ooru thiruvizha (village festival) is on the Friday after next Friday,

Do you not want to stitch a nice shirt for yourself?"

And so on.... Ambi would smile listening to all the stories.

In between their conversation, Selva would say "Mani, konjum andha bit thuniyelaan andhe dabba le podreya, (can you collect all the small strings and pieces of clothes in a box)" Mani would collect the scraps of clothes quickly, he loved doing it, especially because of something that followed. Nila and Mani played with the colourful – red blue green multi-coloured discarded strings of clothes from that box. Selva would heave a sigh of relief, after emptying his mind of all the stories he carried in his heart.

This would usually be Mani, Nila and Ambi's last stop before Mani returned home and Nila and Ambi returned back to the temple.

One summer morning, after Mani's morning visit to Nila at the river, and fetching water for his neighbor Meenakshi Amma, he had now just brought a kudam, a pot that his Amma sent him with to collect water. After collecting water, something in him told him to visit the temple. He felt like seeing Nila. Ambi wasn't around when Mani met Nila. They played and spoke and spoke and played. Until, Nila pointed to the pot and Mani sensed that Nila was thirsty, Mani had stroked her, played with her, fed her leaves and fruits and all of that, but had never fed her water. He had seen her drink water at the river and it would always be Ambi at the temple. What do I do, what do I do, what do I do, Mani wondered. Then, seeing his friend's tired face, Mani quickly placed his kudam near Nila.

"Indha Nila, kudi, (here you go Nila, drink)", he told her and he sat opposite to Nila on a big rock in the temple premises. Nila looked at the pot and tried to insert her trunk into the kudam to reach the water as Mani watched. It was a struggle to do that because the neck of the pot was narrow and somehow she managed to do it. But, just when she tried to lift her trunk from the pot, she couldn't. Her trunk was stuck in the pot. Mani ran towards her. He saw a look of anger, despair on her face that he had never seen before. She was tired and thirsty and now, her trunk was stuck.

She let out an angry roar and with her front left foot stamped the kudam and released the trunk.

The water was all out and the kudam smashed beyond imagination. Mani burst into tears. Ambi reached them at that instant. He placed a big bucket of water in front of Nila and comforted Mani in a hug.

"Amma yenne thittuva, Appa yene thittuva, (Amma will shout at me, Appa will shout at me)", he kept mumbling in a singsong way , crying bitterly. And after a few minutes, he finally set home.

Mani reached home and yes his Amma Appa were angry, but not so much for the pot but because he was late and they were very worried. They heard the complete account of what happened and comforted him. Mani was happy to eat his favourite mulangi (raddish) sambar and rice and went to take a nap. It would not be easy for his family to buy another pot right away, but they couldn't bear to see their son sad. And things became okay too, for the most part. But, yes there was something about that look on Nila's face -that angry violent look that scared Mani now.

He stopped meeting Nila. The Sunday strolls stopped too. He still continued running errands, but he couldn't bring himself to see Nila.

Ten months passed, and Mani's parents were blessed with a sweet baby girl and Mani and his brothers were elated beyond measure to be blessed with a younger sister. On the twelfth day after Lakshmi's birth, the entire family dressed up in lovely clothes for her first visit to the Vinayaga temple. As they went around the temple together, they went close to Nila. Nila looked at Mani, as he hid behind his parents, tugging at his Amma's brown with red spots chungudi saree and very slowly peeped to see his friend whom he had not seen in a long time. He watched Nila, she isn't scary, she is so sweet. That day, she was afraid, and even if she was a little angry, don't I get angry too sometimes, he told himself.

"Nila, nila odi wa," Mani sang as he started walking up to her, and she came forward too. Mani stroked her gently like he always did, Nila nodded in joy and brushed his trunk on him. They had missed each other. And Mani then noticed how she was looking at Lakshmi and all of them. "Nila, I'll see you tomorrow, I am sorry my friend", he told her as his family left for home.

That night, Mani couldn't sleep well. He kept tossing and turning. What was that look of sadness on Nila? Yes she missed me, but it was something more. Somewhere in the middle of the night, he woke up from a bad dream drenched in sweat. In the dream, he saw Lakshmi being taken away from them by some scary looking beasts. He woke up, went and checked on Lakshmi paapa – she was fine. He then went back to bed. In the morning, while walking towards the temple, a thought came to him. Nila, Nila is sad, because she misses her family. Yes, that was it. Mani went straight to Ambi at the koil (temple) and asked "Ambi mama, where did you bring Nila from."

Smilingly Ambi said, "Wa inge, (come here) I'll tell you. When Nila was very young, we found her in a pit at the outskirts of the forest area near Trichy. She looked very tired and hungry and we brought her here. Mani, she got so attached to us and we to her, our darling, Nila. That we kept her with us, as part of our village family. And you, you have given her such a lovely name."

"Ambi mama , but we are not her family , don't you think so ? Mama, can we not take her back to her home, her family, her herd in the forest?"

Ambi's face looked flushed, Nila was like his daughter. But he knew Mani was speaking the truth. He had stopped himself from thinking about it all these years.. He knew though that it wasn't fair.

"Yes Kanna (dear one), you are right. Let me think about it. You come tomorrow"

A big smile broke on Mani's face, as he hugged Ambi and went to Nila , gave her a hug before returning home.

This night, again, Mani couldn't sleep, but this was out of joy and excitement and little bit of anxiety. Early in the morning, he went running to the koil. Ambi had a big smile on his face.

"Mani, you have such a big heart, I know how much you love our Nila. I spoke to Ganesh Sir, he is Meenakshi Amma's son who is in the forest department. We will try to take Nila to the forest area where there is a big herd of elephants and it is not far from where we found her. If we have Vinayagar's blessings, they will take our Nila in and give her the family love that may be we can't".

Ambi's voice shook as he spoke and his hands trembled. Mani held his hand and shed some tears Himself.

"Mani, neenum vareya (would you like to come too)?"

"Nejamma, really can I come? Super Ambi Mama."

"I'll speak to your Amma Appa, kanna"

And so the date was decided, and that Saturday morning, in a truck, Mani, Ambi, Nila, with Ganesh. Sir would set out to Nila's new home.. And the day before that on Friday everyone in the village, including Meenakshi Amma, Thaayi paati with her special garland, Tamarai with bananas, Gopalan, Chandramma, Selva, everyone came to offer love and respect to their Nila. It was like a ooru thiruvizha. Mani could tell Nila was looking confused, and gently stroked her "Nila, don't worry all will be well, it would be wonderful, you will find your family, your home". And just for one more time they went to the river for some fun.

When they reached the forest area, some people from the department were waiting with a vehicle and slowly they drove up to a green clearing in the middle of the forest, very close to the river. There was a big herd of elephants, big and small , some feasting on leaves and others splashing water on themselves with the river water happily, just like Nila would do. Mani felt this was the most beautiful place he had ever seen in his life. They were asked to wait at a certain distance. And the forest officials slowly took Nila near this herd. Everyone waited and watched, watched and waited, and slowly as if a magic unfolded, the older matriarch slowly came close to Nila, guiding her to the herd and everyone could tell, Nila was now one of them, and maybe she already was and reunited. It didn't matter. She had a family now who loved and cared for her.

Ganesh mama took Mani and Ambi to Nila one last time, before they set off for the village. Mani broke down as he hugged Nila and Nila looked forlorn too. And Ambi emotionally comforted both of them. And there in the distance Mani noticed a small hairy baby elephant an infant, just like Lakshmi. "Aww, Nila has a baby brother or sister now too".

That brought a big smile to his face and the vehicle turned to go back to the gate. It was late evening. And till a distance, Mani and Nila looked at each other, till she blended into the moonlight in the beautiful forest, her home, now. When they reached the gate, before they left, Ganesh mama let in a secret in Mani's ears. And Mani's face twinkled even more. At home, Mani told his Amma Appa, Chithi, Chitappa, brothers, Paati, Lakshmi paapa, all the mamas, mamis, thathas, paatis, paapas (all uncles aunts grandparents children) from the village had gathered at his place, he told them all every little thing about this most magical day in his life.

"We are so proud of you Kanna." they told their adorable Mani.

Next morning, Mani reached the temple and went to meet Ambi. "Ambi mama, are you okay? Did you miss Nila too much last night, let me tell you a secret. Ganesh mama told me that every summer, he will take me to see Nila, you come too".

That's such wonderful news, thank you. And I know when you see her, you will sing your favourite song to her, Nila Nila odi wa won't you? And she will come sprinting to you", smiled Ambi. And they hugged each other, dreaming of a good life for their Nila and of meeting her soon. For theirs, was a love beyond...

***

Ramya believes in the strength of a warm, holding and healing space. She finds herself working towards bringing people closer to themselves and connected to each other through story and expression. She is fascinated by the magic that every moment, every day, every person story holds and that of dreams! She loves soaking in nature and loves to sing like she breathes. Her storytelling initiative is called 'The Bright Lamp Storytells'. She is trying to live a fulfilling life one breath, one step, one day at a time.

Love Knows No Bounds

Madhavi

Karnagni was watching the herd of wild elephants closely as they approached the bank of the river. It has been three days since he watched each one of them. He was the only Mahout who never used any tool to tame the elephants. He also chose the elephants after careful observation. Even a baby elephant showed peaceful tendencies and calmed down in his presence. He had a calming aura surrounding him that a charging elephant would stop in his tracks and try to find another target exhibiting anxiety.

He liked one particular baby elephant; it was always snuggling with its mother and running around playfully. The other mahouts tried luring the elephant with food and toys, but she would cling to her mother more at the mere sight of them.

Karnagni approached the herd and stood watching them with a look of admiration. The wild elephants didn't mind his presence and went about their washing and playing in the water. The herd did not panic at the sight of Karnagni.

He slowly approached the baby elephant and caressed her trunk; the baby responded by coiling its trunk to his hand and snuggling to him. The mother rebuked the baby to move away from Karnagni. The baby obeyed reluctantly, and Karnagni let her go.

Every day, he would come to the river bank and spend some time snuggling and caressing with the baby elephant. A few days later, he brought toys that she could play with. Gradually the herd trusted him and allowed him to offer them fruits. It then became his ritual to give the herd a basket full of fruits and played with the baby elephant for some time.

One day, he bought a piece of jewellery that dangled from the baby elephant's ears. The baby liked playing with it. No sooner Karnagni put the ear danglers than she would shake it vigorously and throw it to the ground and roll over to express happiness. He would playfully join the baby elephant and play for some time.

The next day, he bought the brocade scarf and decked the baby elephant in it, fastening it securely, so that she did not trip or fall when walking. She loved it so much that she ran around trying to shake it off her body. Each day, he brought ornaments and played with the baby elephants. The herd would wear the ornaments soon after the baby elephant was done playing with it.

The villagers heard that Karnagni had become friends with the wild elephant herd, and started coming to watch him handle them. To their surprise, the herd did not bother even when other people started coming near them. They had become friendly with Karnagni and assumed the rest of the crowd to be like him.

Karnagni had instructed them to stay far away and not to panic or fear them. They followed his advice and remained perfectly calm, which is why the herd became comfortable with them. The baby elephant, who Karnagni now addressed as Airani, would be super excited seeing the people. It was a welcome change; earlier, the baby was always scared of seeing people, now she gets excited seeing them.

Soon, the mother elephant and the rest of the herd started playing with the ornaments, and the villagers clapped and cheered for them. The herd initially panicked, but as soon as Karnagni told them,

"It is fine; I am here; all the people are happy that you liked your playthings," they calmed down.

Airavata

The herd now behaved as one unit and listened to Karnagni's every instruction. He achieved all this without using any of the tools like the chains, ankusha or sticks.

The villagers were now confident that Karnagni would have the herd ready for the upcoming festival to carry idols. The next day, Karnagni bought a tiny Shiva's idol for Airani. She loved the idol very much and clutched it with her trunk and pulled it close to herself. She tried eating it at first, but when Karnagni gently showed her that it hurts if she eats it, she let it go.

Karnagni put the idol on his head and started to walk carefully, showing how to balance the idol on the head. The herd watched him intently. Airani wanted to copy him and took the idol from his head. She tried balancing it on her head. Karnagni helped her place it correctly, and soon she was walking around in circles just like Karnagni walked around.

Soon, every elephant tried balancing it and allowed Karnagni to sit on them, holding the idol while they circled and paraded proudly.

It continued for many days, and soon the villagers were cheering the elephants that carried heavy idols in cradles. Karnagni also trained them to play tug of war with a rope. The elephants enjoyed playing while the villagers cheered them on. The village sarpanch was elated to see that the whole wild herd was ready to participate in the celebration.

The challenge now was to take the elephants to the village for the parade. Karnagni spoke with each elephant and told them gently to follow him where they could play with idols. Airani followed him without hesitation; the mother elephant also trusted Karnangi and followed him. The herd was hesitant but eventually followed the baby and the mother elephant into the village. Karnagni bathe the elephants and decked them with jewellery telling them soothing words.

Once ready, the idols of gods were tied securely on each elephant. This job also had to be done by Karnagni because the elephants tended to become anxious whenever any stranger approached them. They were now accustomed to strangers cheering them, but they did not like them close by.

Just when everybody thought it was going fine, the musicians started blowing the trumpets, and the herd panicked and started running wildly. Karnagni signalled the musicians to stop the music at once and went to every elephant and spoke soothing words.

The archaka of the temple was now disappointed,

"What is the use of the Ratotsava if there is no auspicious sound of the trumpets?" he asked Karnagni.

Karnagni bowed down before the holy person and said,

"Oh, revered sir, if it is possible, request the musicians not to play it loudly or to play only near you while I take the elephants with idols around the village. It is the question of the lives of many innocent people. Also, the elephants are not harmful; they are scared of loud noise. It is my fault I could not get them accustomed to the trumpet sound. Please do not trouble the elephants, or else all the villagers will have to suffer the consequences.

The procession went around the village. Airani was very excited to see the children coming near her. She carried the smallest Utsava Murthy and was leading the parade with joy.

***

Having imaginary friends in your childhood is a common thing. Madhavi believes that the writers retain their imaginary friends and keep noting down the tales they tell. She is a published author who loves to read and write Science fiction tales. Her short stories are available in Kindle editions.

The Dancing Elephant

Misna Chanu

Once upon a time, there was a white elephant named Elle who lived in a dense forest somewhere in India. Elle knew how to dance well by swinging her trunk and her heavy body beautifully twisting, circling then rounding herself with the flow of the wind.

Elle spent almost every day dancing. Sometimes she danced near the river, sometimes in the middle of the forest to the music created by the rustling of the trees , to the chirping of birds during dawn and dusk, then to the whispers of insects in the night and to the sound of water flowing in the river and streams of the forest.

All the other elephants ignored Elle, thinking she was different because of her white coloured skin and her dance. They didn't want Elle to be in their group. But Elle didn't mind because she was always content within herself and lived always happily, no matter what.

When Elle's parents were getting older, they started worrying about Elle more as they knew one day they would die and Elle would be left alone in a world where she was treated differently and not accepted by the majority.Elle had her siblings too but they were not as white as Elle and they didn't danced the way she did ! They were grey in colour as all the other elephants of the forest. Whenever her parents advised Elle to behave like all the other elephants, she told them that she wanted to be who she really was and not as others wanted her to be.

Years passed and finally, the dreaded day came when her parents left the world leaving Elle alone. Being alone in the world where no one expects anything from you and you don't expect anything from anyone was in a way liberating but getting lonely at the same time. After the death of her parents, Elle became totally alone but she kept saying to herself again and again that it's going to be fine. She believed that her parents were watching over her as spirits and she was loved by them always. But no matter how hard she tried to console herself, she was sad. She couldn't dance anymore like the way she did before the death of her parents.

One day, Elle finally left the forest where she used to live with her family wandering into the woods alone in search of a melody that she could dance upon and live in content with herself once more.

She walked aimlessly for many days, many weeks, maybe months. She crossed many valleys, hills and rivers. After wandering for many months, one day she felt too exhausted and worn out .Spotting a fountain in the middle of the North eastern forest she paused for water. She was hungry and thirsty too. Quickly, she drank the water from that fountain and slipped into a sweet slumber, waking up only after two days.

On the second day after sleeping near the fountain she woke up and found herself surrounded by a group of elephants. They too had white skin like her !

Elated, Elle stood up and watched them with astonishment . All the elephants greeted Elle by swinging their trunks in the wind. And they started beating their feet on the ground, first slowly, then faster and faster. It started sounding like the beating of drums .The beats and the rhythm made them dance, and they started moving and jiving to their own beats, swinging, circling and swaying with the wind.

Elle realized that this is where she belongs. She found all the lost melodies and her will to dance back.

Airavata

***

Writing is not her hobby or passion but a call of her soul. Misna Chanu was born in Assam, she loves art and literature with her heart and soul. She loves almost all kinds of art but poetry, painting, dance and photography are her favourites. Since she was a little girl, she started writing poetry in her mother tongue, Manipuri language. Some of her Manipuri poems were published in Manipuri magazines of Assam. Her first poem in her mother tongue was published in a Magazine called "Yening" when she was 15 years old. She started writing in English after marriage and published many poems and short stories in national and international journals, magazines and Anthologies of poetry and short story.

He poems have been translated into eleven languages. She has published her two poetry books named "A little Piece of Melancholic Sky" and "Many Shades Of Love". She also has published three international anthologies named "Under The Azure Sky' (Bilingual), "May Love Heal The World" (English) and "Beyond the Language" (Multilingual).

The Elephant in the Room

Soumya Torvi

"Papa there's an elephant in our backyard", cried Siya as she ran into the living room from the backyard. She had a petrified look on her face but was also excited at the same time. "It's not an elephant in the backyard, dear it's an elephant in the room. Now, calm down and tell me what you want to talk about," said her father, Mr Patil, who sat on the sofa, unmoved by his daughter's expression.

"No Papa, I mean there is an elephant in our backyard", cried Saanvi. Her father shifted his gaze from the TV and looked at his daughter. He held her hand and made her sit next to him as if preparing for a long conversation, still unperturbed by the child's mixed emotions of awe and fear. Her mother, who was unpacking the groceries in the kitchen and arranging them on a glass shelf, decided to stop her chores and take a look at the backyard out of curiosity, least expecting anything unusual.

As Mrs. Patil walked towards the backdoor, Mr. Patil began by saying," The correct phrase used is 'the elephant in the room', and it indicates that you want to talk about something that we may not be comfortable about. Now tell me, have you done something you shouldn't have done, is it about your test grades…." Naveen, Naveen….." Mrs. Patil came calling as she ran towards the living room just as her daughter had done a while ago. "What's the matter, Preeti?" Mr. Patil asked as he stood up and looked anxious. " There's an elephant in our backyard", Mrs. Patil gasped and spoke in horror. " Now, now, I understand you both want to talk to me about something, but why don't you get straight to the point and….." Before he could complete it, his wife and daughter held each of his hands and led him to the backyard.

Now it was Mr. Patil's turn to be horrified; he stood there in complete silence, his limbs numb from shock. He saw a baby elephant moving its head and trunk in full swing, trying to stretch its trunk beyond the high compound wall in an attempt to reach a banana tree from the adjoining farm. " How ….I mean…..when…." Mr. Patil muttered.

A while later, the Patils were sitting in the living room of their farmhouse. The holiday was certainly nothing like the one they had expected. Siya had just finished her 3rd-grade exams and wanted to spend some time in their farmhouse. It was located on the outskirts of Bangalore, away from the hustle and bustle, in a peaceful location. They had just moved into the farmhouse and were settling down before spotting the elephant in the backyard! Mr. Patil had summoned Nanja, the caretaker of the farmhouse, and his wife, Manda, the house help. Mr. Patil was wondering how the elephant got into his backyard and was questioning them. Mrs. Patil, who had been anxious since she saw the elephant, suggested, "We should worry about what to do next instead of crying over spilt milk!"

After a thorough round of questioning, which sounded more like a rapid-fire quiz round, Mr Patil finally concluded, " On our way to the farm, our tyre got punctured and I called Nanja to fetch someone from the nearby mechanic shop and asked him to make it fast. Nanja took his two wheeler out from the backyard and in a haste, forgot to lock the gate. The baby elephant which may have strayed from the forest nearby walked into the gate. It was able to do despite the strong bordering wall and fence guarding the forest as the recent rains had destroyed and damaged a small portion of the wall facing the street opposite our house leaving a gap enough for the truck to move out and maybe the elephant squeezed through." " Why didn't we hear the elephant when we came in?" asked Siya. "That's because of the strong glass wall between the backyard and the room but that still doesn't explain one thing," said Mr. Patil. "How did the gate get locked?" asked Mrs. Patil as she was wondering the same thing. " I checked the gate, Ma'am. It has been locked and the lock doesn't belong to us. Maybe someone saw the elephant entering the backyard and locked it inside so that it doesn't wander out into the nearby village," replied Nanja.

After considering the suggestions from all the members in the room, Mr. Patil had called the police. They had asked him to contact the forest department. The forest officials had said that it would take a while, as a nationwide lockdown had been announced due to the pandemic. They would reach the place only the next morning. He had also sent Nanja to fetch as many bananas that he could find from the neighbouring village market. Nanja had taken Mr. Patil's car to stuff as many bananas as he could. The villagers were amazed by the number of bananas Nanja was buying. " Is it for a grand wedding? Are you calling the whole city?" the vendors at the marketplace had asked. Nanja, obeying his master's orders, hadn't revealed anything but replied with a grin that revealed his yellow teeth.

"Where's Siya? " asked Mrs. Patil as she put her mobile down after explaining the details of the entire event to her mother. Mr. Patil was on the phone, too, discussing the next steps with a forest official who had advised against breaking the lock and letting the elephant loose. He excused himself and cut the call, and ran towards the glass wall overlooking the backyard. But Siya wasn't there. The elephant, however, was gulping down water flowing from a big pipe that was hanging from the wall. "How did that happen?" Mr. Patil was awestruck. A few seconds later, he was running up the staircase that led to the terrace.

Siya and her mother were indeed on the terrace. Siya managed to connect a pipe to the overhead tank, let the water flow through it, and reach the elephant. Mr Patil leaned over the compound and looked at the creature but with different eyes." The poor darling," he said, " it must have been really thirsty!" After quenching its thirst, the elephant looked at the humans on the terrace longingly. Siya jumped up and down, blew kisses in the air towards the elephant, and cried out, "Don't worry, your food is on the way!" As if hearing Siya's words, Nanja parked the car.

With the help of Nanja and his wife, the Patils unloaded the car, which was filled with bananas on the roof, rear, and inside. But how would they give them to the elephant? They decided to go by Siya's suggestion and went to the terrace. They lowered the banana using two ends of a rope tied to a big bamboo basket that Manda had fetched from the storage. They lowered the bananas one basket at a time. The baby elephant hungrily ate the bananas. At first, it was plodding up and down the backyard, restless with hunger and panic. Siya had cried to it, "wait my dear, you are getting food", and had gestured to the elephant giving it a big hug in the air. The elephant seemed to wait patiently as if understanding her gesture.

The elephant was full after emptying more than three-fourths of the overhead tank and many Kgs of bananas. Its tired eyes looked in the direction of the humans who were watching from behind the glass door. It quietly folded its big feet and prepared to go to sleep. It fell asleep in a few seconds. "Isn't that incredible? " said Mr. Patil who was in awe despite being tired and hungry. "There isn't enough water", Manda had declared. " We will not take a bath", Siya had offered. " Let's not cook," declared Mrs. Patil. " We have some snacks remaining from what we packed for the journey. Let's eat that and rest a little," Mrs. Patil had offered.

After munching a few snacks, they had all fallen asleep almost instantly on the living room floor. Siya had made frequent trips to the glass door to watch over her new friend. Nanja and Manda had sneaked into the neighbouring banana farm to collect as many fresh bananas as possible. They returned with nearly three baskets of bananas wrapped in Manda's old saree, which they had used as a bag. They thanked God that Muniraju, the farm owner, was snoring away and hadn't heard them. But they knew that he would make a trip to the southern end of his farm early the next morning and would make a ruckus of a scene when he would see the missing bananas. He would summon the entire neighbouring village.

Siya enjoyed her ride on the elephant, which was happily swaying from side to side majestically paving its way through the jungle. She awoke with a start. ' Oh, I was only dreaming, she thought. She looked at the clock. It was only 4:00 a.m. She looked at her parents. Her father was snoring away on the sofa, and her mother was fast asleep on the carpet. They were so exhausted. They looked like they had climbed Mt. Everest in a day. Siya tiptoed to the glass door. She stepped back in shock and almost slipped. The baby elephant was moving its trunk restlessly against the glass door.

"What if it breaks the glass door? " Siya thought and shuddered, but something that her friend did made her think otherwise. On spotting her, the elephant stopped moving, stared at her through the glass door, and slowly raised its leg. " Oh my God!" she said, "Is it trying to break the glass? Should I wake up my parents?" she wondered. As if answering her questions, she stood still and looked at it calmly. She looked at its eyes and saw the pain in them. She held out her hand as high as possible and touched the elephant's paw, albeit from the other side of the glass door. " I know what you want, " she said softly.

Mrs. Patil stretched her hand to caress her daughter's hair, but it hit the hard ground next to the carpet. She opened her eyes and sat up, startled. Siya wasn't by her side. The clock showed 6:30. "Siya, where are you?" she called out. Mr. Patil woke up due to the noise. Mrs. Patil ran to the glass door instantly. The view that lay ahead was both worrying and incredible. She would never have seen such a delightful thing all her life. She looked at Mr. Patil, who was now standing beside her and staring out the glass door. A few seconds later, they dashed out of the front door, which was just shut and not latched, waking up Nanja and Manda, who were sleeping in the kitchen.

The Patils now stood at the locked gate guarding the backyard. " How did you get in there? " asked a baffled Mr. Patil. Siya, who was now sitting on the back of the elephant and riding on it with a big smile on her face, answered, "I just climbed over!" The gate, which was relatively high to keep up with the high stone walls of the backyard, would have posed quite a challenge for an average adult to climb over. But Siya's tiny legs could fit through the openings between the vertical bars to reach it would have been almost impossible for her unless…..Mr. Patil looked around and found a stool lying near the gate.

Siya explained to her parents how her dream had woken her up early in the morning and how her friend had explained to her about his hunger. She had considered moving the bananas up to the terrace, but it would be difficult for her to carry so many of them. So she unlocked the main door, loaded the laundry basket with bananas, and pushed it to the gate. The elephant had moved towards the gate in excitement. It had started to shake the gate with its trunk, but Siya had moved the basket just below its trunk, which was now lowered on the other side of the gate.

After filling its tummy, the elephant stood there, cheerfully looking at Siya. She had patted it on the trunk with a tinge of fear. The elephant had responded by wrapping her around with its trunk but slowly. After a little bit of cuddling and patting and talking, which of course was one-sided, Siya was now devoid of the little fear she had of her dear friend, whom she had by now, decided to make her pet. She had decided to convince her father to move to the farmhouse, enrol her at the school in the nearby village, and spend her time after school with her pet. A little later, she tried to climb over the gate but failed. She hadn't given up though and fetched the stool from the house.

The sound of vehicles approaching was quite disturbing in the otherwise peaceful neighbourhood of Mr. Patil's farm. The forest officials had arrived. Six men, some carrying arms, had come in two vehicles. One was a jeep in which the main forest officer was seated with an assistant. The other was a large truck-like vehicle that was used to transport animals. After pulling Siya to safety and moving her inside the house, the forest officials had tranquilised the animal and, with great effort, had moved it to the vehicle. By now, Muniraju and almost the entire neighbouring village had arrived to view the scene.

Siya watched her dear friend being moved away with tearful eyes. At first, she had been inconsolable on seeing the forest officials shooting the elephant. But her father had explained to her that it would only put the elephant to sleep till it was carried away to its original home - the forest where its parents would be waiting for it. Realising that her friend would be happier back in her home with its near and dear ones, Siya had stopped crying, but she could do little to stop the last tear that rolled down her cheek as she bid goodbye to her friend.

***

Soumya Torvi is a software Engineer turned author with a passion towards writing for children. Her works include the 2019 book, A Princess's Quest for Knowledge which received positive reviews by readers across age groups. Her short stories and children's stories have been published on platforms like kitaab, Story Mirror and children's magazines.

Pintoo in the Temple

Airavata

Sudha George

"This is our room Dave." said Thatha, unpacking the bundle

Dave said nothing, he looked sad and pale

"What happened to you Dave, don't you like this room?", Asked Thatha

Dave's family has shifted to a new house and Dave was in tears, he missed his old house and his friends from the neighborhood Thatha understood his state of mind and gave him a consoling hug.

He said, "Don't worry Dave, there is a park on the next street we can go and play there.

Dave remained silent, he was too upset. He had many friends in his old house and never thought he would come here, leaving them all. He never liked the idea of shifting the house in the first place. When appa announced that they have to shift to a new house, he thought all this would take some time, but everything happened so quickly. Thatha and Nana had vacated their village house to live with Dave but their old house wasn't big enough.

After arranging the books and clothes in Dave's room, thatha took Dave to the park. Dave played in the park for sometime but soon lost interest.

He said, "Thatha let's go back home."

While returning back home they heard a bell sound from a temple next to the park. They kept walking, yet again there was a jingling sound- 'ding- ding- ding, ding- ding- ding.' Along with the jingling sound came some screaming and running sounds that got the grandfather and Dave curious and they headed towards the temple. On reaching the gates of the temple they saw a baby elephant running all around the temple, a pundit and one more person chasing the elephant. Dave started giggling as He found all the running and chasing funny.

Thatha and Dave got hold of the little elephant, he had a naughty eyes yet he looked so adorable. When the pundit and his helper came closer to hold the elephant, he immediately hid behind Dave. He was the same height as Dave, and flapped his big ears. His tiny poking hair tickled Dave enough to make him giggle again. Dave lovingly touched the elephant, he had rough skin and he was so strong. Dave pampered and started playing with the baby elephant.

The Pundit informed them that this baby elephant was brought from another temple and he shall live here for some time. Dave was so happy to hear this. Suddenly , there was something to look forward to for Dave and so Dave and Thatha started visiting the temple on a daily basis to meet this baby elephant.

Everyday his grandfather bought some fruits from the market and some of them were always reserved for the elephant by Dave ! The little elephant loved bananas the most, he would gobble up dozens of bananas which Dave lovingly fed him.

Dave said excitedly, "Thatha look, he is eating the bananas without peeling the skin!"

Thatha laughed and said, "Yes Dave, that's how elephants like it".

Dave wanted to give a nice name to this baby elephant. So he asked amma, appa, thatha and nana to suggest a few names.

Amma suggested the name 'Pinky'

Dave said, "Noooo'… that is for girls!"

Appa suggested the name 'Jumbo'

But Dave thought it didn't suit the baby elephant.

Nana asked, "Isn't Ramu a nice name for an elephant?"

But Dave thought it was old-fashioned.

Thatha said, "How about Pintoo"?

Dave instantly liked the name and started jumping with joy. He had finally decided upon the name for his elephant !

The next morning, Thatha and Dave went to the temple and Dave announced to the pundit uncle that he has a name for the elephant and going forward the elephant shall be called 'Pintoo!' Pundit uncle smiled and agreed to the name Dave had for the elephant.

Dave enjoyed spending time with Pintoo, the same way Pintoo also waited for Dave everyday in his temple. On a few occasions Thatha, Dave and Pintoo went to the park to play. Pintoo loved going to the park, he would run all around the park and when Thatha would announce that it's time to go back home, he would turn adamant as he was always reluctant to leave the park. Dave and Thatha always had a hard time pulling him out of the park and had a tough time convincing Pintoo that will come again tomorrow.

As days passed Pintoo and Dave became best of friends. Dave started liking his new house just because of Pintoo. Dave wanted to take a picture along with Pintoo, so he thought of asking Appa for his phone so that he can take a picture with Pintoo, but Appa refused as he was busy but promised Dave that he would come along with him this sunday and take some pictures of the two.

Thereon, Dave was impatiently waited for Sunday. He kept asking Thatha

"How many more days for sunday thatha?"

Thatha would patiently tell him, "Today is Wednesday, then Thursday, Friday, Saturday and then Sunday. So we need to wait for 3 more days."

And everyday this would happen, till Sunday..

Finally, Sunday morning after breakfast, Dave and his family went to the temple to see Pintoo. They took some nice pictures along with Pintoo. Pintoo joyfully posed for all the pictures. They even went to the park to take some more pictures and it was a lovely day. After the photo shoot they all left home tired..

Dave wanted to frame a picture of him and pintoo and hang it in his room. He already made up his mind which picture he would frame. The same day he went with appa and got it printed and framed it so that he could hang the picture in his room. He thought how nice it would be if Pintoo could come and see this, but he also knew that no animals were allowed inside the flat. So he took the photos with him the next day to show them to Pintoo. Pintoo lovingly touched the Photos.

Seeing all this, Pundit uncle said, "He is giving his blessings to the photos."Dave was thrilled that Pintoo also liked the photos, after all Pintoo was now a part of Dave's family.

One fine day Dave's family planned for a picnic near the lake which wasn't too far away from their place. They decided to pack some lunch and snacks for the picnic as well. Appa was busy cleaning the car, amma and nana were busy planning dishes for cooking,Thatha was ironing the clothes, Dave was sitting quietly thinking about Pintoo.

Dave knew how much Pintoo liked playing in the water thus he wanted to take pintoo along with them for this picnic.But he was not sure if that was possible, because Pintoo won't be able to fit in their car ! Oh, how he wished that only if Pintoo was small like a puppy he could easily carry him.He rushed to the temple to inform Pintoo of their picnic plan and saw that Pundit uncle was busy talking to a few people in the temple.

Dave stepped closer to Pintoo and said, I'm going to miss you, Pintoo, it would be so nice if you could come with us for the picnic."Pundit uncle overheard what Dave was saying to the elephant and told him, "Hey Dave don't you worry, we are also going to the same place for a picnic tomorrow!"

Dave was puzzled and asked "Who all are going uncle?"

Pundit uncle said, "Pintoo and all of us."

Dave looked confused and questioned, "But uncle, how will Pintoo fit in the car?"

The Pundit laughed and answered, "No Dave, we are taking him in the tempo, there is a temple near the lake and we are having a special pooja in that temple."

Dave was elated and jubilant.He hugged Pintoo and ran to his house to inform everyone about this good news and Just like Dave, all the others in the family were also happy.

It was a bright sunny day, Dave and his family left in the car early, he waved to Pintoo on the way and shouted, "Come soon Pintoo." Pintoo shook his head in excitement as he too sensed that he was going out somewhere.

Airavata

As soon as the tempo arrived, Pintoo got into the vehicle and danced all the way till they reached the spot. Pundit uncle and Pintoo met with Dave's family who reached the lake much earlier. It was a beautiful scenic picnic spot surrounded by the lake and a garden. Dave and Pintoo jumped in joy, but Pundit uncle reminded them about the pooja at the lake temple and how Pintoo must be ready for it.

They took him near the lake and bathed him with the clean water. Pintoo loved playing in water and started splashing the water on everyone, they all laughed and played along with Pintoo. Soon, Pundit uncle and the other helpers hurried Pintoo and got him ready and took him to the temple which was not very far from the lake, while Dave and his family went ahead for boating, Dave chose a pedal boat which was quite spacious, he sat with amma and appa and was holding tight. He was quite scared when they started pedaling but after sometime he started enjoying the ride!

He cheered appa and amma "Fast appa fast, fast amma fast."

They completed two rounds of the lake, enjoying the water ride.

Dave saw Pintoo coming out of the temple, he ran and hugged him and told him about his boating experience. Pintoo kept staring at the lake as he wanted to play in the water for some more time and started pulling Dave towards the water.

Pundit uncle tried to stop Pintoo, but the little elephant was too strong and adamant.

They stepped inside the water which didn't look too deep. Dave was advised by everyone not to go too far. They happily splashed water at each other and played while the elders kept an eye on them.

Apparently, nobody noticed that they went a little further towards deep water while playing and Dave slipped and fell into the water. Hearing his screams his family rushed inside to save him but Pintoo was quicker than everyone of them, he grabbed Dave with his small trunk and pulled him out of the lake.

Dave was shivering, he had gulped a lot of water, Pintoo was by his side and he was terrified. They made him spit all the water by pressing his stomach and changed his wet clothes. Dave slowly came out of this shock and regained his strength. All were all relieved and left for home. They thanked Pintoo for his timely help.

Dave was too tired and slept on their way back home. For the next two days he was home bound and was asked to rest. On the third day he went to the temple to thank Pintoo, but Pintoo was nowhere to be found. Dave was furious, and inquired from his Pundit uncle about Pintoo.

Pundit uncle said, "Dave please don't get upset, Pintoo has been taken to the other temple where his mom lives, he will live in that temple from now on.."

Dave was shocked to hear that, he ran home crying, he was so upset that he didn't even ask which temple was it that pintoo was sent to. He was sobbing so badly and everyone at home panicked seeing Dave like this. He told his family all what Pundit uncle said and they were equally shocked but they didn't know how to console Dave.

Dave kept looking at the picture of him and Pintoo and cried day and night thinking of him.

Thatha tried explaining to him "Look Dave, Pintoo is a small elephant and he also needs his mom just like how you need your mom. Don't be sad, I will get the temple's address where Pintoo lives now and we will visit him sometime."

Days and weeks passed, Dave's school reopened and he made new friends in school, he got busy with studies and new friends. However, whenever he saw the picture of Pintoo in his room he became extremely sad. He missed him and longed to see him.

Every now and then he would ask Thatha, "Thatha when would we go and visit Pintoo?"

Thatha had something in mind and he would just reply, "Soon Dave, soon!"

Dave couldn't force thatha as he didn't want to trouble him.

And finally the day came. It was Dave's birthday,

Thatha told him, "Dave you can skip school today, we are going to meet someone"

"Whom thatha?"

"That is a surprise"

Dave was clueless and went along with Thatha. On the way when Thatha stopped to buy dozens of bananas Dave knew that he was going to see Pintoo today !

He was bursting with excitement and he just couldn't wait to see Pintoo. But, he had his doubts, whether Pintoo will remember him or not.

'What if he had forgotten me?' he said to himself.

They reached the temple and this temple was a big one. As they entered they heard the same bell jingling ding-ding-ding..

Dave's heart was beating faster now and he started looking for Pintoo everywhere.

Thatha tapped Dave's shoulders and pointed to the corner of the temple and there he stood -Pintoo with his mom. He had grown taller just like Dave and was quite big now.

Dave slowly walked towards Pintoo, he was scared how Pintoo would react. He went and stood in front of Pintoo. Pintoo started shaking his head and then his body, he was almost dancing and touched Dave from head to toe with his trunk. He embraced him and Dave snuggled in the little elephant's warmness. It was evident how both missed each other.

Thatha stood still with tears in his eyes and mommy elephant was enjoying the entire scene from a distance as if she understood everything. Thatha gave the fruits to Dave to feed Pintoo, they stayed in the temple until evening and then it was time to leave.

Dave said,"I promise you Pintoo, I will come and see you often."

Pintoo understood and shook his head in agreement. Mommy elephant blessed Thatha and Dave. Pintoo and Dave hugged one last time and they said good-bye to each other with a promise to meet again soon.

***

Sudha has been working as a story teller for 5 years and she is also the Author of the book "How Dave met the stars". You can check the book on https://www.amazon.in/dp/1639574018#

Kokkitu's not-so-secret Gift

Anugraha Venugopal

Kokkitu has a gift from his grandmother. He uses it every time someone needs it. He uses it even if no one needs it, just to keep it alive forever. No one sees the immense power of the gift like Kokkitu does. Not that he deliberately hides it. It's just not something Kokkitu himself saw as a '*gift*.' It's just what his grandmother – whom he refers to as grammy – taught him as a baby elephant and he's been doing it since.

Airavata

Kokkitu and his best friend Munna were both eight years old. These young elephants lived with their family and friends in the picturesque jungle of Gajaburi. Kokkitu was known to be mischievous but not so much a troublemaker. Munna, older by only a few months, enjoyed wandering the jungle and playing with Kokkitu. They leisurely accompany their mums who meander through new places for food and water. But this was possible only during the weekends because they were busy as the bees on weekdays!

They were schooled at the only school in the jungle where all kinds of young animals mingled and studied together – Gajaburi Union Higher Secondary School (commonly known as GU). There are a few other schools in the jungle as well, but they don't accept all kinds of students. For instance, there's the exclusive Gajaburi School of Spots where the preference is for the little ones of the leopards, cheetahs, giraffes, jaguars, spotted snakes, deers, and hyenas. Then there's the Soar High Academic Center where young birds and insects with wings learn the ways of the jungle. The ancestors of the tigers and zebras wanted to build their own school, so came along The Success Stripes School – but their plan did not go through. They hoped that the honeybees would join them in running the school but the honeybees preferred the school of insects instead of stripes! So now, the zebras and the tigers started sending their children to the all-welcoming GU.

Here's how a week would generally pan out for Kokkitu and Munna- they attend their daily classes at GU. After school, they take up music lessons taught by Ms. Kuyili, the jungle's well-known birdie who had a soulful voice! Even after three months of classes there was hardly any progress to be seen.Ms. Kuyili recommended that they practise daily even though her classes were held only on Mondays and Wednesdays. On Tuesdays and Thursdays, they had the Maths tuition class, handled by the gigantic Mrs. Mambo (who wasn't a native of Gajaburi). She came from Central Africa many years ago along with her husband Mr. Picquer and made Gajaburi their home. Although all the elephants in this land had extraordinary memory power, Mrs.

Mambo liked to blow her own trumpet often! The young elephants still enjoyed visiting Mrs. Mambo as she owned a library! It had a vast collection of books! Kokkitu and Munna choose books randomly and read them during their weekly reading sessions on Fridays! This is how the best friends spend their days in the jungle – learning, exploring, activity time and play time!

It was Tuesday evening. Kokkitu and Munna were attending their Maths class. Mrs. Mambo conducted a surprise test for all. Munna hoped that he had written most of the answers correctly. Kokkitu is certain that he aced it, but he isn't bothered about the results as he attends these Maths classes just to accompany Munna. Kokkitu has been the reigning champion in the annual Spellathon and Math-oh-mate competitions organized by the Gajaburi Association of Schools for two years now. The students, apart from Kokkitu, just can't wait for Mrs. Mambo to announce their results. She announces that Paloma- the parrot has received full marks. Kokkitu claps loudly for Paloma. Jenny, the jungle's beloved deer, had received the lowest marks and so she was visibly disappointed. After the class ended, Kokkitu walked up to Jenny and placed his little trunk on her head and offered a warm smile. Jenny was distraught. Taking his trunk off, he enquired, "Jenny, how about I help you study for the next test? Munna usually prefers to study by himself. So, I could teach you… I mean, if that's okay with you?" Jenny, who felt desolated till now, is thrilled and happy to hear this.

She asks eagerly, as if seeking reassurance, "Really, you could do that?" He flapped his ears in excitement. Munna observed what happened from a distance, but didn't think much of it. He was not the one to ask too many questions, anyways.

On their way back from the tuition class, Kokkitu and Munna noticed the old giraffe Humu by the mango tree, with mangoes strewn all over the ground. The otherwise chirpy Humu aunty seems dejected today. Kokkitu rushed over to probe if she needed any help or maybe, a big ear to simply hear her out. Humu told him how she was craving for mangoes but since

Airavata

she's been ill, her mouth isn't helping her pluck the mangoes from the tree. She didn't have to explain any further, as Kokkitu understood her problem. He glanced at Munna and they both started picking up mangoes from the ground with their trunk for Humu aunty. The old giraffe was ecstatic and humbled. She bends down and devours a few mangoes in quick succession. Watching her eat tempted both the little elephants and they too joined in the mango fiesta. After downing a good number of mangoes, Humu thanked them profusely and blessed them, happily bending her head all the way down. The young fellas take her blessings and run away *thud, thud, thud, thud*.

The next morning, on their way to school, they see Razi uncle, the wise parrot, setting up his shop for the day. He is the jungle's most trusted fortune-teller. He also worked in a faraway land for some humans a while ago. Since then, all the other animals from the nearby jungles came up to him for advice on important decisions. He would just describe to them what he saw in the cards and also reminded them that he cannot 'advise' but he can point to a direction the fortune-seeker needs to look into. Nonetheless, he was revered by the animals. They were elated just seeing him by the shop with his pack of cards. Today, however, Razi seemed upset over dwindling customers in the past few weeks. This was a cause for concern as this diminished his food stock as well, as he got paid with fruits, fruit seeds, nuts, grains and even flowers in return for reading the fortunes. He notices young Kokkitu and Munna walking by the shop and greets them. Kokkitu gazes at Razi uncle who seems sluggish, just like he's been over the last couple of days. He dashes towards him and says, "Uncle, I hope a lot of customers visit you today and you get tons of food". Razi uncle prances in joy as soon as he hears little Kokkitu's words. He gives him and Munna a banana each and wishes them a good day at school.

In the classroom, Kokkitu tells Ryan-the jackal, that his new pencil box looks beautiful. Munna whispers to Kokkitu, "Why are you talking to him? He makes fun of your trunk almost every day." Munna gives him a recap of the jackal's nasty behaviour. He recalls how Ryan deliberately teases Kokkitu on his physical appearance and doesn't seem bothered that his comments are hurtful. Munna growls that the jackal can never be a friend to them.

Kokkitu smiles and responds to him, "I hear you, Munna. I don't consider him my friend either. I strongly believe that friends must love and respect each other. So, Ryan is not a dependable friend. But we can still be nice to him. Don't you think so? My granny told me that being nice to other people is like throwing a stone into the water."

Munna still couldn't understand what it had to do with Kokkitu being kind to Rayan. He seemed puzzled.

Kokkitu continued, "Once the stone hits the water, the water drops touch each other to form beautiful and continuous waves. That splendid pattern is called a ripple. All it takes is just one stone to form that ripple." He goes on to explain further, "Did you see how Razi uncle was happy when I told him he would get lots of customers today? And did you see how Humu aunty blessed us for helping her? They are both happy now. So, they will do something nice for someone else they meet today. And those people will go on to make two more people happy, I hope! Do you understand now, Munna?"

Munna replied, "Oh, is that why you were nice to Jenny last evening and to Rayan, today?"

Kokkitu replied , "Yes ! You are right, Munna! When we are kind to someone, they will be kind to another person. If our kindness can make one person happy, then that happy person will make someone else happy. See how it works? Being kind is like a circle. It has no end point. We can only go to the starting point again and again." Now Munna was able to understand Kokkitu's point.

Kokkitu added further, "My grandmother says everyone can make so many people happy just by being kind to them. We don't have to try hard or be fake to show our kindness. We simply need to look around and see how we can cheer up someone. Kindness is a terrific gift that keeps on giving, Munna." His friend nodded his head in agreement. He was astonished when he saw Ryan sharing his stationery with the rabbit- Putty. He never did such things in class.

Munna couldn't agree more with Kokkitu's words on kindness. 'It really is a gift that keeps on giving.' he tells himself. Thus, the not-so-secret gift also fascinates Munna who now joins Kokkitu in creating ripples of kindness.

Gajaburi now has two young elephants who shall keep the Gift Of Kindness alive...

***

Born in Kannur and raised in a multicultural community in Chennai, Anugraha Venugopal (She/Her) prefers her world to be a mix of variety. She enjoys the adrenaline rush in a commotion as much as the deep breaths for a moment of calm. She's a freelance Writer who feels lively when writing on Personal Growth, Self-Love, and Mindfulness.

Little Jumbo's

The Fall of Insunisi
Aniya Burse

"Can you tell me a story about the guardian using her powers?" asked Isla.

"Of course, which one," I said. She tapped her finger on her chin.

"Hmm...Maybe the storm one." She said.

I nodded. "Before the Great Wall of Insunisi was built, there was a great storm that tormented our island. Hundreds of people died. They were the darkest days of our time. Those days would still be happening if it weren't for our guardian. She walked through the island, Inner Circle, Middle Ring, Outer Ring, and all the forests in between. Her energy declined within seconds of holding back the storm, pushing away the roaring waves and wind. She did this for days until the storm passed, saving the remaining lives while putting her own at stake. When the storm was over she built our great wall" Isla nodded.

"Is it possible that people can take away someone's energy?" She asked.

"No. People don't have magical abilities. They wouldn't be able to do it even if they tried," I said.

"But what if we *could* do magic, would we be able to do it?"

"No, our goddess wouldn't ever give us such destructional power," I replied. Isla nodded. "So you're going to be queen now?" asked Isla.

"Yes."

"So, when are you going to get your blessing from the guardian?"

"Tomorrow at my coronation."

"When you pass, father will take the throne, after he passses, I will be the queen, right?"

"Yes, but that's a long time away, you have plenty of time until you become queen."

"Why do the monarchs have to get a blessing from the guardian when they have their coronation?"

"Go to sleep. You will see everything tomorrow." I loved my niece, but her ability to ask questions no matter what gets exhausting. She started stomping away. "Do you want me to walk you to your chamber?" I called out. She didn't look back, she kept on marching. I went back to my chamber. There was nothing I could do about anything now. I was to be the queen. I was to take on all the responsibility of the kingdom. It wasn't unexpected. I stared at the portrait of my late parents which was hung on the wall. I would take the position that I had been preparing for my whole life.

It was morning, and I was shaken awake by an extremely frantic maiden. "You are still in bed? We need to get you dressed for the blessing ceremony! You must start your day now!" I arched my eyebrow. Her eyes widened. "Forgive me, my lady," she stammered, "I did not mean to disrespect you. not at all!"

"It's fine. I understand your agitation. Shall we go?" She nodded, taking my hand and leading me out.

I was led to the bathing chamber. There sat a bath which they were still preparing, a gown, and more and more. It wasn't everyday that the bathing chamber was occupied with servants. I had thought the ceremony wouldn't last more than a few minutes. I hadn't realised the ceremony was of this much importance. The maiden walked me to the bath, stripped me of my garments. I sat down in the bath. Maidens immediately started washing my hair and face. Pouring liquids of different aromas on my head.

After they were done with the bath, they pulled me out. As my body touched the cold air, I shivered. I was instantly covered with towels. In a matter of minutes, I was getting 'fitted' in my dress. It was in ivory and green color. The sleeves didn't stick to arms, instead they hung low. The train was a few feet long, nothing I would trip over. I remembered my brother's wedding. The train seemed like it went on for miles, the amount of times I stepped on the train and almost landed on my face was infinite. A maiden ran her hand through my hair, combing it back. She weaved flowers of all kinds through my hair. The maiden let the rest of my hair sit on my shoulders. The rest of them were giving the so called 'final touches' to the dress. Eventually, they took their hands off the dress.

"You look fit to be a queen." I turned around. Adonis, my brother, was standing at the door, smiling. My cheeks flushed.

"You're too kind."

"What Lord Adonis says is true, my lady. You look gorgeous," said a maiden, adding necklaces, bangles and rings. I grinned.

"My lady, a message," I looked behind to see a messenger. I took the scroll from his hand.

Dear Princess Amani,

It has come to our attention that other life, who call themselves Antineres, have come to our lovely island.

We welcomed them with open arms to the wall, but they weren't peaceful. They had come to claim the land for themselves, and demanded our immediate surrender. We refused. They killed all the fishermen at the docks. Though some were lucky enough to escape with their lives. We may have an unavoidable battle ahead of us. Unless, you can persuade them to leave our Insunisi peacefully.

Sincerely,

The Outlookers

My smile faded. These disgusting intruders. My people welcome these Antineres with respect, and they kill those innocent fishermen like barbarians. Adonis put his hand on my shoulder.

"I'll get the palanquin ready, we will leave right after your coronation." As I nodded, he left.

"Write this," I told the messenger. " Gather the peacekeepers, I will be arriving soon. Address it to Arccius." He bowed and walked out.

Don't worry about the letter right now, you have something else to attend to. I told myself. I walked with a guard to the temple.

The temple was made completely out of white marble, all the pillars, even the statue of the savior goddess, even the guardian elephant, who lived in there camouflaged with the temple being completely white. There was the head priest, the guardian, and the seminarians, waiting for the ceremony to begin. I climbed up the steps, sitting before the guardian. She was enormous. Her ears were beautiful, decorated with gold earrings bedazzled with gems. She was beautiful.

"Princess Amani of Insunisi today presents herself before the great guardian of our island, who has been with us to receive her blessing," the priest said, "Princess Amani, you are allowed to choose to be able of whatever our loyal guardian is capable of, of course, if she gives you acceptance. Give her this offering." I hand her the bowl of fruit. Her trunk grabbed it and dropped the fruit into her mouth. She leaned down and put her trunk on my head.

"The guardian has accepted you," said the priest. "You can request the blessing now. Do not say it out loud."

Airavata

I closed my eyes and thought. I could be capable of anything she was capable of, she could control water, air, earth, and can bless the worthy with her powers. I want all your powers, I thought.

"So be it," she said. I opened my eyes. She glowed golden. I felt something warm at my fingertips and it went all over my body.

"Thank you," I said. She rose from her leaning position, and started walking back into the temple.

"The ceremony is over, I suggest you return back to the palace, the guardian is to sleep now, she won't come back," suggested the priest. I nodded. Isla tugged on my dress, I don't know where she came from.

"Can you answer my questions, now?" She asked. I watched the priest walk away. Once the priest was out of sight, I took Isla and ran to the elephant. Once I had reached the guardian, she was already lying down on the floor, sleeping. I knelt down, placing my hand on her trunk. Give me permission to bless her, invaders have come to our island and have threatened the safety of our people. My brother and I are leaving tomorrow to send them away, but in case we don't come back, you, along with her, will have to take the charge. I know she is young, but she should be able to protect herself and the kingdom if no one else can. The elephant became alert, she nodded.

"Isla, I want you to listen to me closely, I am going to give you a blessing, you cannot tell anyone what we did here today." Isla nodded. I put my hands on her head and closed my eyes. "I bless you with all the powers of the guardian." I felt the warmth of the blessing leave my hands and to her head. "Now go," I told her.

"Please, If something happens to us, protect the kingdom," I asked. The guardian's golden silhouette illuminated the dark room. It was nearly dusk. I left the temple and rushed to the palanquin where Adonis was waiting. Adonis and I traveled for three days. I looked out of the palanquin, there was a wall that touched the sky, and along the bottom of the wall were men dressed in colorful metal plates pointing their swords at me. The Peace Keepers advanced towards the colorfully dressed men, they didn't move. Both of us got off, they got closer.

"Address yourself," demanded one.

"Amani, queen of Insunisi, and this is Adonis, my brother, and I demand to see your leader," I said. They laughed, resting their weapons.

"And why are you so eager to see our leader? To ask us to leave? Trust us little girl, we aren't going anywhere."

I gritted my teeth. I raised my hand. Dagger-like stones came out of the ground. The Peace Keepers took them, the remaining daggers stayed in the air. "Take us to your leader now, or I promise I won't hesitate…"

They shuffled back a few steps, but didn't agree. I pointed the stones at the men, they weren't fazed. I turned the stone daggers into swords, they raised their swords. Mine attacked the men. The Peace Keepers and the men battled. Some from both sides fell, others kept on fighting. One had escaped the wrath of my sword and fallen out of my sight. I looked to my side for Adonis but he wasn't there.

I tore my eyes from the fight and looked for Adonis. He was dueling with the escaped man. I turned my attention to my swords, and more men had fallen. I looked back to see my brother and the man still dueling. I ran over to assist him. When I had gotten to Adonis, he had many stab wounds and was bleeding profusely. I was surprised that he was still standing. I made another stone sword and stabbed the man in the back. The sword cut through the metal and through the flesh. He cried out in pain. I stabbed him in the same spot again, and then pulled out my sword. Adonis limped to my side and leaned on my shoulder. We walked to the wall, their leader had to be stationed somewhere near. I looked back at the palanquin, all the Peace Keepers and the Antineres had died.

"Where do you think the leader would be stationed?" I asked Adonis. He weakly pointed at the woods surrounding The Outer Ring. I studied the area where he was pointing, then I saw that there was a forced opening in the forest. I followed the path of broken trees, trying to slow down Adonis's bleeding, at this rate, he would be dead by the time we find the leader of these repulsive creatures. I tore some leaves off the remaining trees, using them to cover his wounds. We walked through the woods until we saw tents surrounded by the same looking people.

Airavata

They pointed their weapons at us.

"We come in peace," I said. " We want help for my brother, he is deeply wounded." They glanced at him, and charged. They targeted Adonis. We dodged their attacks, pushing them to the ground. They all tripped over each other, falling on the ground. I made holes where they fell and buried them alive. We ran into the camp. It was crowded, so it was easy to hide. Just then, someone took me by my hand and dragged us somewhere else.

The tent we were dragged to looked big from the outside but was enormous on the inside. The tent was filled with beds, women healers, and wounded men. The person that dragged us here took Adonis and set him on the bed. Adonis looked unconscious, maybe dead.

"How long did you wait before bringing him in here? He's almost dead," she said, wrapping him in bandages.

"Um, the people escorting us ran away, and we were attacked," I said. She believed it.

"I know, I know. It has happened to many of our people that have come here. For people so ignorant they were unaware of any other life beyond this island, are skilled in tearing out the flesh of the enemy." I smiled. "How long will it be until he wakes up?" I asked.

"*If* he wakes up," she said, "He has lost too much blood. He's most likely to die." My smile faded. I couldn't let him die. He is my brother. I didn't say anything, I just nodded. "Now, now. You can just go to the general for the money of a dead relative. He'll most likely give it to you. He bribed people just to come here. Most thought the voyager was a mad man, talking about some faraway island that was filled with riches of many kinds, and then we found this place."

"Where is the general?" I cut off her rambling. She frowned.

"He lives in the largest tent. I don't know why he needs that tent. It's bigger than this tent."

"Thank you!" I told her, running out of the tent." I ran through camp, searching for the tent, until I was halted by a man.

"What is a woman doing in enemy garments running around the camp?" I froze. The healer didn't notice anything, how is it that just one man noticed the clothes? I had to lie.

"I…" I faltered. Nothing I had thought of was good enough..

"You're coming with me."

"What? No!" I pulled at his firm grip. Shooting air and rocks at him as well as I could with only one hand. He somehow managed to still hold on to me and drag me into a tent.

In the tent there was another man. He was dressed differently. There were no colorful metal plates, he was dressed in complete blue.

"General, here is the enemy." He let go of me.

"So, the queen of Insunisi has decided to pay us a visit," said the general.

"How do you know who I am?" I asked.

"You think that healer wouldn't recognize you?." He waved at the man. He went.

" Leave immediately, and peacefully. Or else."

He chuckled, " Or else what, little girl?" I felt heat rise from my feet to my face.

"Or else I'll bring…"

"Your guardian? She's dead." I felt a lump in my throat, the guardian isn't dead. She couldn't be. "Don't believe me?" He pulled out a small box. He placed it in front of her.

"Open it."

I opened the box. I gasped. It had the jewel inside it. The jewel on the goddess's statue that the guardian protected with all her life. "The elephant put up a good fight, thrashed her feet, shot some rocks, blew some air, splashed some water, but nothing wins against me." I lunged at him, he blocked me with his hands. I suddenly felt tired. I was fine a moment ago, now I felt like my energy was sucked out of me. Sleeping felt like a nice idea. I shook the idea out of my head. I shot a tiny, but sharp rock at his arm. The arm didn't budge. It was like his arm was made out of steel. I was getting extremely tired, so I forced my drooping eyelids to open. I created a small tornado around his body. I kept him there until the air started giving out. He stumbled back slamming his head on the floor. He groaned. I rubbed my eyes again, it was like I was under a sleeping spell. It all clicked, these people could reduce someone's energy by touching them. I can only fight him from a distance. I ran out of the tent, instantly there was a sharp pain in my hip. The pain was unbearable. I placed my hand where it hurt. There was a knife in my hip. I was bleeding. I felt a hand on my shoulder. I tried to fight the urge to close my eyes, but my eyelids closed anyway.

"Bye bye, little girl." Was the last thing I heard. I hope Isla is safe. She is the only one that holds the powers of the guardian, she is our only hope.

***

Aniya Burse is a 12 yr old girl who loves to do a lot of different things after school, read, play flute, learn Sanskrit, Coding, play Chess and now also write! She got her one poem and a story published in anthology books Beyond the Verses -2 and Box of tales-2 this year.

Eela's Experience: Exasperated-to-Elated

Disha Kumar

"Hey that tickles! Please Sanskriti, stop… Ah! That was close! Hey, hi! I am Banwari, the Banyan tree. This is Sanskriti. Oh yes! She is a squirrel and yes, she tickles me a lot!!

You know, we banyan trees are so old. I am 210 years old and I have seen thousands of creatures moving around, so we have expertise when it comes to storytelling. Let me tell you a story!"

Well… Mmm… Once upon a time, a cheeky, chubby, plump and fat elephant was born in the Gir forest. She was named Eela. Just after she was born, she felt a touch, a touch of a big fat male elephant and a big fat female elephant. **(Did you know- elephants are born blind!)**

"Gugu Gaga!" She blabbered.

"Aww!" Said Elvika, the big fat female elephant.

"She's so cute!" Said Keshavan, the short male elephant.

And suddenly she could hear thousands of elephants behind saying, "Oh my!"

When she was 5, her parents enrolled her in the Gir Forest International school. The moment Eela opened the classroom door, many voices could be heard.

"Who's that? Looks like a wandering wall!" Said Sneha, the snail.

"Looks like a rugged rope to me!" Said Haru, the horse.

"Looks like a waving winnowing basket to me…"Said Pipilika, the ant.

"Looks like a dirty dagger to me!" Said Zubeidah, the zebra.

"Looks like a tall tree to me…" Said Sunaina, the Southern birdwing butterfly.

"Looks like a slithering snake to me!" Said Monisha, the monkey.

Airavata

"Mmmmmmprrrrffffrahhaahaha HAHAHAHAHAHA! Now that's what we call a rowinning- dagrenake." Druti the deer said.

"Oh my!! I can't stop laughing, hahahahahhah!" Drhti continued.

Eela went and sat on the back bench, so that she won't have to hear more. Soon Snigda, the snake ma'am entered the class.

"Good morning my ssssssweeet and ssssssssuper children! Don't worry. I consume only chilllllld milk. I am your prinssssssipal!" Said Snigda ma'am.

Later that day, Eela met Sanskriti, who would jump around, entertaining her with gymnastic skills and make music with nuts in the break time. With Sanskriti around, Eela would spend her day jumping and laughing. But, without her she would always spend her days in gloom and tears.

One day, Sanskriti took Eela to Mrs. Oorjitha, the owl. After listening to the entire story, Oorjitha said in her stern British accent. "So, you want to stop getting teased right?"

She nodded. "Yes!" Mrs. Oorjotha said clearly. "Listen carefully. Ahem! Go to nature's goddess. She owns a bank you can't withdraw money from and she has a bed, where you can't sleep. She will show you one of the most powerful creatures, who has extraordinary features. The magic will happen on its own."

Eela knew exactly what to do! She went to... hey before I reveal the answer, can you guess? Oh, you are smarter than I expected! Absolutely, a river. Well, Eela had a big brain and knew exactly where to go. **(Did you know- elephants have a big brain!)** She climbed up many hills, until she reached a valley, where she saw the Godavariji River. It had a river bed with a beautiful bank.

"Oh Godavariji! Can you please help me! Mrs. Oorjitha asked me to come to you!"

Godavariji said, "Oh, my dear child! I'm k-k-quite old now, s-s-so now I might stammer a bit. I hope you don't m-m-mind my dear. I know what you want. Just look at my beautiful water. You will see s-something. You will d-d-define…"

"Splash! Splish! Sploosh!" Interrupted the sounds coming from the water, caused by Eela's trunk movement.

"Eela, Eela, Eela… My dear. P-P-Please keep some patience my child! You see… First you must close your eyes. Come on, c-c- close your eyes! Yes, that's like it, n-n now feel the pleasant air coming into your lungs. Then take a deep breath in and a deep breath out. Do this for 3 rounds."

Godavariji continued. "1, 2 and 3! Yes, now check the river. Don't wave it with your trunk like before. Just look into it."

"But, I can't see anything! Is it a problem with me? I am the one who always creates problems." Eela said, rubbing her eyes.

Godavariji chuckled, "Oh my child!! Eela dearie! Just close your eyes again and forget everything. 1, 2, 3. Yes, now rub your trunk on your body, gently place your trunk on your eyes and then open them slowly. Now look at my water. You will define…"

"I got my answer now!" Ella interrupted. "I see a huge… me! I can see it. Thank you Godavariji!"

Godavriji smiled, "Oh god! This generation has so little patience. In my generation you know! It was just so different… anyways! Welcome dear and bye! See you next time!"

When she turned back, she saw a big silhouette that was looking a bit blurry because of the sun's scorching heat and Eela's poor vision. **(Did you know – All elephants have a poor vision and are colour-blind.)** She took water in her trunk and squirted it. She sucked some mud in her trunk and smeared it all over her body. This acted as a natural sunscreen. She then went forward and could see a little better. It was a figure she hadn't seen since years! It was Lipilika, the leopard.

She crept as quietly as a mouse and headed towards the classroom's back bench. Most of her classmates, Druti the deer, Sneha the snail, Snigda ma'am,

Airavata

Zubeidah the zebra, Monisha the monkey and Haru the horse were sitting there. She had to alert them, that too quickly.

She got an idea.

She took a raspberry, a blackberry, a mango, a dandelion and a banana leaf. She used the leaf as a canvas and smashed the raspberry with her feet on the right of the leaf, which produced a blood red colour. She smashed the mango to get a sunny yellow colour. Then she picked up the dandelion

with her trunk. Using the dandelion as a paint brush, she quickly painted a leopard in the centre of the banana leaf. She then took the blackberries and smashed them with her legs to get a beautiful black colour. She used that to make spots on the leopard.

It was an alert message.

She passed it to Sanskriti. Sanskriti scurried and passed it to the baboons, who climbed on my topmost branch and made an alert sound, "Kiiii! Kichak! Kwiiii!" All got alerted. Lipilika needed at least 45.67 seconds to arrive there, so they sneaked out before she even knew!

The next day, when Eela opened the classroom door, everything was… empty. But when she checked the right side, she saw a group of ants, led by Pippilika making a heart GIF. Oh yes, we're advanced- we know what GIFs are! When she went inside further and turned left, baboons started welcoming Eela with bananas falling from the east, west, north and south. Then, a sound erupted as all the animals jumped and screamed, "Eela, the eeeemazing elephant!" I am sure that was Eela's most memorable day.

Hey, that was an elephantastic story! Wasn't it? And most importantly- I had been a great storyteller. Storyteller Banwari! Hahahhahahahhah!

You know, as I am standing next to the school's break bench, narrating this story to you, I can see Eela's daughter- Elisha carrying her school bag and entering the classroom. Maybe, someday I will have stories about her adventures too! Hey it's cooking time now; better go to cook some oxygen in my kitchen. Bye for now!!

Disha Kumar is a creative soul and loves to write. She has her books published and available to read on sites like Storyweaver and GiftAbled. She has also won storywriting, drama and storytelling contests like:- Nandini Nayar's Writing Contest 1st prize, Bhopal Tribe Storytelling Contest 2nd prize, Beliterate Writing Contest 3rd prize, etc. She passed Drama-Level one of Trinity College, London with distinction. Besides writing, her hobbies are to tell stories, acts, sings and dances among others She enjoys working as a team, too.

Heroic Han

Prisha Gupta

The music boomed. The announcer roared. Hannibal barely bothered to listen for his cue. He knew Mark would come backstage and call him up anyways.

Backstage was a chaotic place, with the panicked employees and the thundering applause and the smell of firecrackers waiting to go off. Yet Han quite enjoyed it. For an elephant, he tremendously loved performing.

Bobo squealed excitedly, 'All the best, Han!' Poor Bobo. He never understood what he was supposed to do. And barking chihuahuas aren't very crowd-pleasing.

Mark was there shouting over the music, that Hannibal had to get ready. He was ready. As ready as he could be.

'PLEASE WELCOME OUR FINAL ACT…THE HEROIC HANNIBAL!'

Han confidently sauntered onto the stage. He adored his audience. Throughout his act, they gasped, laughed, whooped, and applauded at all the right places.

*

Alisha was waiting for him backstage. 'Wondrous as always, Heroic Han,' she said sarcastically.

Alisha despised the circus. She claimed that performing was rotten and never bothered to put up an act. She wanted to get kicked out of the show, hopefully get sent to a *'wildlife sanctuary'*, but being a tigress, even her looking bored would entertain the watchers. In fact, she'd earned a bit of a reputation as 'Angry Alisha'. She despised Han a little, too, for enjoying the show so much.

Hannibal decided not to respond. She seemed in a worse mood than usual.

'You know,' she persisted, 'Mark said he'll cut off my skin and sell it if I don't get my act together.'

That piqued him. 'Mark would never say anything like that. He's…'

'He's not the person you knew, anymore! He's greedy and *cruel!*'

Their conversation was brutally interrupted by a loud, pained squeal from Bobo.

*

Han couldn't sleep.

Well, being an elephant, he rarely slept, but even for his species, he was restless. His brain was having trouble comprehending the fact that kind Mark could ever be *un*kind. Surely, he'd been hallucinating when he saw Mark…*kicking* Bobo?

'You don't know half of it, Han. He'd never harm you, you perform too well,' Alisha had told him solemnly before she laid down to sleep.

After that, something felt horribly wrong. The walls of his enclosure, once so cosy, were now threatening to suffocate him. The rumble of the moving caravans was no longer soothing, it was threatening.

For the first time in his life, Han was not content.

*

The next morning seemed a particularly miserable one. Even more so as Han didn't enjoy travel days. As a circus they were always travelling, never in one place for long. He was dull, until he learnt their next destination.

Han had overheard a few employees chatting about how excited they were to get to 'Yellowstone' and put up the show there. 'Yellowstone' was a name familiar to him. He recognized it from Alisha's ramblings about all the different amazing habitats for animals. Yellowstone had been her favourite.

Yellowstone *Wildlife Sanctuary*, to be precise.

Perhaps…

He casually wandered over to Alisha's enclosure, where she was snoring. 'Alisha!' he hissed. Then a bit louder. She snapped awake. 'What?' she growled. Han hated to wake her up, but this was important. He quietly told her about their destination, and more urgently, his plan.

Her eyes grew larger as he spoke, and finally she was grinning widely. 'I *knew* you'd come to your senses! I'm ready to go, Heroic Han!'

*

Airavata

Alisha was excited. Nervous, too, because what if something went wrong? But mostly excited.

After so many days of longing for freedom, her dream was going to come true.

She only vaguely remembered her life before the circus, but she knew she'd been *happy* then. Something she wasn't now. She was determined to escape, and hopefully return to a free life.

Hopefully.

Which brought her back to the plan.

It was quite a good plan. Han had thought it out carefully, and she was proud and he was using his clever head. They would of course free all the other creatures, too, who were in on the secret. The past few travel days had been spent 'training' for their act, but also secretly forming a brilliant seven-phased plan that involved leaps, ropes, growls, dramatic reveals and a whole lot of feathers.

What could possibly go wrong?

*

A few minutes later, Han was ready. *As ready as I could be*, he thought.

Alisha had just left for her 'act'. Phase One was in motion. Mark came up to Han to tell him it was a big day and he was not to mess anything up because the official sanctuary people were watching.

Ha! If only he knew.

Suddenly there came a yell from outside followed by a lot of screaming, which marked the beginning of phase two. Mark grew pale at rushed on stage. Han 'panicked' as per his role and caused a lot of pandemonium indoors. But then he felt a sharp prick on his right fore-leg... and the world went awry.

And then *everything* went wrong.

*

'Poor Han. You missed all of the action,' Alisha said. She wasn't very upset, however. Even though nothing had gone to plan, she was quite satisfied with the end result. 'Tell me about it,' Han grumbled. 'Some hassled employee stuck a tranquilizer in me and suddenly I was out for the day. Tell me what happened, anyway.'

So Alisha told him. After she leapt into the crowd, there was a lot of chaos. Of course, she hadn't meant any harm, but the crowd didn't know that. 'And you tromping around backstage didn't help with the matter either,' she added gleefully. But there had been the sanctuary people who were experts in dealing with crazy animals, and they'd unfortunately chained Alisha. An employee of Mark Johnson had tranquilized Hannibal.

Before they could tranq Alisha too, however, a nice-looking lady wearing the Sanctuary's uniform had angrily exclaimed, 'But this is a Bengal tiger! Why do you have a member of an extremely endangered species in your *captivity*, Mr. Johnson?'

Thus followed a heated debate among the humans. It wasn't much of a debate than an interrogation by the Sanctuary lady, however, and she fired questions, to all of which Mark was left speechless. 'Apparently a lot of the stuff Mark was doing was behind the scenes and also *illegal*. Bobo very helpfully showed himself and whined a lot. The lady got even angrier,' explained Alisha.

Eventually they came to a conclusion and now Mark was facing a trial. Also, the circus had been permanently disbanded.

'So what happened finally?' asked Han. 'Why are we in a moving truck again, if there's no circus?'

Alisha rolled her eyes. 'Use your brain, Han. The Sanctuary people decided to take us all in! We're going to the wilderness!'

Han started. 'Really? That's amazing!' He wanted to jump for joy, but as a pachyderm he might just break the truck. Also…he found it quite impossible to jump, actually.

'Yeah, and they're even going to hold a few shows once in a while starring the Heroic Hannibal. They've seen some of your shows on tape and they think you might enjoy it.'

Han didn't think his day could get any better.

Prisha Gupta, a 13-year-old bookworm, loves to read more than anything. She loves to be creative and artsy and makes beautiful, colourful and fluid art pieces. An evolving writer, she writes poems and stories without any boundaries and is open to all sorts of ideas! She learns Kathak and also enjoys playing sports such as basketball and badminton. She co-wrote and illustrated her first book, 'Verses and Strokes'.

Jumbo's Happiness Formula

Shrija Karthik

Once upon a time in a vast green city called Enmento, there stood a huge statue of a metal elephant at the Town Square. It looked as though a real elephant was standing, so calm and splendid. Everyone who passed by the Town Square admired its magnificent body dipped in grey paint and dark small brown eyes. Its enormous trunk, broad ears and tiny tail were moveable and looked very attractive. The metal elephant was fondly called 'Jumbo'.

The Town Square became so lively especially during the Spring season. The climate was very pleasant with trees flooded with fragrant flowers. Cool breeze added more charm to this place. So, many kids visited the Town Square from all the nearby villages. It was very busy in the evening when the sun sank in the west behind the green mountains. Children used to swarm around the elephant and play with its trunk. They used to sway Jumbo's trunk to and fro like a swing. Their bubbly gurgles and joyful laughter were a melody to Jumbo's broad ears.

Goes my trunk swish, swish
Kids swing as they wish,
Their joyful smiles make my dish
Cause I don't eat any fish.

Jumbo's heart sang in delight.

Jumbo's only friend was Toto, the parrot. She was a colourful bright parrot with a curved red shiny beak. She had dark black eyes, soft fluffy feathers and brown strong feet. Everyday when the moon and stars were set in the sky Toto used to spend a few minutes with Jumbo. Jumbo liked its company very much and would share his happy moments with kids he experienced that day.

Everything was smooth and flawless until one day when a group of children visited Jumbo from a nearby village. As soon as they saw Jumbo, they fell in love with him. Every word that fell from their lips was in praise of Jumbo. They were all so excited that they swung the trunk of the elephant with lots of excitement. They played to their heart's content. When the sky became dark, all the kids returned home. The Town Square became silent.

Airavata

The sky looked like a shining lamp with twinkling stars scattered all over. Jumbo was standing all alone with tears streaming down from his eyes. That day turned out to be a gloomy day for Jumbo. As all the kids played vigorously, Jumbo's trunk loosened. He was so worried. His sobs were heard by Toto who flew by at that time. She swooped down from the sky and asked Jumbo, flapping her wings. "What happened my friend? Why are you weeping?"

"Many kids visited me today and they all played with me in full zeal. As they swayed my trunk very fast a lot of times, my screws became loose. My trunk might get dismantled tomorrow. How can the kids play with me without the trunk?" Said Jumbo with a long face.

"Enmento officials will get your screws tightened tomorrow. Why should you worry?" Comforted Toto. But, as soon as Toto finished speaking, the weak trunk fell down with a clinking sound. Jumbo became too nervous.

Oh, my trunk is broken,

My eyes are swollen,

Can you fix the trunk, please?

Till then, my tears wouldn't cease.

Toto consoled Jumbo and said "I shall seek my friend's help to fix you before dawn. No worries Jumbo." Jumbo stood still like frozen ice.

Toto flew to the nearby forest and headed straight to Molly's burrow. Molly was a young rabbit with light pink ears and white fluffy body.

Molly asked "What happened? Why are you panting?"

"My friend Jumbo's trunk got dismantled a few minutes ago. We have to help Jumbo recover before dawn." said Toto, breathing heavily.

"Let me seek help from my friend Babloo," said Molly comforting Toto.

Babloo was a big brown bear. He had just returned from his walk. When his grey eyes saw Molly in the wee hours of night. He understood the emergency and ran towards Molly. Molly explained everything.

"Help, we must,

Upon us Jumbo has trust,

Let's all hurry

And stop Jumbo's worry!" Said Babloo.

All of them rushed to the Town Square.

Jumbo was moaning in grief "Oh! How unlucky I am? How can I bring smiles on children's faces with a broken trunk?" He lamented.

Babloo wore his thinking cap and whispered to Molly to get the screws and screwdrivers to tighten. Toto flew up in the air in search of a shop where screws can be got. Molly started to hop as fast as he could. Drops of sweat trickled down from Molly's face. Since Molly became exhausted soon, Toto swooped down and carried Molly in its feet and flew.

Meanwhile, Babloo sang songs of hope to Jumbo to motivate him.

"Hold onto hope always

You 'll never be in a maze

To come out from grief, there are ways,

Wait for bright days." Sang Babloo.

The sharp eyes of Molly saw a man tightening the screws in a car. Toto flew lower and let Molly hop. Molly silently scuttered near the car and when the man did not notice, he grabbed screws and screwdrivers from there. Toto lowered again to carry Molly into the air. Within a few minutes, they reached the Town Square.

Seeing them, Jumbo's eyes twinkled in delight. Babloo immediately fixed the screws and tightened the trunk by rotating the screwdriver. The trunk got fixed. Jumbo swayed its trunk so beautifully and thanked Molly, Toto and Babloo for their timely help.

"You fixed my trunk at last,

So strong like in the past,

Without delay so fast,

Am happy. Am happy

Am very happy." Jumbo sang with loads of happiness.

Jumbo looked grand and majestic again. His eyes gleamed in delight because Jumbo was happy only when he could make kids happy.

***

Shrija Karthik, a cheerful little girl studying in 5th grade loves to read, listen and narrate tales.Stories are her favorite entertainers.She has participated in many Storytelling contests and won prizes.

A Case of Collective Nouns

Aniruddha Iyer Bali

In a community of people

A gang of cronies

Stole a string of ponies.

This incident was seen by

A party of children

And a herd of elephants.

Out of eleven children

Airavata

Only six wanted to
About this….
Start an investigation.

Whereas, the elephants
Mama, Papa
Decided that they
It is dangerous
And not just by half!
Other than the eager calf.

The children had heard
A patter of footsteps
Also had smelt
Peculiar and fishy scent
The calf decided to investigate
And be part of the parade

They went to scrutinize
In the farm nearby
They saw a
Bike of bees
In the pig-sty.

One of the children
Saw honey on the floor

While the others in the barn
Noticed a secret door.

They went inside
Holding the trunk of the calf
And
Lo! Behold

They were surrounded by
A battle of artillery
They also saw a sack full of
A rouleau of money.

They opened
A chest of drawers
In which there was
A wad of notes
And a bouquet of flowers.

They were about to cross
The verandah
When they spotted
A pack of thieves.

The thieves were standing
Under the shade of an orchard of fruit trees

In the crook's hand

Was pots of gold

The children then heard

Let's run away ….

Master Archbold.

Out of the blue

The thieves went to

The trap door

While the children ran back

To the shed they were

In before.

Billy, the youngest lad

Had stumbled upon

A ream of paper

On the top sheet

Was written

A collection of alphabets and numbers.

On that paper, was written

In code

12'ness Yellow-wit 121413 costume

All 19 goods

Bit low, in a smaller font

Airavata

There was something scribbled
"Drawn is a screw of hawks. "

Roxy, the oldest
Added,
The 12th letter is "L"
And wondered
What is L-ness ?

After, a couple of minutes
"It could be Loch Ness "
Jim, said

Trevor, exclaimed
"That could be it!"
But we don't have
Enough money
Thus, to go there
We won't be able to
Buy tickets

Andy quickly interjected
My caretaker is taking me
To Loch Ness, tomorrow
And, I am allowed to take
A group of friends

Airavata

Yes, even you our calf

I guess, this is not where

Our investigation ends !!

On Wednesday,

The chaos of children

And our calf

With their suitcases and trunks

Boarded a Ritzy plane

And sat in cool bunks

The sandwich they ate

Was totally insane.

They reached Loch ness

And were amazed to see

A crowd of people

They also saw

Acrobatics in motion

Of a swoop of seagulls

They went inside the hotel

To see a Rookery of front desk clerks

In smart attires

They also glimpsed at

An alley of clowns

Out of 4, 2 were performing

Topsy turvy gymnastics

Our calf too did a jig

And he got a cheer

And a piece of jaggery

That for his mouth

Was a bit too big!

Going forward, they saw

A dapper mime

In an elan suit

On reaching the room

Saw all their selection of shampoos and soaps

Stored in a bag made of jute.

The party of children

Had bunk beds on

Both sides of the room

And were served High-Tea

With an array of muffins and scones

At sharp 3pm

In the afternoon.

The calf ate some cakes

And drank juice

Enough to fill the lakes!

They went to boat

At the Loch

Airavata

And spotted
A romp of otters
On reaching the shore
Were next to
A parcel of deer.

The next day
On their own
The youth's went sightseeing
On the lake
They saw a boat
Gently sitting and rocking.

Swimming to the boat
They came across
A boil of hawks
Drawn on it
And on the boat
Was carved the inscription
YELLOW -WIT.

In a flash
Sam helped his friends
Aboard the boat
Luckily, inside the barque
There was lying

Airavata

A pile of coats.

The children came back
Soaking wet
To the lodge
After, bathing
They were happy to
Eat a box of chocolate fudge
The calf nudged them a bit
And asked for a wee bit more.

At night, Jim stepped out
To take a stroll
And he heard some voices talking
"Tomorrow, we can do the Loch ness monster-Master Archbold"

After a couple of minutes
He heard
"Hmmm… good idea Brokium
You have given me
A nest of ideas
About how at 10.57 pm
Tomorrow, we could rob the museum."

Jim had recorded this event
On his cell phone

Running quickly back to his friends
He showed it to
The hunch of detectives
(The children)
While they were in
Yellow wit alone.

At 10.56 p.m.
the next day
Armed with
A babel of cell-phones
They went to the local gallery.

They saw the thieves
Coming to rob the exhibit
On a herd of ponies
They quickly called
The village police station
The thieves were caught
By a posse of policemen.

Stealing an ancient coin
That costed Euro half a million
The now called suspicion of detectives
Were still not satisfied
As they had not found

The other loot.

So, they went back to the boat
And saw a piece of parchment
Which said ….
"Steeple, Hill, Well and Field of wheat."
Below in a larger font was scribbled
" SWIM TWO HUNDRED FEET "

Because, they could see everything
Written on the paper
Hence, Trevor and Roxy
Dove into the water
Two hundred feet
In full diving gear
The calf waited on the banks
As, he wasn't wearing
His swimming trunks.

Down, on the sea bed
They found a secret door
They beckoned the policemen
To come up to the bed of the river.
Aided by the calf
They all fell on the banks
Dripping wet

And had a good laugh.

In the secret portal

Was the loot filled

Loch ness monster

That is how they stole

The artifacts

By distracting, said the

Now angry crew of museum workers

The children and the calf

Exhibited the goods

In the farm

Some of the artillery

Were fire-arms.

The party of youth

Were awarded

100 Euro's each

And a free vacation

To British Virgina beach

The calf got a juicy farm

Full of sugarcanes

And some bees in a swarm.

Moreover, they received

A KNIGHTHOOD

The children formed

A company of detectives

Wearing their own

Monogrammed suits

The little brave calf

Got a majestic bell

So, they could hear him

And beckon him as well.

They henceforth were known as

The Greatest Investigators

But, this crime file was officially christened

THE CASE OF A CALF AND YOUTH-I-GATORS

***

Aniruddha Iyer Bali is a 09 year old who loves to think and write in verses.

Chadanese Reunion

Srikar Chitta

There was fog, smoke, and fire everywhere in the Serengeti! I was searching for my family, "Mama?" I screamed, searching for her. "Mama, can you hear me."

But there was no sense of her; everywhere around me was fog, then I saw in one corner an exit from this dreadful flame.

I thought everyone went in that direction, so I decided to go in that direction and rescue myself. At the same time, I had a second thought, what if my family didn't make out of this dreadful flame.

What should I do? I had no time to search and wait, so with hope, I just ran. When I came out of the fire, I lost consciousness because I swallowed too much carbon dioxide. Also, there was a temperature difference I couldn't sustain for a long time.

The next day when I opened my eyes, I was surrounded by metal rods instead of fire, from one daylight nightmare to another. I looked around the metal, and I realized that I was in a cage with other animal species. I checked for any Chadanese elephant species. There were none except me.

However, no members of the Chadanese elephant species made it out of the fire except me or at least what I thought. Breaking my thoughts, there was a monkey who was laughing at me, and he said, *"Human beings are really primitive, you know, they don't even understand the language we speak, and yet they call us unintelligent species."*

I said, *"I am not ready to speak about anyone because I am lost. I lost my family, I lost my mom, I don't even know whether they are alive or not!"*

The moment I stopped speaking, the cage owner opened the door, which made a creeeeekity-cric noise. He just unlocked all of the cages and made us walk on a ramp, leading us to more giant cells. I was kept with other species which I never knew about. I sat alone for the rest of the day. Then I saw a fascinating creature, sort of like a Hyena. However, it had grey fur with no spots; I enquired him, are you a fox.

He replied, *"No, foxes and wolves are of different kinds. For instance, wolves are more intelligent than foxes. But anyway, Welcome to the paradise hell for animal species, The great Zoo. You may wonder why I said paradise hell. It's basically 'HELL', some species think it's paradise and some species think it's hell, it's up to you."*

Even though the wolf talked to me about the place, my heart and mind thought about my family.

Interrupting me, the wolf said, *"Hey, you look pretty dull. Why?"*

"Do you know how it feels to lose a family and move one to a place where you know nothing about it?" I replied with a blind furry taking hold of me.

To my shock, the wolf replied, *"I don't know about my parents' loss, but I was tranquillized by humans, and I was brought here. I thought that both my parents were killed by poachers, and that's why I am here."*

Oh my! I gasped.

I asked, *"By the way, what is a poacher?"*

"A poacher is a person who kills animals for money," was said by a parakeet in a cage behind me.

"Hey parakeet, let me answer," the wolf said to the parakeet.

Continuing the conversation, I asked the wolf, *"Did you ever try to go and check on your family or just your thought that a poacher killed them."*

Wolf replied, *"No! I am happy here because I am safe from being killed."*

I said, *"My instincts are telling me that my family is alive. We are Chadanese elephant species. We can survive for many days without food, and we can even survive in hostile temperatures! I am sure they are alive!"*

Parakeet asked me, *"I heard that a wildfire raged across central Africa, and you were the last remains of the Chadanese elephant species. Is it true?"*

"Wait a minute, from where you heard this news of near extinction," I enquired.

The parakeet replied, *"The BBC news!"*

"No way, I am not going to believe or rely on this news." I said to the parakeet.

The wolf said, *"What are you going to do now? Can you escape? Of course, you can't escape; this zoo is strictly under surveillance. How can you check on your family, dude? You have no option; you need to believe the BBC news."*

This made me cry. And that night, I couldn't sleep at all. Then like lightning, an idea popped into my head. What if we escaped? The following day, I told my opinion to the other two. Hearing this, the parakeet almost died, laughing at me. It chuckled. *"There is so much surveillance, and the guard would come with shotguns; if you try to escape, you would be shot before you ran a yard! Also, it is not THAT bad here; you get lots of free food, and there is no need to worry about dying!"*

I replied, *"We should Never give up! We should try and try again! We shouldn't be lazy, or we should not become addicted to these human tactics. These human beings go to any extent for their greed! They use us for earning money in the name of ZOO. We should check on our family, as they are not necessary; they are **EVERYTHING** to us!"*

Hearing this, the wolf said the entire timetable of the activities in the zoo. The exciting facts said by the wolf were, *"The evening shift ends at 10:00 p.m. and the night shift begins at 10:15 p.m. One of the monkeys in the cage is good at opening doors, but the only thing is we need to convince him."* With these facts, all of us formulated a plan.

At 10:00 p.m. all the security guards left their duty, and for 15 minutes, the zoo was void of humans. As soon as this happened, the wolf told the monkey to open the doors. Even though we convinced the monkey, it started to shiver.

I screamed at the monkey, "You monkey, you agreed to open the door; why are you not doing it? We have a few minutes. Do it fast." Now, even more scared because of my words, the monkey unlocked the door and then he fainted. Carrying the monkey on me, we ran towards the exit. Somehow, we managed to escape into the van, and the wolf drove us to the forest.

It was covered with ash and bones when I left the woods, but now it was totally an opposite scene as if the fire was erased from history. The forest was now covered with lush green bushes, waterfalls, big trees, and so many chirping birds around us. I trumpeted, rumbled and roared! Sound of happiness came out through me. *'This is my place.'* I stared around the forest.

I saw a blur of big, gigantic species coming towards me; one after the other massive species count increased. At first, I got scared! *'Are they humans with shotguns?'*

Slowly my vision was clear; it was not the humans; it was my species, my *Chadanese* species, and my family. I trumpeted louder than ever, and finally, I saw my mom with tears of joy in her eyes. My instincts were right; I yelled and hugged my mom.

Seeing all these, the parakeet, the wolf and the monkey were lost in joy. The monkey returned to its home in India, the parakeet returned to Brazil, and the wolf went back to the Arctic. Everyone lived happily ever after! Except the zookeepers, of course.

***

Srikar Chitta is an imaginative Indian-American sixth-grader now at Birla Open Minds International School, Hyderabad. He enjoys reading, learning new technologies, and studying science and nature—but what he loves doing most of all is writing! He writes enthusiastically, and his stories are award-winners—a prize in the 2020 KidEngage short story competition, and he is the BTB Storyteller of the Year 2020. Two of his prize-winning stories are Devil in Disguise and Three Sides of a Coin. He won Literoma Junior Star award for the year 2021 and Won first prize in 'The Little Scoop International Creative Writing Competition'

Just Another Horrible Year is Srikar's first published book, and another of his stories will be published in the upcoming Box of Tales—Volume 2: A Beyond the Box Series Anthology.

Not all of them...

Golpo Nodi

Whoosh!

Water splashed on me as I and my best friend, Ivor, playfully sprayed water on each other.

The autumn breeze blew past my ears. It was pleasant weather.

"It's getting dark. We should go home" I said.

"Aww...bummer"

"You have to be home by 6, remember?"

"Yeah, right. Of course. You just had to remind me." He said with a sad face.

"Let's go," I replied, marching through the Elephanta trails that lead home.

It was already dark. I shivered but my skin kept me warm.

I walked and walked for about fifteen minutes until I realized Ivor was missing.

I frantically started searching around me. Where did he go? I couldn't even recognise where I was.

The wood looked unfamiliar; the fresh smell of pine trees was missing. So was the boundary between the elephant housing area and the human world. The lush green pillars covered with vines weren't there either. There was dead silence, no chirping of birds and not a single trumpet of an elephant. And the grass under my feet felt prickly and different. This was a different forest.

And it was then when I realized... It wasn't Ivor who was lost. But it was me.

I groaned. This has happened to many baby elephants from our village multiple times; but can we really call a teenager like me a baby! My parents would probably punish me from having sugarcane for a month. But that wasn't really the urgent matter at this point.

I looked around everywhere but couldn't find anyone.

"Ivor! Omma! Appa!" I called out. Nobody responded. I started to panic.

No! It's alright, nothing's going to happen, I said, trying to console myself.

I wandered for a long time, trying to figure out where I was. I called for Omma and Appa some more until my throat dried up. There wasn't even a small pool nearby.

Oh no. Oh no. Oh no no no no no. Could… it be?

Was this the place Omma always warned me about? The…human world?

I instantly felt my heartbeat rise. There had been countless encounters where elephants had been lost in the human world and never been seen again. The very few that returned were either half dead or badly injured. But how could it be? I had clearly stuck to the trails and as far as I remember, Omma told me there should have been a barrier before entering the human territory.

But all over Elephanta was the unique smell of sugarcane and pine trees; but here that was completely missing. As I was pondering on all of this, I had the sudden feeling that someone was watching me. I turned around and lo behold…there was no one.

I heaved a sigh of relief. I hadn't encountered any human beings yet.

I walked for a while, trying to find at least a small pool or some food. Before that, let me tell you why we were precisely so scared of humans. From oral knowledge passed down by the wise elephants, humans are peculiar little creatures with a large amount of power which they misused to slaughter animals like us. So now you understand, why am I so worried!

With a heavy and anxious heart, I walked for a whole 4 hours until I slumped down under the shade of a tree. The trees here were different. They were so small that barely two baby elephants would be able to rest under it. I sat there for some time.

Airavata

Troo, the elephant who has never once missed a chance to go for an outing, a chance to get away from her boring home, was now engulfed with the feeling of homesickness.

Concentrate, Troo! You need to get back to Elephanta, I scolded myself.

After walking for a while, the forest started to disappear and I came to a small clearing. The first sign of human habitation I had found. So, this was what a human village looked like. I was grateful that now I had a source for nutrients but was still lost and afraid of the humans.

I took cautious steps towards the village centre and saw a little pond not far away. But when I reached there, it happened to have muddy water. I looked for food but the fruit-bearing trees all looked poisonous. What if people kept them there to attract innocent elephants? I immediately shuddered at the thought and shut my eyes.

Other than the petrichor emitting from the wet grass, there was no distinctive scent there. Now that I was actually looking around properly, I noticed how tiny the human houses looked.

I tried tasting the grass. This grass seemed so different from the dry straw we used to have in Elephanta! But I liked the taste of the grass here. I immediately fell for its chewy softness. The squelchy mud felt pleasant to walk in. But I couldn't really hear anything around there. As it was night, I assumed the humans were sleeping too. I deserved a quick nap too after all that walking I did. I slept peacefully all through the night.

In the morning, I woke up, startled by the crow of the roosters. Soon after, all the birds started chirping cheerfully and my face immediately lit up and my mood was brightened. I had lived in a forest all my life, so I wasn't used to the sun's bright rays falling directly onto my face. The scorching heat was very unpleasant. I wondered how humans lived every day in this climate.

This place was dangerous. I should've been going back after collecting resources like food and water for the journey home. But something seemed to draw me here. As I was debating with myself in my head, I heard a sound that I would be stupid not to recognize.

Ivor's muffled trumpet sounded behind me.

There he was! But he wasn't alone; he was surrounded by lots of human children. Strangely they were not at all harming or disturbing Ivor, rather they were very friendly, whispering sweet nothings in Ivor's flappy ears, feeding him the most nutritious food I have ever seen and singing the most beautiful melodies I have ever heard.

There was no cage around Ivor. Why? Those are the only stories Troo had heard about humans before- how unkind, cruel and unjust they were! While I was thinking, children whole-heartedly started singing a farewell song for Ivor.

After those difficult goodbyes, Ivor came almost running towards me, swaying his trunk. The first thing that he whispered in my ears was, "Not all humans are bad, rather mostly aren't!"

***

'Golpo' means story and 'Nodi' means 'River', and she can be called as 'River of Stories'. She dreams to quench the thirst of her readers and listeners, being an author and a storyteller. My Amphan fund-raiser story 'Sunodri's Red Boots', set in the Sundarbans Mangrove Forest, showing the difficulties of common people during the double whammy of Amphan Super Cyclone and Covid-19, was featured in multiple International Festivals. When she is not into stories, she is a baker or a Drama Queen.

Daredevil Pintu

Sanvi.P

Airavata

In the outskirts of a town called Crystal there was a huge jungle. In that jungle, a baby elephant was born and his name was Pintu. What do you think was so strange about Pintu? Well, Pintu had a short trunk! Really! All of you know how useful trunks are for elephants. Even though Pintu had a really short trunk, he could manage his activities very well. But there was one disadvantage. Pintu was always teased by the other animals.

"Hee! Hee! Hee!" cackled the monkey as Pintu wandered near the tree on which the monkey lived.

The hippos boomed with laughter as soon as they saw Pintu lumbering towards the pond.

Once Pintu asked his mother Kaya, "Mother…Will I have a short trunk forever?"

"That… Depends…" sighed Kaya.

One day, when all the animals were having a meeting in the middle of the forest, Pintu went in too. When he got there all the animals started giggling again. This was too much for Pintu. He bursted out in anger.

"OK! You want to make fun of me? Then so be it! There are many things you can't do while I can!" Pintu yelled.

"Many things that you can do but we can't!? Ho! Ho! Tell me more!" Boomed one of the humongous hippos.

"Oh ho! So, you challenge me now Hippo, do you? You know about the Khatarnak Crocodile, right?"

"Khatarnak Crocodile, you mean the oldest crocodile in the crocodile pond?" interrupted the squeaking mouse.

"Yes..." Pintu continued.

"Wait a minute are you talking about the fiercest crocodile in the crocodile pond, the one our Lion king fears too?" Asked the zebra.

"Hey! Watch it!" Growled the lion. "Or I'll throw you straight to Khatarnak Crocodile's mouth!"

"Yeah. Now…", said Pintu, getting irritated.

"Wait… Is the Khatarnak Crocodile the same crocodile who bit my Great Grandfather?" Asked the lion's cub.

"Quiet!" The lion barked. "Pintu, what about the Khatarnak Crocodile? What are you going to do that we can't?" Asked the lion curiously.

"Hee! Hee! Hee!" Pintu snickered.

"Ummm… Pintu?" All the animals gaped, puzzled.

"Wait and watch!" Said Pintu and walked towards the crocodile pond.

"I think he's going to challenge Khatarnak Crocodile!" whispered the deer.

"I might not look good. But I can hear very well." Pintu whispered back.

"Huuhhh!" Gasped the deer.

Pintu walked towards the crocodile pond and spotted Khatarnak Crocodile lying in the water with eyes closed.

"Hey, Khatarnak Crocodile! Wake up!" Pintu trumpeted.

"WHO DARES TO DISTURB MY SLEEP!" Snarled Khatarnak Crocodile.

All the animals gasped and moved back. They were very scared of the Khatarnak Crocodile.

"Well, today is Pintu's last day on earth." The tiger whispered.

"We better find a huge spot to bury him." Said the giraffe.

"Duh… we need to make a coffin to bury him." Hissed the snake.

"STOP TALKING! Look! Pintu is pulling Khatarnak Crocodile's tail!" Yelled the lion cub.

Indeed, Pintu was pulling Khatarnak Crocodile's tail! Then he also wrapped his tail around Khatarnak Crocodile's mouth. The ugly elephant had done it! He had proved to everyone that he can do what the others can't. Khatarnak Crocodile was stunned because he had never seen anyone so courageous. Everyone in the forest knew how Khatarnak Crocodile had bitten the lion's grandfather.

"Aooowww… this fearless elephant! He has wrapped his trunk around my mouth. I'd better get away from him," the Khatarnak Crocodile thought.

Thinking fast, Khatarnak Crocodile said "Hey elephant let me go I'll never come in your way again. If that satisfies you…"

"Ok! But, if you ever come in my way…" Started Pintu.

"No! No! I won't, don't worry." Interrupted Khatarnak Crocodile hastily.

"Then, you're free to go now!"

"Thank you", said Khatarnak Crocodile and ran as fast as he could.

"Ok! So, did you see how I scared Khatarnak Crocodiles?" Pintu asked proudly.

"Yes…yes. We understand now." Replied to all the animals.

Since then, the animals never teased Pintu again about his short trunk and he was renamed as "Daredevil Pintu."

Once Bhalu, the bear had a dare for Pintu. Bhalu wanted Pintu to bring down honey from the fiercest honeycomb in the forest. As usual, Pintu agreed.

Pintu went to the tree where the fierce bees lived. He stored some water in his trunk. So, when Pintu was right below the tree, he sprayed a jet of water to the beehive in which the honey was stored. The bees got a little scared. But didn't fly away. So, Pintu inhaled deeply and let out a gush of wind through his trunk. The bees were really frightened now so they started flying away.

Pintu, brought down the honeycomb from the tree and took it to Bhalu.

Bhalu was stunned! He had attempted 50 times to get down the honeycomb. But, Pintu took only a minute! This was amazing!

One day, some humans started building a factory on the outskirts of the forest. The lion was sent to scare away the humans. But he was unsuccessful. When Pintu heard this, he started laughing.

"Hee hee hee! Ha ha ha! The lion failed to scare away the humans! Oh, what a shame!" chuckled Pintu.

The lion was furious. "Oh! then let's see how you scare the humans. Go scare them."

"Ok, I'll go! I've got no problem." Saying this Pintu went to the factory area.

There Pintu quietly sneaked in when there was no one around. It was lunch-break for the humans. So Pintu walked in calmly. When he reached a big shutter door a human pressed his remote that made the shutter door close slowly.

"Oh no! The big thing is closing! If I don't get in, I won't be able to scare the humans." Thought Pintu.

He started jogging and after some time, he broke into a sprint!

Thump! Thump! Pintu's footsteps thundered the ground.

"NO! NO! I can't lose the bet! If I do, then all the animals will start teasing me like before."

Yelled Pintu while running. The shutter door was almost about to close, when Pintu tripped and slid on the ground before he was face to face with the shutter door!

"Humm…" sighed Pintu. "I guess I should have kept quiet when the lion had failed. Now how will I face them? They'll start making fun of me again. I'll go back and tell them I wasn't successful."

When he tried to get up, he was being pulled down! He tried again, but couldn't. Then he noticed that his trunk was stuck under the shutter door. He tried to pull his trunk out but it didn't work. He started trumpeting loudly, so his friends could hear him.

Soon in the forest his friends heard him and rushed to his rescue. The animals spotted Pintu lying on his tummy close to the shutter door.

"Hey Pintu, why did you call us? Were you so tired after scaring the humans that you slept here?" Grinned Bhalu.

"No, no," gasped Pintu. He was tired from trumpeting and found it hard to breathe since half of his trunk was under the shutter door. "Get me out of here!"

"Huh…aren't you sleeping? Can't you get up by yourself?" asked Bhalu.

"No! I'm not sleeping, my trunk is stuck under this stupid door." Squeaked Pintu.

"So…you didn't frighten the humans?" All the animals gasped.

"No! I didn't. Now please help me… please!" Cried Pintu.

All the animals agreed to help him. They all tried to grab Pintu so they could pull him out. The only thing they could hold on to was Pintu's tail. So, they all caught hold of his tail and pulled.

"Yieeeee!" Pintu shrieked, "Owww! Stop pulling my tail. It hurts."

Since the lion was right behind Pintu, he caught hold of Pintu's back.

"Yieeeee! Your claws are digging into my skin lion, stop clawing me!" Yelled Pintu again.

The animals pulled and pulled. Finally, Pintu's trunk was free.

"Huff! Huff!" Pintu puffed. "Thank you dear friends".

"How on earth did yoooooooouuuuuuuuuuuu Pintuuuuuuuuuu?" The tiger's mouth hung open.

"What happened to the tiger?" Asked Pintu, surprised.

"Y… yo… your trunk!" Stuttered the tiger.

"What? Huh!? My trunk!" Gasped Pintu.

Indeed! Something was wrong with Pintu's trunk. It had lengthened! When the animals were pulling Pintu, his trunk had stretched and had become as long as a normal elephant's trunk! Pintu thanked his friends for having given him a normal trunk and the animals thanked him for taking the dare on their behalf and risking his life.

***

Sanvi a 11 year old, likes to read stories and writes short stories. She can code and design apps and play keyboard too.

Kuki & the Elephant

Aadya Sethi

Once upon a time there was a young girl named Kuki. She lived in a village located near a dense forest. Her favourite animal was an elephant and had wanted one as a pet for so long but her parents were poor and could not afford one. Every day, she used to go to the forest and collect some fruits for her family. One morning when she was ready to go to the forest, she called out to her mother and said, "Ma, I am going to the forest to collect some fruits". So saying this she took a jute basket and headed towards the dense jungle. Her Mom told Kuki to be careful in the forest and return before it is dark.

Airavata

She was somewhere in the jungle, picking up the fruits that had fallen from the trees and putting them in her basket when she heard the loud trumpet of an elephant. Excited, she started walking in the direction of the sound. At a distance, she spotted a beautiful grey baby elephant.

The poor little elephant was crying out in pain as one of his paw was entangled in an iron chain with thorny edges jabbing out of it. Kuki could not bear to see the elephant in pain and ran ahead, trying to free him but the elephant didn't allow her to come anywhere close to him. Kuki stood back and thought a lot. After thinking for a while, she had an idea. She sensed the elephant was not only in pain, but must be very scared and hungry too. It turned out that her guess was correct because he gladly accepted the fruits given by Kuki. Once his hunger was satiated, the elephant allowed Kuki to remove the thorn from his paw. As soon as the thorn was removed, the elephant was relieved of the pain, felt happy and his stance softened towards her.

The elephant knew the jungle very well. He made Kuki sit on his back and took her to an area of the jungle densely covered with different types of fruit bearing trees. Kuki was very happy to see such a big source of fruits and picked up some more fruits for her family. Before long it was time for the sun to set and for them to get back home before dark. Sensing she would like to go back, the elephant carried her back to the place where they had met first. Kuki smiled and caressed his big back as a way to say bye and started walking towards her home. After reaching home, she narrated the incident of meeting an elephant and how they both had helped each other to her mother who was proud of her nature to help others. She asked Kuki what she would like to name him. After thinking for a long time, she decided to name him Pintu.

Next day, Kuki was eager to get back to the jungle. She had hoped she would be able to meet Pintu at the same place. She was delighted when she saw him actually waiting for her at the same spot. They became good friends. Kuki had always wanted an elephant as a pet. She was able to fulfil that desire of hers because she got to feed and play with the elephant every day. The elephant never allowed any other animal to hurt Kuki. He was also fond of her.

One day Kuki had gone to the marketplace with her mother when she heard an announcement being made by the king's soldiers. One of his beloved elephants was missing and whoever would get him back or share any information about him would be rewarded. She wondered if it was the same elephant whom she had met and became friends with in the jungle. She was in two minds whether to tell the whereabouts of her new friend or continue enjoying the company and playing with Pintu in the forest. Not only was she afraid of losing a good friend and protector but also facing the wrath of the king if he came to know that Kuki knew where his elephant was.

She was silent on her way back home. She also got to know from her mother that the soldiers were searching for the baby elephant in the jungle again. They had tried once but could not find him. She too wondered if it was the same elephant. Kuki was sad on hearing this from her mother too. She thought about it a lot and finally made a decision.

She asked her mother to take her to the palace. Once there, she told the king that she could help find the elephant. However, she had a small condition. She did not want any reward but if the king could let her meet and feed the elephant everyday. The king, who had been sad about his missing elephant, became happy to hear Kuki's words and readily agreed to her wishes. On their way back home, her mother shared with her about how happy she was with Kuki's decision.

Next morning, the king's minister and a few of his soldiers accompanied Kuki to the forest. After reaching their favourite place, Kuki called out for Pintu and shortly after, the elephant came running to her. The courtiers immediately recognised the elephant and were really surprised to see how Kuki and Pintu had become good friends. When the soldiers tried to capture him, he got irritated and started trumpeting and moving back but then saw the minister and remembered him. He calmed down after that. Kuki caressed his ears and tried to make him understand that it would be good to go back home. They all headed back to the

palace after that, where he was happy to meet his family and friends. Happy to get his favorite elephant back, the king not only kept his promise but also gave a lot of money to Kuki and her family.

Pintu was back home, the king was happy. However, the happiest was Kuki for not only she got a big reward but also her friend was here to stay in her life.

***

A grade five student and an avid reader, Aadya Sethi has always had a creative streak, be it writing or drawing. Kuki marked her debut on the published media platform. Apart from writing, playing with her younger brother, games, and the outdoors interest her.

The Night-flower Quest

Shruti Tripasuri

In the dense jungle of Assam, by the river and under a small roof made of haystack lived an elephant with his herd. The elephant, Jumbo, was a calf whom everyone loved because he was a helpful, cheerful and hard-working elephant. He loved playing around with his two friends by the river.

One day, when Jumbo was helping the woodcutters carry the load of logs, Ramu came running to him. He said, "Jumbo, Meera is not keeping well! Let's go meet her."

Ramu was a small boy, aged about ten. He was the son of one of the woodcutters and thus knew the jungle well. Jumbo kept his load down and plucked a few flowers from the nearby bushes and Ramu helped himself to Jumbo's back. The two of them left for the village in no time. The flowers looked gorgeous and smelled heavenly. On reaching the village, they went around the green hedges, and reached Meera's house.

Over there, they found Meera lying on the cot and her mother tending to her; Meera was a girl, about the same age as Ramu. On seeing her best friends, she gave a smile and gestured to them both to come in. Her mother offered them some water and delicious fruits.

"Thank you for coming, Jumbo and Ramu! It feels much better seeing you both. Thank you for the adorable flowers, Jumbo. I have to tell you both something." Said Meera.

While Jumbo was munching over the apples, Ramu helped Meera's mother to fill the jug of water. He meticulously listened to Meera. She said with interest, "Do you both know, when I was reading a book the day before, I read that there is a beautiful flower which blooms only at full moon. It's known as the *Moonflower*. Legend says that seeing it bloom brings luck for the person viewing it. I would really love to see it! Shall we all go together to see it this week as there's going to be a full moon?"

Jumbo trumpeted in agreement and excitement. Ramu said that they would set off once Meera would feel better. All of them agreed in unison. Meera added, "It would take us a few hours to reach the cave where it grows."

"We will first bring a bag containing a small flask of water, fruits and some food for Jumbo," said Ramu with ebullience.

"A mat as well and oh, we shouldn't forget the book from which I read about the flower. It'll help us find the correct location of the flower", added Meera.

"Okay then! Let us know if you're feeling better by tomorrow evening Meera. We can then meet near the banyan tree by the river," replied Ramu. They left once all the planning was done. Meera whispered in excitement, "Can't wait!"

*

The next day, Meera was feeling much better. She packed everything in a jute bag as planned the day before. She left her home exhilarated. After taking some sticks along with him, Ramu gave a little pat on Jumbo and left for the river along with him. He reached the designated meeting point to find Meera waiting there, impatience evident on her face.

"All set?", he asked.

Nodding her head in answer, Meera said - "It is written in the book that *this flower grows on the other side of a cave which is in the forest near the villages of Assam.*

I've been wondering if it is the same cave in which we had taken shelter from the rains once?"

"Yes, even I thought so... Do you remember that Jumbo was also with us at that time! Maybe he can guide us how to get there; Elephants have an amazing memory after all!" Ramu said with a wide grin. Meera agreed. She showed Jumbo a picture of the cave and Jumbo made a deafening sound and pointed his trunk to one of the pathways leading deep into the dense jungle.

On the way they both sang various folk songs and hymns and at times when they were tired, they would sit on the mat under a tree and have water and fruits which they had packed. They soon reached a point where the path diverged into three directions. Jumbo sensed and led them to the right path. At a distance, they saw the figure of a large, rocky cave.

They ran as fast as their legs could carry them. They thus reached the cave. The cave was pitch black. There was a feeling of gloom and dullness in. Jumbo found a stick and Ramu found two stones and rubbed them until they ignited. He lit the stick which Jumbo held in his trunk and started walking. As the cave was lit, they could see a whole lot of foliage clung to the roof and sides of the cave. Soon they reached a place where there was a huge opening and below that, was a tiny island surrounded by shallow waters. The moonlight shone on it and that's when all of them realized that the Moonflower grew there. But there was a problem –

"Meera, how do we reach that island? Was there anything written in the book about that? It is surrounded by water and the moonlight will shine anytime soon," asked Ramu, who was enchanted by this sight. Both Jumbo and him were staring at Meera as she was flipping through the pages of the book in search of that article.

"Nothing is said about it here Ramu," she kept scanning the pages. "I think we must overcome this obstacle ourselves," she added.

Jumbo then pointed his trunk to some rocks by the side and a ton of mud next to that. The two kids understood that they must build a bridge in order to reach the isle.

Taking a rock was a tricky job; of course, those rocks were heavy! When Ramu tried placing the rock on water, the rock had sunk in almost no time. Meera suggested that they put some mud and then place rocks on them. They knew that it would take a long time, but they got on to it at once. It took them a good hour and a half to make a bridge with mud and rocks.

Happy with their success, the three of them walked on the bridge they had made over the shallow waters and reached the other side on the isle. The isle was somewhat average in size. There were rocks and bushes on the edges of it and on the bushes were the tight shut white buds which were of the moon-flower. It was very soft to touch and tickled Jumbo. In between the island, there was an open, grassy space on which Ramu laid the mat and Meera sat on it. It was time when the moon was shining above them! After gathering around the bushes, the three of them saw it bloom and were amazed to see their beauty.

"Doesn't the flower look lovely?" asked Meera who was still gazing at the flower.

"Yeah," replied Ramu. He was still awestruck by the beauty of the flower. "Let's stay here for a while and then we can go home," he added. Jumbo nodded his head happily.

They sat together on the mat and had some of the leftover fruits. They washed their faces from the waters and started packing up to go home.

*

The cave was lit by the moonlight and thus went out of it and back into the woods. They were still reluctant to leave the place though. They kept Jumbo in his shed and went to their homes back in the village at nightfall. It would always be their favourite and unforgettable trip they'd ever been to.

***

Shruti currently studying in grade 7. Some of her hobbies are playing the keyboard, drawing, painting and listening to music. Sometimes she bakes and read. Also she likes to play badminton.

Airavata
The Compiler

Meera, a wandering dinosaur, roars her day with 20 Surya namaskarasanas and ends with 20 push-ups by her minion, well it's on her. In between, her sanity is kept alive by the Writing and Storytelling communities she runs on Social media: LetsMakeStoriesDino and Mayaakatha, where Stories Dance. Her 99% of madness can be read in her 2- self-published books and 12 co-authored journeys. And, she blogs 1% of goodness on Neuro Linguistic Programming and Storytelling/words maze on meeeasoasis.com

To sum it up, this Dino writes/blogs/creates content, publishes/compiles anthologies & Poetry book, runs online communities on Storytelling and Writing, Trains and Coaches Teachers, Children, Parents on Storytelling and NLP. She has won Women Achiever and multiple awards for her work on writing/ running initiatives and being an Influencer.

You can find her leaving her words and nose in an ocean of topics.

The Editors

Deepti Sharma, is a management post graduate and a former entrepreneur. She has worked as a sub-editor of a woman's magazine, and presently is working as a freelance editor. She is a Language coach, a blogger, a poet and a mini fiction writer. Her work has been published in anthologies like 'TSL's Roseate Sonnet Anthology', 'Towers of Inspiration' 'Arising from the Dust' et al. She has won many poetry and fiction writing contests, a mother of three, she resides in Punjab.

Preeti S Manaktala is currently serving as in-house Poetry Editor of a reputed publication house and online journal called **Chrysanthemum Chronicles.** She is also a published author, poet, blogger and a contributing writer to various online sites. She has won many accolades and recognition for her poetry contribution to various online contests. She calls herself a writer in progress and believes that life is a melange of learnings. She is a firm believer in the age-old saying **"My Life is My Own Making."**

Her Latest books –

Indian Summer In Verses- A Poetry Anthology.

Macabre Tales – A Thriller Anthology.

Shristee Singh is a believer of one world family, She loves to write songs of the soul. She had won copper medal for an All India Creative Writing competition while in school. She was also recognised for her contribution for English poetry in Youth festival of Lucknow Mahotsav. She had been a nominee for the Author of the Year-2019 at StoryMirror for her contribution towards English literature. Currently she is based out of Hyderabad and besides writing in her free time, works as Associate Editor with Chrysanthemum Chronicles.

The Illustrator

Satinder Ahuja is a self taught artist, in fact, thanks to the pandemic, she found time to discover her passion. She is an MBA, worked for more than 20 years as an HR professional. Currently a Homemaker and a full time mother to her princess. She is married to a Cardiac Surgeon. The cover page is an Elephant Mandala, using acrylic paints, on 8*10 canvas board.

www.ingramcontent.com/pod-product-compliance
Lightning Source LLC
LaVergne TN
LVHW091629070526
838199LV00044B/992